HUNG UP

Bennett Security Book 5

HANNAH SHIELD

HUNG UP

Chapter One

Danica jogged up the marble steps of the West Oaks Natural History Museum. A Dua Lipa song blasted through her Air Pods. The salt-scented air filled her with energy, and she paused just outside the entrance to soak up the golden sun.

It's so good to be back, she thought.

New York was home now, but Danica would always be a California girl at heart.

Unfortunately, an annoying shadow would be following her around on this trip. A glance over her shoulder confirmed that her security detail was still hovering. They'd parked their Range Rover in the circular driveway, right in the red "no-stopping" zone.

Ugh. She'd have to find them a better spot next time. Something less obtrusive.

Her family's chief of security had insisted the bodyguards pick her up at the Burbank airport and drive her here, which was ridiculous.

They'd caved to her request to connect her phone to the car stereo, but they had clearly not enjoyed her favorite playlist.

None of them had cracked a smile. Not even when *Levitating* came on.

She'd outright refused to let them tag along inside the museum with her. No, thanks.

Danica didn't have devoted bodyguards in New York, and West Oaks wasn't New York. There were no photographers stalking her here. No pushy investors clamoring for meetings or access, or journalists angling for a quote, all of which she normally managed just fine on her own.

In West Oaks, she'd be safe and free from distractions. These days, a streamlined work schedule or her morning run were the only things to get her blood pumping. A little sad? Yes. But she had no time to deal with men and all their demands and drama.

But I'm going to check-mark the hell out of my to-do list. Just see if you can stop me.

The glass entrance glided open as she approached. A spacious atrium overlooked the oceanfront beyond. The garage-style doors were open, letting in the afternoon breeze.

A well-groomed man in a tailored suit looked up from the ticketing desk. "Welcome."

Danica tugged out her Air Pods. "Am I too late for the five o'clock tour?"

"Considering you're the only taker? Then no, not late at all." His name tag read *Anderson*. A curator, according to the profile she'd requested of the staff here. He looked more relaxed than his photo.

She waited for some sign of recognition, and was pleased when Anderson's smile remained distant, though friendly.

"Perfect." Danica paid for a ticket, admiring the beige stone of the lobby.

"Shall we?" Anderson picked up an info guide and handed it to her.

"We shall." She accepted the pamphlet with a smile. "Is anyone going to take over at the desk? In case other visitors turn up?"

"That's unlikely this late in the day." Anderson strode across the atrium, gesturing for her to follow. "There's only one other guest here, and he chose to go self-guided. I much prefer the quiet, to be honest."

His tie was loose, and she noticed the button at his collar was undone. So he couldn't be *that* straight-laced. A good sign. Maybe he'd be easier to work with than she'd thought.

Anderson glanced back at her. "Speaking of visitors, I'm afraid I might have to cut the tour a little short this evening. We're closing a few minutes early. *Big* VIP coming." He didn't roll his eyes, but she could hear it in his voice.

"Oh? Who's this VIP?"

"Daughter of William Foster-Grant. The billionaire. Heard of him?"

"I might have." She worked to keep a straight face. "I take it you're not a fan?"

"I wouldn't say that." They walked along a row of sea creature fossils. "But…"

"But?" She grinned at him encouragingly. "Come on, share."

Anderson pushed back his shoulders. "His daughter is in charge of his nonprofit foundation. Fancies herself a reformer, which is fine, but it hardly makes her a museum expert. Wants to make this place more interactive. Child-friendly." His expression conveyed his distaste for that idea.

"You mean, bring it into the twenty-first century?" Had the guy not visited a modern museum lately?

"This museum is about appreciating nature's past in a serene environment. Soon, it's going to be nonstop running and screaming and grubby little fingers on the glass."

"That does sound like a change."

"You're more diplomatic than I."

No kidding, she thought, suppressing a laugh.

They passed by a broad-shouldered man in a dark overcoat, who was the sole other visitor. He was milling around next to a display of Paleozoic bivalves. A black ball cap was pulled low over his eyes, but Danica could've sworn he did a double-take when his head turned toward her. Anderson hadn't recognized her, but she wondered if this guy did.

The man's jacket collar was up, but she spotted a large tattoo on his neck. A black bird with its wings outstretched and an oddly curved head.

The image was almost menacing. Danica shivered as she looked at it.

The guy didn't seem like the typical museum-goer, but she figured she was being unfair. If only more people from West Oaks were showing interest in this place.

They headed back into the atrium, where fresh marine air drifted in from the open doors.

How long had it been since her last visit to West Oaks? Five, six years?

She'd been avoiding certain memories, but it was time to set the past aside—so to speak. It was a little ironic to think of letting go of her past while in a history museum.

This would be a small project as far as the Foster-Grant Foundation was concerned, but it had outsized significance for her. Danica had grown up here, and she was finally ready to reconnect with her hometown. She wanted to show off West Oaks at its vibrant best.

In just a few days, she'd get the chance: an invite-only gala for top donors. An event she'd been anticipating for months, and it was almost here.

"Danica? Is that you?" Lindley Colter's voice rang out across the atrium. "You're so early! What a lovely surprise."

The new executive director of the museum walked toward them, stiletto heels clicking.

"Danica?" Anderson choked out, staring at her. "Danica Foster-Grant?"

"Guilty as charged." She gave him a sheepish smile.

"I am *so sorry*. I didn't—I mean, I—"

"Sorry for what?" Lindley asked. She was every bit as well-dressed as Anderson, yet Lindley's broad smile was disarming. She'd styled her red hair into a sleek bob.

"Just a little mix-up. So good to see you." Danica gave Lindley a hug. "Anderson's been showing me around and giving me the insider view. I appreciated his candor."

He was buttoning his collar, though the poor man looked like he needed more oxygen rather than less.

Danica put a hand on his arm. "I'd much rather get honesty than have you tell me what I want to hear. And if you're willing, I'd love to explain my vision for the museum in more detail later. I'll make a believer of you yet."

"Of course, Ms. Foster-Grant. I'll just close up the office and the computers. If you'll excuse me?" Anderson strode toward reception, apparently eager for the excuse to end their conversation.

"What did you *do* to him?"

Danica laughed. "I might have misled him a little. He didn't recognize me, and I just couldn't resist. But now I feel bad."

She didn't usually dress the way someone might expect for a billionaire heiress. Today, she'd worn straight-legged jeans, a lightweight linen blouse, and Converse hi-tops. Her dark hair was back in a ponytail, her messy bangs falling over her forehead. Gossip columns would talk about her whatever she wore, so she preferred to use her energy more productively.

Lindley dismissed the concern. "Anderson's part of the problem around here. No sense of adventure. You and I are shaking things up, and I can't wait."

About six months ago, Danica had joined the natural history museum's board of directors, promising a major infusion of funds from both the foundation and West Oaks donors. Hiring Lindley had been one of their first steps toward transforming this place.

"Will Anderson forgive me if I invite him to dinner?"

"You're not letting the poor man off the hook?" Amusement danced in Lindley's eyes.

"Oh come on, I'm not that scary."

"I know it. But you *do* have a fearsome reputation. The no-nonsense philanthropist who refuses to compromise, and is just as cutthroat in the nonprofit world as her father is in the corporate one?"

Danica laughed. "You read that *Vanity Fair* profile? It was a bit over the top."

"But you looked gorgeous on the cover."

And nothing like my real self, she thought.

Danica's attention caught on the other visitor she'd seen earlier. The man in the black ball cap with the creepy neck tattoo. He was standing near the exit talking into a phone.

His face was turned to the side, yet she had the sense that he was watching her. And that he'd just been listening to their conversation.

Was she imagining it?

That shiver from earlier was back, but it had blossomed into a genuine sense of unease. There was something she really didn't like about this guy. And it wasn't the weird neck tattoo.

It was the uncanny impression that he was studying her.

His body was tense. Bulky with muscle beneath the overcoat. A coat, though it was hot outside and the patio doors were open.

Just a few minutes ago, she'd been annoyed about having a security detail following her around. But at the moment, she figured a bodyguard's presence wouldn't hurt. She texted, asking one of them to come inside.

But the message didn't go through.

For a moment, she was confused, until she noticed she had no service. Was the museum a dead spot? She checked for public Wi-Fi, but no networks came up. Which was even weirder.

But the guy with the neck tattoo had just been on the phone. If he had service, why didn't she?

Immediately, her nerves went to a higher state of alert.

When she looked back toward the exit, the man in the ball cap was gone. Danica breathed out with relief.

False alarm.

West Oaks isn't New York, she thought again, sending off another message to her security so they wouldn't freak out.

"Should we head to dinner early?" Lindley asked. "I have the latest design renderings for the renovations, and I have the feeling we'll want some cocktails to celebrate. I can drive us."

"That would be great. I just have to let my security detail know."

Danica checked her phone again. Her messages to the security team had finally gone through. She told them she was heading out, and they agreed to meet her by the museum's back entrance.

Lindley grabbed her things from her office, and Anderson closed up the patio doors.

They went out the back exit into the employee parking lot.

Danica glanced around. "My security team should drive up any minute." In fact, she was surprised they hadn't beaten her here.

Then the sound of metal crashing into metal cut through the air.

Lindley grabbed Danica's arm. "Oh my god. That sounded like a car accident."

Danica's eyes searched frantically for the Range Rover, but she couldn't see the main road from here.

Tires screeched. A white SUV with dark tinted windows came into view, accelerating down the narrow side street.

Something bad was happening. She felt it in her gut.

Danica pushed Lindley and Anderson back toward the museum. "We need to get back inside. *Now.*"

Lindley kept looking from Danica to the approaching SUV and back again. "But—"

They weren't moving fast enough. "Come on. *Hurry.*" Danica's hand dove into her purse, closing around her canister of pepper spray.

Anderson tried to unlock the door to get back into the museum. His hands were shaking, and he dropped the keys.

She heard the revving of an engine right behind them. Brakes squealed. As she turned, a door opened.

A face in a ski mask reared out of the shadowy interior.

Danica didn't think. Didn't hesitate.

She aimed her pepper spray at the now-open doorway of the SUV, hit the trigger, and unleashed a jet into the person's eyes.

The guy screamed, shielding his face.

"Let's go!" Danica grabbed Lindley's arm and pulled the woman away from the SUV. "Anderson, come on!"

She'd drilled kidnapping attempts before. That had to be what they wanted—to get her into the car. But she'd never thought this would actually happen. Her heart felt like it was choking her, beating wildly at the base of her throat.

Danica pushed through the row of decorative hedges, ignoring the scrape of the branches, and emerged on the patio.

The engine revved. The car was probably rounding the building, trying to cut them off via the road on the other side.

Danica looked frantically for a means of escape. They had to get away from the street. That meant going toward the beach.

Dragging Lindley along with her, she raced down the patio steps and into the sand.

"Where are we going?" Anderson asked.

"The water." They'd swim to get away if they had to. Anything to make it harder for those men to get her into the SUV. "Get rid of your shoes."

"My *shoes*?" Anderson whined. "They're Ferragamo."

"Then I wouldn't recommend getting them wet."

Anderson toed off his loafers. Lindley had already lost her stilettos during their run, and her face was streaked with tears.

As soon as they splashed into the surf, the wail of sirens reached her ears.

Danica looked back and saw no sign of the white SUV. Anderson's deep tan had gone pale. Lindley seemed like she was in a daze.

A wave swelled, soaking their pants to the knees.

Danica put her arm around the other woman as police vehicles roared down Ocean Lane. And finally, her lungs relaxed enough to take a full breath.

Chapter Two

*N*oah Vandermeer tightened the knot on his neck tie. He cast a longing glance across the Bennett Security workroom, where morning sun glinted across the ocean through the windows. If not for his boss's urgent call half an hour ago, Noah would still be out there right now, getting a nice runner's high.

Instead, he was on his way to woo some mysterious new client. At least he looked damn good in this suit.

Max Bennett strode toward his desk. "Aren't you ready yet?"

"I thought I was. But you said I should look professional. You look *fancy*."

Max was dressed in a suit, too, but he'd opted for a three piece Noah recognized as a Tom Ford and a silk tie. Bringing out the big guns, apparently. Who the heck was this client?

"What?" Max looked down at himself. "This is how I dress."

Right. "I could've worn something nicer if you'd told me." Well, *nicer* wasn't the right word. More expensive.

"It's not a competition, Vandermeer. Enough preening. We can't be late."

Noah grabbed the paper bag sitting on his desk. Most body-guards didn't have an assigned space in the workroom, but as a captain, he had administrative duties to deal with. "Want a bagel? I picked them up on my way in."

"Do you have any idea how many carbs that would be?"

"Hey, I ran five miles this morning. I would've kept going if you hadn't called me in." Noah pulled off a chunk and took a bite. Salmon cream cheese on pumpernickel. Delicious.

Devon Whitestone met them by the elevators, his gray suit perfectly squared away, shoes shined. He was only a few months out of the army and was one of the more uptight Rangers Noah had ever met. Though Devon had loosened up a bit since meeting his girlfriend.

Noah held out the paper bag. "Bagel? I offered it to Max, but he's watching his figure."

"Can't blame him. Metabolism drops in old age." The paper crinkled as Devon grabbed one.

"Fuck you both. I'm only thirty-five."

And Noah wasn't far behind, but he didn't point that out. Age snuck up on you and bit you in the ass like everything else. Nothing lasted forever. *Especially* the best stuff.

But he was going to enjoy the good times while he could. Noah took another bite of his bagel.

The three of them got into the elevator.

"Eat fast," Max said. "I don't want crumbs on my leather seats. And check your teeth for poppyseeds and shit before we go into the meeting."

Noah snickered, shaking his head. It was funny when Max got this worked up. "Seems like you're nervous about getting this contract, Bennett. Who's it for? Some celebrity?"

"I don't know for certain. But I have a few guesses."

"Such as?"

"There was an incident at the natural history museum yesterday."

"I heard about that," Devon chimed in. "Billionaire's daughter almost kidnapped in broad daylight."

Billionaire's daughter? That description made him think,

automatically, of a certain name. A certain someone he'd used to know. But Noah hadn't seen her in West Oaks in years.

All the same, a pang hit him square in the chest. Always did, whenever he thought of her.

Max nodded. "I got the call this morning from a concierge service. They keep their clients anonymous. They said someone needs a bodyguard team urgently, and price was no object. Preference for ex-special forces."

"No wonder." A brazen kidnapping wasn't the kind of thing that happened here every day. But West Oaks had its share of one-percenters, many with second homes, who traveled in and out of the seaside town. They provided Bennett Security with ample business.

The elevator doors slid open on the lower level, and they walked toward Max's black Lexus.

"I can see why you're trying to put the best face of Bennett Security forward." Noah gestured at himself, and Max snorted.

"Right. Or maybe Tanner didn't answer when I called him first. When somebody wants a bodyguard, they usually picture a giant who benches 700 pounds. Like him. I had to bring you and Devon both to make up for it."

Noah laughed. "Oh, come on. Nobody benches 700 pounds."

"We know *you* definitely don't."

Max liked to give Noah shit for being the "lesser" of the two former Navy SEALs on their bodyguard team. Noah and Tanner were as tight as brothers. And although Noah looked small in comparison to his co-captain, he was still six-one and over 200 pounds of lean muscle. He didn't have any trouble reaching things on the top shelf.

"Then it's too bad Tanner didn't answer the phone," Noah said. "I could be eating my breakfast in peace after finishing my run." He slid into the shotgun seat beside Max, while Devon got into the back.

Joking aside, he didn't mind working weekends. Unlike

Devon or Max, he didn't have a significant other taking up his time.

Noah preferred having a relationship to dating around. He enjoyed getting to know someone, finding out what made her laugh. What made her moan. But unlike some of his teammates, he wasn't a romantic. Once upon a time, he'd believed in "forever," but the universe had only laughed.

"We don't *need* this contract," Max said as he drove, one hand resting casually on the steering wheel. "But what can I say? I'm a competitive bastard. And so are you, Vandermeer."

This was true. Noah and Max got their motivations from very different places. But they both liked to win.

Sometimes, Noah wished he could give a shit about starting companies or running a business empire, like Max did. Max was a former Green Beret who'd started Bennett Security from nothing and grown it into a top security company in Southern California, serving an elite clientele and consulting with law enforcement.

But Noah had seen firsthand that leading a successful corporation and making gobs of money didn't guarantee happiness. Neither did being in love. His parents were case in point. But he had experience of his own.

Noah had been in love twice in his life. First, with a girl. Then, it was a job.

Both times, Noah had gotten his heart broken.

It was far wiser not to fall in love at all. Better to make peace with whatever you had, safe in the knowledge that you could bear to lose it.

They pulled into a nondescript office building. A guard took their IDs, wrote down their license plate, called to check they were on the list, and then *finally* waved them into the garage. More armed guards watched as they parked.

"You sure they need more security?" Noah muttered. "Looks like they've got plenty."

"But we do our job with a smile. Makes all the difference." Max said this with a sardonic frown.

They got out of the car, and a man with a salt-and-pepper flat top came over to meet them. He looked like he could play a four-star general on TV.

"Max Bennett? I'm Blake Halston, chief of security for the family. Formerly with the 7th Special Forces Group."

Family? Noah thought. What family was Halston talking about?

Max turned on the charm, flashing his grin as they shook. "I was with the seventh as well."

Fellow Green Berets. A good sign for getting this contract, Noah figured.

"Though a few decades apart, obviously?" Blake said with a chuckle.

"I wasn't going to point that out."

Blake gestured for them to follow, and they got into an elevator. "We can head straight up. Mr. Foster-Grant is ready for you."

The elevator doors slid closed just as Noah felt the urge to bolt.

Foster-Grant?

Oh, fuck.

No, no, no.

Danica.

His heart pounded like it was repeating her name. *Danica. Danica.* His chest felt like a vise had closed around it.

Had she been the target of the kidnapping attempt? Had she been hurt? Was she *here*, in this building, right now?

He'd instantly gone into protective mode, wanting to demand answers though he had no right. Not as far as Danica was concerned. If anything, her day would get even harder if she had to see him.

I have to get out of here.

Blake and Max were chatting loudly at the front of the elevator about their army days.

Noah leaned over to Devon. "I can't be here."

"What? Why?"

"Nobody said who the client was. I…I know this family."

Devon's eyes widened. "You know William Foster-Grant? The billionaire?"

Somewhere in the top ten richest people in the world, depending on the day and the stock market. "We were neighbors. I used to be best friends with his son, Soren."

"Used to?"

It was too complicated to explain in the time they had. Which was minutes. Maybe just seconds.

Noah glanced at the two men in front of them, sweat breaking out over his skin. Bad guys with AK-47s didn't faze him, but it had been over twelve years since he'd last seen her. His heart wasn't ready. *Especially* because she wouldn't want him anywhere near her.

The elevator stopped, and the doors opened. Blake stepped out, followed by Max.

Their boss glanced back and noticed them hesitating. His gaze was stern. *What the hell are you doing?*

"Come on, guys. Hop to it."

The elevator doors were starting to close. Noah had no choice but to get out alongside Devon. But he pulled his boss toward him and lowered his voice even more.

"Trust me, the Foster-Grants won't want me in that meeting. I need to go."

Blake had turned around. "Gentlemen? Something wrong?"

Max's eyes locked with Noah's for a moment before he faced Blake and spoke, an easy smile returning to his face. "Not at all. It seems an emergency has come up with another client, and Noah's going to handle it. I apologize. It'll just be Devon and me."

Blake nodded brusquely, and they resumed their path down the hallway.

Noah exhaled. That had been close.

He spun around and hit the elevator button. He'd find a coffee shop nearby to wait. Just as long as he was away from this building and from anyone named Foster-Grant.

But when the elevator dinged and the doors opened again, a vision from Noah's past stood inside.

His ex-best friend's older sister. The only girl he'd ever loved.

And now, here she was, standing in front of him.

His heart started up its rapid-fire chorus again.

Danica.

She was in a loose top and jeans, looking down at her phone. Effortlessly beautiful, as she'd always been.

Immediately, his mind called up his last memory of her.

His mouth on hers. Arms around her waist. Promises about when they'd see each other again.

I'll be thinking of you until then, she'd said. *Every second.*

His most intense feelings for her had faded a long time ago, but the last thing he wanted was to upset her. Could he disappear into the walls somehow? Evaporate into the air?

But by then, she was already looking up.

Danica froze. For a moment, the two of them just stared.

She looked confused, like she was trying to place him. Then recognition hit, and shock overwhelmed her features.

"*Noah?*"

Sweat rolled down his sides. "Danica. Wow. It's been a while. How are you?"

Maybe she'd play along. Pretend this was a normal, chance meeting between old acquaintances and not completely excruciating.

But no such luck. She was still gaping at him. "What are you... Why are you here? *How* are you here?"

"I was just leaving." He cleared his throat. "Are you getting out on this floor? Or going down?"

She looked around as if just remembering where she was. "I'm going down. Yeah."

"Okay. So am I."

Danica shuffled to the side as Noah got on the elevator. He felt the skin at his neck jumping as his pulse jack-hammered.

The car started moving. His eyes watered, unblinking,

watching the numbers tick slowly down. Noah was holding his breath, trying not to breathe in her scent.

Jasmine, like the scent of summer in the hills.

Had the elevator been this slow before? Or had time itself literally stopped, stranding him here?

"Could you answer my question?" Her voice was careful and even. "What are you doing here? The entire building belongs to my dad, so don't act like it's a coincidence."

He took a breath, and jasmine filled his nose.

"I work for Bennett Security. My boss got a call about someone needing bodyguards."

"Um, yeah. I was almost kidnapped yesterday."

"I'm so sorry. That must've been terrible."

She wiped a hand over her face. She looked almost the same. Dark hair framed her delicate features. Her cheekbones were more prominent, and shadows lay beneath her eyes. That made him worry about how she was doing.

Which he had no right to do.

"It sucked," she said. "But honestly? Right now, I'm just trying to get used to the fact that you're here."

"I didn't know you were the client. If I had, I never would have presumed."

She looked over at him, but he didn't see anger. She'd never been afraid to hold eye contact. Yet that didn't mean she was easy to read. This woman had more than one master's degree from Ivy League schools. No wonder she was leading a major nonprofit these days, making waves in the media and changing the world.

The elevator doors had opened on the ground floor. Danica still hadn't said anything. Those mesmerizing gray eyes seemed to be studying him, deliberating.

Noah stepped out into the lobby, then turned back to face her. "I apologize again. We have a great team at Bennett Security, and I promise they will take very good care of you. You won't have to see me again." He smiled with his lips closed, planning to head toward the nearest exit.

But Danica hurried after him, placing her hand on his elbow. "Wait a second. That's all you have to say to me? Seriously?"

"What else do you want me to say?"

"You could explain what the hell happened."

His brows knit. "You mean, with Soren?" Didn't she already know?

Annoyance crossed her features. "You're a dumbass, you know that?"

Noah couldn't help laughing. The front desk security guard looked over.

Danica huffed. "Come on. We need to talk."

She pulled him by the arm down a hallway. Her grip was firm and brooked no argument. But if she wanted to see him, even just to unleash a tirade? He wasn't about to refuse.

Chapter Three

*N*oah was here. Really here.

Danica had never expected to see him in West Oaks again, or anywhere, really. Even though she'd thought of him often enough.

Noah Vandermeer. She was torn between elation at seeing him and frustration that it had taken this long.

He followed her into her office, and she closed the door. There wasn't much furniture inside yet, just a desk and a small couch. A window overlooked an outdoor courtyard, with palm trees, bushes, and flowering plants creating a tangle of green with bright splashes of color.

Her father owned this building—a recent acquisition, part of some merger or other—and she was just borrowing the space.

"You can sit, if you want," she said.

They both remained standing. Noah tucked his hands into his pants pockets, his shoulders tense in his jacket like he was ready to flee.

"I'm not going to attack the minute you let down your guard. If that's what you're worried about."

"You *did* just call me a dumbass."

"If you can't guess why, then you *are* a dumbass."

Noah tilted his head, the corner of his mouth lifting, and there was that dimple. She felt a tug in her stomach.

Where to even start with this man?

There was too much history to unravel between them. Danica liked to be prepared, and she hadn't remotely been ready to see him again.

But that didn't mean the surprise was unwelcome, as he seemed to assume.

There were questions she wanted answered, but that could wait until the ground wasn't shifting beneath her. Between the kidnapping attempt yesterday and seeing Noah again, she'd had too many shocks in a short period.

Danica leaned against the wall. Her knees felt weak, and she didn't want Noah to notice. In her family, weakness was something you kept to yourself.

"So you're a bodyguard now? I didn't even realize you were still in West Oaks." This wasn't entirely accurate. But she hadn't known for sure.

"Came back after I left the Navy. I was a SEAL."

"I know. That was what you'd always wanted."

Danica had kept in touch with Mrs. Vandermeer, who'd sent a picture of him in his dress whites at his Trident pin ceremony. Danica had been proud of Noah. Worried for him. She'd *ached* for him.

But he'd been nothing to her then. Just a neighbor. Someone she'd used to know.

"You look different," she said. "I mean, it's been a long time, so of course you would."

Despite the new lines around his eyes and mouth, he still had that boyish charm. Light brown hair parted to the side. Clean-cut and preppy, with that mischievous dimple when he smiled, hinting that he could break the rules when he wanted. A few freckles on his nose from the sun, though more than in her memory.

But he must've grown two or three inches and gained thirty or forty pounds of muscle since his sophomore year of college.

He looked...wow. Good was an understatement. He'd gone from boy scout to Captain America.

"You look the same," he said. "Mostly."

She remembered watching him at swim meets when he and Soren had been on the same competitive team. Her younger brother's best friend. That tiny Speedo, hugging Noah's ass.

Her skin heated as she pictured it, then imagined how well he would fill out that swimsuit now.

Danica started to laugh. Which was cathartic, considering what her last twenty-four hours had been like.

"What's so funny?"

"Nothing. I'm wired. Didn't sleep much last night."

"I can imagine. Do you want to talk about what happened yesterday?"

She pushed out a breath. This was a topic she could handle. She'd retold this story a dozen times at least, so it was getting easier.

"I'd planned to meet the director of the natural history museum, Lindley Colter, at six o'clock yesterday evening. But when my flight landed, I decided at the last minute to head to the museum early."

"Very spontaneous. The Danica I remember would never have changed her schedule."

She rolled her eyes. "I'm a little more flexible now." Though he was right. She liked to keep a strict routine. Danica needed that structure to keep herself focused and productive. Otherwise, she'd fall behind on her work.

Every morning, she woke up early for yoga, went on her run, then went over that day's agenda while she had coffee. She had playlists to match every task and every mood, whether she needed to concentrate or kick back.

Reuniting with your brother's ex-friend, who you fell for one summer and then never saw again...

Yeah, she needed a playlist for that.

"I wanted to visit the museum while it was open. To get a feel for it, since I'd never seen it in person."

"You'd just arrived from New York?"

"Yes." So he knew where she was living these days. But it wasn't hard to find out.

For years, Danica hadn't spent much time in California, even though her father still lived primarily in the house in the West Oaks hills. Usually, William came to visit her in Manhattan. And of course, Soren was there, too.

When her dad had told her the West Oaks Natural History Museum was struggling, she'd seen the opportunity to both help out and reconnect with her hometown. *This would be a perfect project for your talents,* her dad had said. *And I've missed having you around.*

"There was a man inside who seemed like he was watching me, and it made me uncomfortable. When I left, I asked my security detail to meet me at the back exit. But that's when the white SUV drove in."

The crash they'd heard had been another car ramming into her bodyguards' Range Rover. It had all been coordinated. One car to cut her off from the security detail, another to grab her. But neither she nor the police had any idea whether that man with the neck tattoo had been involved.

She hugged her elbows, steadying herself. "When the SUV's back door opened, I used my pepper spray. Caught the guy by surprise. Then, I ran."

"Sounds like you were quick on the draw." Noah had been walking closer as she spoke, a look of careful concentration on his face as he listened.

"Good thing. Otherwise, who knows where I'd be right now." She'd seen two men in the back seat, one in the front. Without a doubt, they'd had guns.

But after she, Lindley, and Anderson had run for the beach, the SUV driver must've decided to cut his losses and flee. Same with the hit-and-run vehicle that had targeted her bodyguards. The police had issued alerts on those cars and plates, but the kidnappers had likely abandoned them.

Noah rested his hand on her arm, then let go, which was too

bad. She'd liked that brief touch of warmth, the reassuring weight.

"I remember you and Soren both had anti-kidnapping training when we were in school," he said.

Danica nodded. "Yeah. Joys of being our father's kids. For the last several years, I've been taking martial arts classes. Jiu-jitsu and Krav Maga. I wanted to learn how to fight."

"Those kidnappers didn't know what they were in for."

"Maybe."

She didn't tell Noah that he'd inspired her. After he'd become a SEAL, she'd thought of him often. How brave he was.

"You're tougher than most," Noah said. "I saw that TV interview last year."

"You did?" She groaned.

There'd been a particular morning show where the TV hosts loved to bring on guests with opposing views. She'd gotten drawn into an argument, and the clips of her biting responses had made the rounds on national news. Since then, she'd had a much higher profile, going from a fixture of New York gossip rags to *People Magazine* and *US Weekly*. Privacy was becoming a luxury, harder and harder to find.

Noah's smile broadened. "It was hard to miss. But I tend to pay attention when I see your name."

"After all this time?"

"It's been a while, but I never stopped thinking about you," he said softly.

Noah touched his lower lip, and she wondered if he was remembering what had happened between them all those years ago.

That kiss.

Her breath caught in her chest.

"Do you think they wanted ransom money?" Noah asked.

She forced her mind back to the present. "That seems most likely. But I don't know." She'd been going over each detail in her head since last night. So far, the picture wasn't clear. Who they were, what they were really after.

"And your father decided to hire new bodyguards for you? What about the team with you yesterday?"

"They're back to running regular security for my father's house. Dad wants me to have bodyguards with special forces military training. Only the best, like you." She rolled her eyes. "I'm supposed to meet the finalists later to make a decision."

Danica had promised she'd keep her new detail close while she was in West Oaks. After her trip was finished, their chief of security would assess whether or not the threat was bigger. She certainly hoped not.

"Bennett Security *is* the best," Noah said. "I hope we make the list. But I assume your father won't be happy about me working there."

She bit her lip. It was tough to say. William wasn't the type to get involved in his children's dramas. But her father also valued loyalty over nearly everything else.

Noah pressed his lips together. "And then there's Soren."

She had a better idea of how her brother would react. He despised Noah. He'd claimed that Noah had tried to ruin his life out of jealousy, which she didn't really believe. But the true story was less clear because Noah had never told her. She only knew her brother's side, plus the pieces the media had reported in the wake of the scandal.

"Soren doesn't make my decisions for me."

"Dani, I've never wanted to come between you and your brother. That's why you and I...cut things off."

She huffed a laugh. "You make it sound like it was a mutual agreement. But you didn't even give me a chance. Do you have any idea how that felt?"

"I tried. I wanted to explain."

"Months later." She'd ignored his voicemail because she'd been too pissed by then. "But here's your chance. You can tell me right now."

He opened his mouth. And nothing came out.

The man was unbelievable.

"Really? You've got nothing?"

"You know most of it," he said. "As for what the media left out, I don't see the point of dredging it all up."

Danica walked over to her desk and put her hands down on the surface. She didn't want to be angry at him over ancient history. But she was so sick of the people in her life not telling her the truth.

Especially the *men* in her life.

"I could've handled things better," Noah said. "But I can't change what happened. Right now, my biggest concern is your safety. I think Bennett Security is the best company to protect you, but only if my history with you won't be an issue."

Danica turned around. "Are we really talking about Bennett Security protecting me? Or you, specifically, being my bodyguard?"

Noah held her gaze. Tingles spread through her limbs. She was definitely not supposed to be thinking about how Noah's lips had felt against hers. The way his fingers had sifted through her hair, while his other hand had pressed into her lower back. The eager strokes of his tongue.

She'd had a lot of kisses since then. Fallen in and out of love. So why did that one kiss with Noah hold such a prominent place in her memory?

Maybe because they'd never gotten to find out where it would lead.

Before Noah could answer, his phone buzzed. He looked at it. "Shit. That's Devon, my teammate. I need to go."

"Oh." Now that he was here, she realized she didn't want him to go so soon.

Even if what had happened between them was long in the past, and they couldn't go back to change any of it, she'd missed him.

"Maybe we can finish this conversation another time," she said. *If you can be honest with me.*

He smiled, his dimple winking. "I hope we'll get the chance."

Chapter Four

*N*oah met Devon and Max in the parking garage. They piled into the Lexus. "How'd it go?" Noah asked.

"Started out fine," Max said. "I gave Foster-Grant our pitch. He was amazingly calm, considering his daughter was almost kidnapped yesterday."

That didn't surprise Noah. When he and Soren had been friends, Noah had almost never seen William. He'd been a hands-off kind of parent. But William's exploits as a ruthless corporate raider were the stuff of legend.

Max tapped his fingers against the steering wheel. "Then I told him you work for me, since you'd said you knew the family, and he was going to find out eventually. A man like him doesn't like being caught off guard."

"And?"

"Things wrapped up very quickly after that. He was eager to get us out of his office."

Noah closed his eyes. Damn.

According to his reputation, William Foster-Grant wasn't the forgiving sort. But Noah had still hoped Bennett might get the contract. He cared less about their company's bottom line than about Danica's safety.

Devon leaned forward from the back seat. "How'd you piss off the guy so much?"

"It happened when I was in college. Soren, his son, thinks I betrayed him. And I guess I did."

"What did you do?" Devon asked. "Sleep with Soren's sister?"

Max glanced back, his scowl a clear warning. Max was still a tad sensitive about that subject, even though Devon and Max's sister Aurora were madly in love and disgustingly happy together.

"No. Nothing like that." Soren didn't know that Noah had kissed Danica. If only that had been the extent of their rift— walking in on Noah and Danica making out. Or even naked together, if they'd had the chance. Soren would've been upset, to say the least. But he probably would've gotten over it.

"Did you steal his girlfriend?"

"God, no. You think I'd do that?"

Devon shrugged. "People make mistakes."

Noah would never have stolen Soren's girlfriend. It was unthinkable. Yet what he'd done? Probably worse, from Soren's perspective at least.

"You know what?" Max said. "It doesn't matter. We know you and your level of integrity. Whatever went down, we're on your side. And if William Foster-Grant still has a bug up his ass about it, I'm good with not taking his money."

Noah leaned his elbow on the passenger door. The Bennett Security building was up ahead on the rocky part of the coast. Waves crashed into the shoreline.

"I'd feel the same if I knew Danica was being taken care of," Noah said.

"I hate to say it, but you guys aren't the only decent body-guards in Southern California. I think she'll be fine." Max loosened his tie.

~

NOAH PARKED by the driveway to his dad's underground garage and walked to the house's back door.

There was no answer when he rang the bell, so he let himself in. "Hey, it's me. Anyone home?"

He wanted to be sure to give his grandpa warning. Otherwise, it was entirely possible Noah would catch Gramps and Ginger in some sort of compromising position. Not something he wanted to witness.

Ginger swept into the hall wearing a flowing silk robe. "I thought I heard the door. It's good to see you, darling boy. So handsome. Did you dress just up for me?" She kissed him on each cheek.

"Client meeting for work."

"Did you see your grandfather on the way in?" She had just a hint of a French Canadian accent.

"Nope. I was going to ask where he was."

"I suppose he's still out hitting his golf balls. Well, have a seat. What can I get you? I was just thinking of opening a bottle of Blanc de Blancs."

Noah smiled. Ginger was as over-the-top as an old-fashioned movie star, and she had the wavy blond hair to match. "I'm fine. But don't let me stop you."

"When have I ever?"

Noah's grandfather had married Ginger two years ago after a whirlwind romance. The two had met at the West Oaks country club. Ginger was originally from Montreal, but she'd been a fixture in the social circles of Southern California since her youth. She was widowed once, divorced twice, a semi-retired professional dancer. At sixty-eight, she was junior to his grandpa's eighty-five years.

The two seemed to be crazy about each other, and despite his cynicism, Noah was thrilled for his grandfather. He hoped their marriage would beat the odds and work out.

Ginger had quite the real estate portfolio, including condos up and down the coast. But she and Gramps preferred staying at the Vandermeer house these days, partly because it was closer to the golf course, and partly because there was nobody else here.

Noah's parents were divorced, both living elsewhere with their new spouses. He had no siblings.

Ginger popped the cork. Vapor rose from the neck of the champagne bottle. "Would you like lunch? It's just going to be a salad and those little spinach triangle things your grandfather likes from the freezer section. Not fine dining, I'm afraid."

He wasn't picky. "Sounds good to me. I know I'm earlier than usual. My boss was meeting with William Foster-Grant."

Ginger put a hand to her chest. "My goodness, does it have anything to do with his daughter, Danica? I saw on the news what happened. Just wretched, what this town's coming to these days. Murders and kidnappings and who knows what else."

"It was about Danica. Yeah." He wasn't trying to be mysterious, but he didn't want this to become fodder for gossip later. He liked Ginger, but her love of sparkling conversation rivaled her love of champagne.

"Are you going to be her bodyguard?"

"No. Not me."

She stuck out her lower lip. "That's too bad. It would've been romantic, don't you think? She's stunning."

"She is." A smile snuck onto his face, despite the disappointment he was feeling. "Heard anything about whether Danica's staying with her father?"

"I did hear a rumor." Ginger's expression turned conspiratorial. "Karen in my bridge club was complaining about work trucks clogging up the road just this past week. Right in front of the Foster-Grant house. So, draw your conclusions."

Noah nodded, like this was just mildly interesting.

Ginger didn't know that Noah had once been friends with the Foster-Grants. But his grandpa would remember the drama of his falling out with Soren. How depressed Noah had been for months afterward. Losing Soren and Danica at the same time. It had been rough.

He watched the bubbles popping in her glass of champagne. "Do you have any regrets, Gigi?"

She tipped her head thoughtfully. "One. That I didn't go on that weekend getaway with John Stamos back in 1993. What a beautiful man."

"I'm being serious."

"As am I." She looked offended. "But all right, let's hear yours. You're feeling philosophical about *something*, and I'm ready to listen."

He'd never really talked with anyone about this. His mom and dad and grandfather knew the general landscape, but not the details. They didn't know how he'd agonized over what had happened.

"Just thinking about some things that went down in college. I lost my best friend."

"That's awful. Why?"

"I found out he was part of a cheating ring." They'd been getting tests early, distributing them to athletes who'd needed a boost to their grades to stay eligible. If the NCAA had found out, their school's teams would've been penalized. Not to mention the fact that it was just *wrong*.

"I confronted him. Told him to stop, and he wouldn't. Finally, I went to our swim coach."

Ginger sucked in a breath. "That must've been a difficult choice."

"You have no idea." Then, the investigation had blown up so much bigger than Noah could ever have expected.

Soren and his new friends hadn't just been trading tests to athletes all over the school. Whenever the tests hadn't been enough, they'd bribed professors to change grades. Bribed school administrators to look the other way.

When the truth had come out, people had gotten *arrested*.

The national media had swarmed, creating a frenzy around the scandal. The fact that the ringleader was a billionaire's son only made the outcry worse. Noah was thankful his name had stayed out of it.

The Foster-Grants had hired the best attorneys, but even his father's money couldn't shield Soren entirely. Soren had ended up pleading guilty and receiving a slap on the wrist. Probation instead of a sentence to federal prison. But he'd gotten kicked out of school.

"Did you try to talk to him afterward?" Ginger asked.

"No. Our friendship was over."

Noah had known his friend could be reckless. Soren had been an asshole about some things. But they'd had so many good times together before that. Laughing, supporting one another.

Afterward, Noah had assumed Danica would never forgive him, so he hadn't tried to explain his side of things. And by the time he'd finally decided to reach out? She'd moved on.

Ginger squeezed his arm. "I'm sorry. Do you wish you'd chosen differently?"

"I don't. I did the right thing. But I wish there'd been another way to handle it." Some way that could've preserved Noah's chance with Danica.

He should've tried harder to talk to her. Shouldn't have let so much time go by.

Or maybe that wouldn't have made any difference, either. Something else would've gotten in the way. It was impossible to know.

"And this is about the Foster-Grants?"

He nodded. "You saw the news reports? There were a lot of stories about the scandal when it happened."

"I can't stand the news, darling. But I've always been able to read men like the Sunday paper, and I knew there had to be a reason you were thinking of this now. It's never too late to fix things. Unless, of course, we're talking about John Stamos and me. That'll never happen. I love your grandfather too much."

Noah laughed and gave her a hug. "Thanks, Gigi. You're one of a kind."

"I know, dear boy. I know."

Chapter Five

*D*anica tried to finish the spreadsheet she'd been reviewing. But her eyes stung with exhaustion. The numbers were starting to blur. And the more tired she got, the more a feeling of panic was creeping up on her, like some creature out of the shadows.

She'd been trying very hard for the last day to remain stoic. Especially in front of her father and Blake and all those bodyguards. In front of *Noah*. Danica hated to look weak or scared.

But she *was* scared. Terrified. So fucking afraid that her body seemed to vibrate from the constant stress of it.

Danica's father had nixed Bennett Security from his list, and she'd decided not to fight the issue. Her history with Noah made things too complicated. But she would've welcomed the distraction of his presence right now.

Her new bodyguard was right down the hall, yet this wing of her father's house felt eerily empty. Like Danica was exposed, and anyone could sneak in and find her.

Last night, she'd woken in sheer terror from a nightmare, covered in sweat. She'd been dreaming of the man at the museum. The way he'd been watching her. The bulky coat. The phone conversation he'd had just before he left.

Had he been looking for her? Did he have something to do with the kidnapping?

How could they possibly have known she'd be at the museum at that particular time?

In her nightmare, the man's eyes had glowed like two red dots. And his neck tattoo had been writhing. Alive.

In reality, she'd only gotten a brief glimpse of the ink. But it pulled at some corner of her subconscious.

What was it about that tattoo that bothered her so much?

Danica grabbed a sheet of notepaper and a pencil. She tried sketching what she remembered. The tattoo had depicted a bird, mostly in black, but there might've been a splash or two of color.

And there'd been something strange about the bird's neck. It had been curved, almost like a snake. She tried drawing it, but it was missing something.

The man's tattoo had been symmetrical.

She added another curved neck facing the opposite side. *Yes.* That was it. A bird with two heads.

An eagle.

Danica had seen this kind of bird before.

She grabbed her laptop and opened the internet browser. *Two-headed eagle*, she typed. Websites and images came up. She clicked on one.

A symbol used throughout history, often by empires, she read, *representing power.*

Danica kept working on her drawing, filling it out as best she could. She even dug around in her desk until she found a set of colored pencils and added red to the beaks and yellow to the talons. Finally she sat back, staring at it.

A shudder ran through her.

She'd seen that eagle tattoo before this trip. Not in some history book or online, but in person.

~

IT WAS LATE, and the lights in the hallways were dimmed. With her drawing in hand, Danica left her room.

Rosalee Consuelo, her new head bodyguard, looked up from her post as Danica neared. "Evening, Ms. Foster-Grant."

"Hi, Rosalee. Just going downstairs to my father's office." She was hoping her dad might recognize the eagle design and tell her where she'd seen it before. William's brain was like a trap for small details like that.

"No need to inform me. I'll follow at a distance."

Danica gave her a polite smile. "I'm not used to having a bodyguard with me 24-7." She started toward the stairs, then turned back. "It's all right if I call you Rosalee?"

"Certainly. Though Rosie is better. That's what my friends call me."

"Perfect. Then you should call me Dani."

"I can try."

She and her father had decided to hire a company recommended by their chief of security, a massive firm called Valoris. Her brother had used Valoris before in New York, and Soren had spoken highly of them.

While her dad's regular, full-time guards would continue to secure the house itself, Valoris bodyguards would be protecting Danica and her father wherever they went.

But Danica had insisted on choosing her own head bodyguard from among Valoris's ranks. After reading through dozens of ex-military profiles, Danica had chosen Rosie.

She was a former Marine. Not special forces, but she had expertise in multiple forms of combat. Plus, Rosie worked among men, so she had to be that much tougher to earn respect.

Downstairs, Danica turned down the hallway that led to her father's office. Rosie stationed herself there at the mouth of the hall.

William's door was cracked open. The light was on inside. As she approached, she heard voices murmuring. She wondered if her father and Blake were discussing the new security arrangements.

But when she got close enough to see into the room, she didn't find their security chief.

Instead, a woman named Tori was bent over the desk, whispering with William.

Tori was their chief of security's new assistant. A pixie cut flattered her delicate bone structure.

William put his hand on Tori's arm. Then he touched her cheek, and the intimacy in the gesture was unmistakable.

Danica startled back, feeling like she shouldn't be watching this.

It wasn't that she minded her dad having a girlfriend. But Tori was younger than Danica herself. Given the age difference, she couldn't blame her father for keeping this affair private.

But it was just one more sign that she was a stranger here.

Danica waited in the hall until Tori emerged. The assistant turned the opposite way down the hall without seeing her.

After Tori's footsteps had receded, Danica knocked on her father's door and went inside. "Dad?"

He looked up, hitting something on his keyboard. Like he was closing a window on his computer screen. "How are you faring?"

"Not bad. Trying to look forward." One of her father's frequent sayings. *Keep looking forward, Danica. Let go of everything else.* "You and I haven't had much chance to talk since I arrived, with everything that's been going on," she said. "Anything new with you?"

A wrinkle sank between his brows. "New?"

"Just…in your life."

"I'm not sure what you're asking."

So he wasn't going to tell her about Tori. Maybe it wasn't serious. More likely, he didn't want Danica to know.

Her father didn't owe her a play-by-play on his love life, nor did she want one. But still, the distance between Danica and her father had only seemed greater since she'd returned to West Oaks, rather than less.

He glanced at his computer screen. "It's late. Could we finish this chat tomorrow?"

"Hold on, there's something else I wanted to ask you." She unfolded the drawing and held it out. "Have you seen this before?"

William leaned forward and accepted the paper. He stared hard at it.

Was that a flash of recognition in his eyes?

"What am I looking at?"

"Remember how I told you about the man inside the history museum, the one who seemed suspicious? He had this tattoo on his neck. I think I've seen it somewhere before, and I thought maybe you'd know."

Again, her father studied the drawing, and again, she had the sense that he saw something there. Something meaningful.

But he shook his head. "I'm sorry, Danica. It's not ringing any bells."

"You're sure?"

"Completely."

She accepted the paper back.

"You should be resting or focusing on your own work," her father said. "Leave the investigation to Blake and the police." His tone was dismissive.

"But wouldn't you want to be involved? If you were in my position?"

"I'd let the experts do what they do best."

"Not sure I believe that."

William shrugged, settling back in his chair. "This has been a terrible ordeal for you. But I'm thankful you were here in West Oaks when it happened. Blake and I will make sure that you're safe. You don't need to worry beyond that."

As she left his office, her uneasiness had only grown.

Had he recognized the tattoo? Or not?

The museum project had been her father's idea. Supposedly, to allow them to spend more time together. To heal the distance that had expanded between them over the years since her mom had died.

If her dad hadn't invited her back to West Oaks to open up about his life, then why did he even care that she was here?

Chapter Six

Noah's sneakers pounded into the asphalt. It was his favorite time of day to run, just as the first rays of sun were lighting up the sky. Trees and hedges bordered the road, sheltering the houses beyond from view. Far below the edges of the cliffs, the ocean was calm. A few seagulls glided by overhead.

Last night, after dinner with Gramps and Ginger, he'd decided to stay over. A morning run in the hills had sounded appealing. It was Sunday, and he had no other plans for the day. Work or otherwise.

Most of the time, he took his morning runs on the path by the beach. His condo was in a tall building on Ocean Lane, and he liked seeing the town wake up at the start of each day.

But during the periods he'd been deployed overseas and had thought of home, these views in the hills had always come first to mind. How peaceful the world seemed on mornings like these.

Danica had used to run every morning, just like him. In fact, they'd been running partners for a few weeks one fateful summer.

And though he'd been doing his utmost not to think about her since their conversation yesterday, he'd failed miserably.

He needed to check on her, make sure she was safe.

Noah's usual running path took him past the Foster-Grant

property. How would her father and her security team react if he just strolled up and knocked on their front door? If he even got past the gate.

This would've been much easier if he had her current phone number.

His speed increased as he neared Danica's house, his breaths rhythmic. His back twinged slightly in protest, and as usual, he ignored the discomfort.

Noah slowed at the gated entrance to the Foster-Grants' driveway. There wasn't a soul around except for a guard inside the kiosk, who glanced up.

"Can I help you, sir?"

"I—"

Then he turned and saw Danica. She'd just jogged to a stop, having come up the opposite side of the road.

"Noah? What're you doing?" A pair of bike shorts and a tank top hugged her curves. Her high ponytail swung back and forth as she tilted her head, and her bangs were pushed back.

Noah's pulse raced much faster than the exercise alone could account for. "Danica. Hey." He held up his hands. "I come in peace."

The guard inside the gate kiosk stepped out. "Do you know this guy, Ms. Foster-Grant?" he asked gruffly.

"I used to." Danica's eyes lit up with amusement as she tugged the Air Pods from her ears. "I don't think he's a threat." She gestured at her running mate, a sturdy woman who so far had remained silent. But from the gun holster she was wearing, Noah guessed this was Danica's new bodyguard.

"This is Rosie Consuelo. She's on my new security team. Rosie, Noah Vandermeer. A...neighbor."

Neighbor. Damn. That was a downgrade. But fair.

Rosie shook his hand. She gave him a polite nod, not revealing whether she'd heard his name before.

"I didn't know you still lived up here," Danica said.

"I don't, most of the time. But I stayed over to visit my grandfather and his wife."

"Oh? What about your mom and dad?"

"They're out of town. But not together. They got divorced."

"I didn't realize. I'm sorry."

"Nothing to be sorry for. They're both fine."

There was an awkward pause. He remembered when it had been effortless to talk to Danica. That summer before his sophomore year of college, they'd spent hours upon hours together. Talking, laughing…flirting.

Danica tucked her ear buds into a small pocket in her shorts, then gestured at the road. "Are you going this way?"

"Do you mind me tagging along with you? Or will your security team try to take me out?"

She smirked, her full lips twisting. "I don't know. You do look like a shifty character. What are your intentions?"

"Entirely innocent. Even if I'm not your bodyguard, I wanted to check on you. As a…neighbor."

"You have a neighborly concern for me?"

"Exactly. Very neighborly."

Her eyes flashed playfully, a glimpse of the Dani he'd used to know, and Noah's body filled with adrenaline.

"All right. You can join me. Let's see if you can keep up." Danica took off.

Noah sprinted to catch her, then fell into step beside her. Rosie lingered a few yards behind them.

"What company did you go with for your new detail?" he said quietly.

"Valoris."

"You're happy with them?"

"I like Rosie. I think she'll be great. And she vouched for the other two bodyguards who're switching off with her."

Then that was good enough for Noah, though he would've preferred that Bennett Security protect her instead. "Any news on the police investigation?" he asked.

"Not much so far. But…" She looked like she was holding something back.

And there was a brief flash of something on her face.

Fear.

"Dani, what's wrong?"

She blinked rapidly, and that glimpse of anxiety was gone. "It's been stressful. All of this. The kidnapping attempt, not knowing what they really wanted."

"Yeah. Of course. Is there anything I can do?"

Danica's eyes remained steady on the road. "How can I trust you if you're not honest with me?"

He felt those words like a punch in the gut.

For a couple of minutes, the only sounds were their footfalls, their breaths, the waves, and the gulls. Then Noah spoke again.

"I want to tell you what happened with Soren. But it doesn't feel like my place." He kept his voice down, not wanting this to be overheard.

"Why the hell not?" Now, her gaze was unflinching. "If you won't tell me, who will?"

A fair point. Back then, he'd wanted to tell her all of it. He'd wanted to ask for her advice. But it would've been impossible and unfair to pull her into it.

A white work van exited out of a neighbor's driveway and coasted slowly past them.

"You already know about the cheating ring at our college," Noah said. "That I reported Soren."

"Yeah, he told me that. And then the bigger scandal came out. The bribery. *Everyone* knows about that."

"But not everyone knows that Soren was sleeping with one of our professors. Apparently, that's how he got the tests he was trading around. And that's how I found out. They were together in the apartment that Soren and I shared, and I walked in on them. She was *married*."

The Foster-Grants had managed to keep those little details private. The affair had been just one small piece of the scandal, and it had been easy enough for them to bury it.

Danica's gait faltered, and she slowed to a walk. "That's unbelievably shitty. But it's almost smaller than what I was imagining."

"What were you imagining?"

"That…" She made a face and spoke the rest of the sentence so fast he could barely catch it. "Soren said you reported him out of petty jealousy. I thought you and Soren were fighting over some girl you both wanted."

"Fighting over some girl?" She'd really thought that? He hated that she'd assumed he could forget her so quickly. "Dani, *you* were the girl I wanted. There was no one else."

There's never been anyone else. Not really.

Flutters spread through his chest at this silent admission.

Two dots of pink appeared on her cheeks. "If I had a ridiculous theory," she said, "it's your fault for not talking to me."

"True. But I was trying to give you space so you didn't get caught in the middle. I thought you'd get in touch if you wanted to."

"But how could I, if I didn't know what really happened?"

They charged up the next hill. By the time they reached the top, they were both breathing heavier. The burst of energy felt good. A way to channel his frustration at his old self for hurting her, though he'd tried to do the opposite.

"You're right. But I'm not sure you realize how much Soren hated me. He said he was going to kill me."

"He *what?*"

"Soren went after me, right in the middle of the quad." Noah didn't feel the need to describe how he'd bloodied Soren's nose and blackened one eye with two vicious jabs. All the fight had gone out of his friend, and Noah had hated seeing it. A hundred witnesses had agreed that Soren threw the first punch.

"Then he said, 'If you ever come near me again, I'll kill you.' Hyperbole, obviously. But his feelings were clear enough."

"Shit. What a mess."

"So you can see why I didn't want to drag you into it."

He hadn't wanted to sully her with all that ugliness. He did regret losing her, even though it probably wouldn't have worked out. As a SEAL, he'd been deployed six months out of the year. And even his periods stateside had been hectic with training.

But he did wonder. Sometimes.

"Will you tell me now what's bothering you?" he asked. "Something about the kidnapping investigation?"

She shook her head as if shaking off a thought. "I'm not sure there's anything to tell. I'm still trying to sort it out in my mind. Might be nothing at all."

"How about I give you my number, and you can let me know when you're ready?"

"All right." Danica took her phone from her shorts pocket. He recited the digits, and she typed them in.

They were nearing his family's house. Noah saw the turn up ahead. He wasn't ready to say goodbye to her yet.

He'd made the mistake of not saying enough before. He wasn't going to do that again. Even if this friendship—if he could call it that—lasted only so long as she was in town, he was glad for it, and he wanted her to know.

"Whatever you need," he said, "all you have to do is ask. I'll make it happen."

"Why? You're just that upstanding and honorable? Navy SEAL swooping in to save the damsel in distress?"

"You're no damsel in distress. And my reasons might be slightly more selfish. I want you to be safe, of course. But I also like being around you, and I'll take any excuse to do it." She'd wanted honesty, so there it was.

Danica pushed out a breath, hands on her slender hips. "Noah. I wish you wouldn't say things like that."

"Am I supposed to pretend I can't stand you?"

Her smile reappeared. "Let's go with that. We're neighbors who barely tolerate each other. Sounds about right. That's how I used to think of you when you were Soren's bratty little friend."

Ouch. That stung. But he was grinning. "How long will you be in town?"

"I have a big fundraising gala coming up this Thursday, and I take off after that."

So little time. Less than a week. "What if I see you out here again some morning?" he asked. "Can I join you?"

"It's your neighborhood, too. I can't stop you."

"Will Rosie?" He glanced back at the bodyguard.

Danica laughed. "I'll tell her to go easy on you. Though I can't promise *I* will."

"I wouldn't expect you to."

Twelve Years Ago

---

*D*anica sprinted up the hill. *Teenage Dream* by Katy Perry blasted through her headphones. Her chest and quads burned.

She'd just finished her last semester of undergrad, and her brother and dad were both out of town for all of June. The house was hers. Such uninterrupted bliss. She really needed this downtime before her graduate programs started.

Danica crested the hill, ready to enjoy the downward part of the slope.

But instead, she ran headlong into someone else. Someone tall and solid.

"Hey!"

"Ow!"

Sweaty arms wrapped around her. The both of them fell into the grass by the side of the road and rolled.

Danica ended on top, with the other person below. The two of them were a heaving mass of limbs and hostility.

It was Noah Vandermeer. Soren's friend.

"What the *hell*, Noah?"

"Your fault, not mine," he said hoarsely. "You're supposed to be running against traffic."

Why did his voice sound like—

Oh. Crap.

Danica realized the unfortunate placement of her knee. She'd racked the poor kid.

"Sorry." She rolled away, and they both sat up. "Are you okay?"

"Probably. I'm sterile now, but aside from that…"

She snorted a laugh. "I did the world a favor. There won't be any more of you running around, slamming into people."

Danica stood and held out a hand. He grabbed it. Then the jerk actually pulled her back *down*. She yelped, and Noah caught her around the waist just before she landed in his lap.

He smirked up at her.

So he had quick reflexes. And more muscles than last summer. So what? He was still annoying.

Once her feet were back on the ground, she asked, "Why aren't you in Mexico right now? I thought you'd be with Soren." Her brother had jetted off to Cancun with his friends.

"Didn't feel like spending a month drinking. I'd fall behind on my training."

"For the Navy SEAL thing? You're still doing that?" She hadn't taken it very seriously, and Soren had given it up.

"That's all I want to do."

"Wow. Okay." She had to admit, she was impressed.

Last summer, after he'd graduated high school, Soren had gotten it into his head that he wanted to become a Navy SEAL. Maybe it was the fact that he was a competitive swimmer, a natural athlete. More likely? It was some comment their father had made about how impressive military special operatives were.

Whatever the reason, Soren had roped Noah into running with him after their swim practices. They'd become training buddies, lifting weights in Soren's gym at the house, doing sit-ups and push-ups out on the lawn with their shirts off.

Not like that had interested her. Nor had her eyes lingered on Soren's annoying friend during the guys' swim meets, noticing his butt. Or that megawatt smile.

The dimple, though, she had to admit was kinda cute.

"What're you doing home?" he asked. They were walking together now, heading in the direction of both their houses.

"My program doesn't start until August."

"Right, I heard you graduated early. Congrats. You're doing your masters next?"

"Double masters. Public policy and nonprofit management."

He grinned, looking at her sidelong. "Typical Dani. What an overachiever."

"Shut up. Like you're not."

While Soren had just squeaked by, Noah had always gotten straight As. She was pretty sure Soren had been accepted into his college because he was a legacy.

They reached the turnoff for Noah's house. "Want to come over?" he asked. "My parents just got back from Napa and brought back half the state's annual supply of cheese."

"What about those cookies your mom got before? The ones you brought over last summer?"

"The brown-butter chocolate ones? Yep. Good thing I saved some. Just in case any girls came over."

Why did his voice sound so flirty suddenly? And why was her body tingling in response?

"Maybe some girls will," she said.

"What about you?"

"No. I have plans."

"Another time?"

"I'll think about it." For the cookies, obviously. Nothing else.

"TAYLOR SWIFT IS NOT GOING on my workout playlist," Noah said.

Danica grabbed her iPod from his hands. "You have to listen to the song all the way through before rejecting it."

"Fine," he grumbled. "Go ahead."

They were sitting on the living room floor at Danica's house, backs against the couch, arms pressed together as they listened to music and argued about the playlist they were making.

And Danica was loving every moment of it.

Noah had a fondness for hard rock with angry, screamy vocals, which he swore by for weight lifting, while Danica liked pop. The more bubble gum, the better.

Three weeks had passed since they'd slammed into one another on the hill.

At first, he'd kept turning up on her morning runs. And she'd kept turning down his invites to his house. But finally, she'd relented. Lunch with his parents had been fun and low key. There was no judgment or disapproval or unnecessary competition in the Vandermeer family. Being around them was relaxing.

And those cookies. Amazing.

So she'd kept going—even after the cookies were gone—and she and Noah had started spending more time together. Longer runs, lingering conversations. Noah had been showing her how to deadlift.

For the first time, Noah was truly *her* friend, not just Soren's. It wasn't something she ever would've expected.

Growing up, Danica had been the serious one, while Soren had been the popular jock. Danica had gotten sick of playing the grumpy, stick-in-the-mud older sister who only cared about school and didn't know how to have fun.

But now, Noah kept texting her and inviting her over. Like *she* was the fun one.

As the weeks had passed, their workouts had morphed into video game tournaments, movie marathons, or music debates.

And, just in the past few days, they'd started hanging out at her house instead. Where it was just the two of them.

Alone.

"All right," Noah said. "That song wasn't so bad. It's on the list. But now it's my turn to pick. Hand over the iPod."

She held it out of his reach. "No Metallica. Or other things with 'metal' or 'death' in the name."

"What? That's not fair."

"It's my iPod."

Noah grabbed for the device, then gave up and grabbed Danica instead. He pulled her into his lap and tickled her until she was breathless and screaming. "Fine, fine, take it!"

But he didn't take the iPod when she offered it. Instead, he grinned at her. Then he licked his lower lip.

Ughn. Arousal sped through her veins, setting off a needy ache between her legs.

She wanted to… But she couldn't. *Crap.* He was Soren's best friend. Soren's roommate.

"I should…"

He nodded. "Yeah."

Still, it took several more seconds for her to push away from him and stand up.

"I guess I'll head home," Noah said. But his tone made it clear he didn't want to go home. He wanted something else entirely.

And *god*, she wanted it, too.

This was Noah. What the hell was she doing?

For a long time, Danica had thought of him as a kid. He'd been a late bloomer. But Noah was very much a man now, not a boy. He was twenty. Their age gap of two years had never seemed so small.

And the way he looked at her? With one heated glance, he could get her blood pumping. He looked at her like she was firing up his body in all the ways he did for her.

Like he wanted *everything*.

The same way he was watching her right now.

But they couldn't. Even flirting felt wrong and forbidden. She knew her brother would be weird about it. Soren would get jealous, say she was trying to steal his friend the way she'd monopolized their father's attention and praise for so many years.

"I'll see you tomorrow?" Danica asked.

"Yep. See you." Noah headed for the door, his disappointment obvious.

When he was gone, she curled up on the couch, holding a throw pillow to her stomach to crush the feelings there.

ONE DAY LEFT.

One day until Soren would return from Mexico, and Danica would leave for school.

She woke that morning feeling panicked. She'd been looking forward to starting her masters since her freshman year of undergrad. She'd worked her ass off and sacrificed to get here.

And she didn't want to go.

Because of freaking Noah Vandermeer.

They met in front of her house for their run, just as they did every morning. The sky was a cloudy gray, and the air was heavy with moisture.

"It's supposed to rain later," she said.

He murmured something in agreement.

Noah was quieter than usual. She could've sworn he felt it, too. That ratcheting of the tension between them. The longing for things that might be impossible, but maybe, just maybe... weren't.

"Have you packed?" Noah asked.

She nodded.

"Of course you're packed. I bet you were packed a week ago."

"Then why'd you ask?"

Instead of answering, he sighed and frowned.

Then, when they were about halfway through their route, thunder rumbled overhead.

And the rain came.

It was like the sky had cracked open down the middle. Huge rain drops splattered on their heads and on the asphalt.

The two of them laughed and shouted as they ran for the cover of a tree. They huddled together while cold raindrops pattered around them.

Water dripped from Noah's hair and down his lips. His T-shirt was plastered against his torso, showing off the channel between his pecs. The ridges of his abs. She couldn't stop herself from staring.

Their eyes met, breaths going ragged.

She knew exactly what would happen, yet she didn't really believe it until his mouth landed on hers.

Noah's kiss wasn't slow and tentative. This was rough. Demanding. She kissed him back with equal urgency. Tongues probing, hands exploring. They both knew they didn't have much time.

He tasted like rainwater and sweat. Like salt and fire and temptation.

Danica felt his erection against her hip. She cupped her hand around it, feeling the heat of him through the wet fabric. His cock swelled even more beneath her touch, and Noah moaned into her mouth.

She broke off the kiss. "Should we go back to my house? To my room?"

His gaze met hers again, and she knew he understood what she wanted.

Him, alone in that big house. Hot, forbidden sex with her younger brother's best friend. Right now, before they could change their minds. While they still had the chance to be this reckless.

"Yes." He dove forward to kiss her again. "Yes."

They splashed through puddles, hand in hand, cutting through neighbors' property to get back as quickly as possible.

As soon as they got in the door, she saw the suitcases on the floor. Heard someone rummaging around in the kitchen.

All the heat immediately fled her body.

Noah launched away from her and clasped his hands awkwardly in front of his crotch as her brother wandered in.

"You're back early." Danica sounded breathless. She hoped her brother didn't notice.

Soren sipped a carton of grapefruit juice. "Yep, caught an

earlier flight. All I was doing was getting wasted, and you were right Noah, it was kinda lame. Why are you all wet?"

"We were out for a run," Danica said.

"Yeah, but in the rain? You're both weird." He walked away, shaking his head.

THAT NIGHT, she and Noah met outside on the porch after Soren went to sleep.

"That could've been really bad," he said.

"Yeah." If they'd gotten home before Soren? Her brother might've walked in on them stripping each other naked. Or her going down on him in the living room. Because she doubted they'd have made it all the way to her bedroom.

"Think he would've forgiven us?" Noah asked. But she could tell by his tone, by his hopeful look, that this was a broader question. *Will he* forgive us?

"I think he would." It was possible. If she broke the news in the right way.

She really, really wanted to think it was possible.

"When will I see you next?" he asked.

"I could come back for Thanksgiving. Will you be here?"

He nodded. "I could try talking to Soren before then. If you think we...should?"

"Yeah, I do," she said, hardly believing they were actually doing this. Trying to make this *real* instead of a ridiculous fantasy. "I'll talk to him. It should be me."

"Okay. But if you don't, I will. I'll see you in November."

"I'll be thinking of you until then. Every second."

He smiled his boyish, dazzling smile, stealing one last kiss. This one, a promise. That the next time they saw one another, they wouldn't have to stop. They'd have as much of each other as they both wanted.

Chapter Seven

*D*anica was toweling her hair dry when her brother called on FaceTime. She accepted the call, and Soren appeared on the screen.

"Hey, how's everything going?" His angular features were drawn with concern. He had wavy dark hair, like her, and in the last few years he'd grown it to his shoulders. Behind him, she saw the expanse of his loft apartment in the Meatpacking district. Soaring ceiling, exposed brick, minimalist furniture.

She'd never been okay with Soren's involvement in the college bribery scandal. But now that she knew the whole truth? It was even worse.

It was hard to even look at her brother right now. But he *was* still her brother.

She sat on her bed, crossing her legs. "Not much to report. My new bodyguard team is in place. Any time I leave the house, I have a shadow."

"I've got security breathing down my neck here, too. It's worse than usual."

Danica nodded, though her brother had never seemed to mind having bodyguards around him. He'd always used them far more than she had. "We've all got tighter security, including Dad."

"You really think this could be a plot against our whole family? They've only gone after you."

"Lucky me."

Was this going to be her new normal? She hated to think she'd have to make permanent changes to the way she lived her life, even when she returned to New York.

Soren wiped a hand over his face. "I'm worried about you. I've been looking at my schedule, trying to see if I can get to West Oaks. It'll be tough. I've got all these meetings…"

"No, it's better that you stay there."

"You sure?"

"You're busy, and so am I."

Since their childhood, Danica and her brother had been fiercely competitive with one another for their dad's attention. Their father had egged on their rivalry, lavishing one with praise only to leave the other in the cold.

But she and her brother had managed to find a balance. They got along well enough, took part in one another's lives. Celebrated each other's accomplishments. Even if they weren't exactly friends.

She hated that her brother had done such despicable things in college. But it had happened a long time ago, and he'd grown up in many ways since then. He'd changed.

"And Dad? How's he?" Soren asked carefully. "I haven't spoken to him since we all had lunch when he was in New York last."

Which had been months ago. She stretched out on her bed, holding the phone aloft. "Dad does what he wants, as always. I think he might be dating someone. She's your age. Maybe even younger."

Soren didn't bite on that tidbit of gossip. "Has he mentioned me? Did he see me ringing the bell at the Stock Exchange last month on the day of our IPO?"

She tried not to roll her eyes. "I'm sure he did."

"You're a bad liar. No matter what I do, he thinks I'm still a fuck-up."

"Then keep proving him wrong."

"I intend to." He gripped the skin between his eyes. "I need to go. Talk soon?"

She'd meant to say goodbye, but instead, she blurted out, "Wait."

"Yeah?"

She didn't want to do this. But she needed to.

"I saw Noah Vandermeer."

Soren's face turned to stone. For several long moments, he just stared at her on her phone screen. His eyes glittered like sharpened flint. "Where did you see Noah?"

"I was out for a run this morning. So was he." She didn't feel like explaining the bodyguard story.

Soren scowled. "And he didn't have the courtesy to go the other way?"

"I wouldn't have wanted him to. Noah was my friend once, too."

"Your friend? Noah was *your friend*? Are you kidding?"

She just shook her head. This wasn't going well.

"He ruined my life, Dani. You realize that, don't you? I got kicked out of college. I have a *criminal record*."

"You're responsible for your own choices," she snapped. "*You* did something wrong, not Noah. And you've worked your way back from it, haven't you?"

His lips were trembling with anger. She doubted it was tears. Her brother didn't cry any easier than she did.

"Why are you bringing this shit up?" he asked.

"I'm just letting you know that I might see Noah sometimes while I'm in West Oaks. And I don't intend to hide it from anyone. Including you."

"Thanks for the consideration. But you'd better not trust him, Dani, because he's a fucking traitor."

Soren's face disappeared from the screen.

She tossed her phone onto the mattress. She couldn't believe Soren had the nerve to talk about trust.

Chapter Eight

*G*inger got up and took a carton of ice cream from the freezer. "So Noah, anything of note to share? New love interests we should be aware of?" Which she always asked over dessert.

They were sitting at the small table in the kitchen, just finishing up lunch. He'd returned to the house after his run with Danica, and he wasn't in a rush to head back down the hill. He liked the thought that she was less than a mile away. Even though the chance of seeing her soon was close to nil.

She'd sounded willing enough to go running with him again. But she hadn't made any promises.

"No, Gigi. I haven't fallen in love since you asked me that same question last time."

His step-grandmother handed him a bowl of mint chocolate chip. "I know you young people move fast. Just trying to keep up."

"Wishful thinking is more like it," Gramps said. "She saw you running with Danica Foster-Grant this morning."

So that explained it. "Dani and I are just…friends."

Ginger pointed a manicured nail. "*Ha*. I heard that pause."

"Only because I almost said 'acquaintance.' Friends might be overstating it."

"Then work on it. Have you seen her on the cover of that magazine? *Va va voom*."

His grandfather groaned. "Gigi, give the poor kid a break."

"A kid?" She grabbed one of Noah's arms with two hands and held it aloft. "Do you see the muscles on this one?"

Noah took his arm back. "You two are like a comedy act from the 1950s."

"*Comedy*? I'm more of a femme fatale. And 1950s? I'm insulted. I was a baby then, thank you." She tossed one end of her gauzy scarf over her shoulder. Noah had never seen anyone look so glamorous while also wearing fuzzy bunny slippers.

"Do you think those kidnappers will go after Danica again?" Gramps asked.

"He must not," Ginger interrupted, "because he's sitting here right now instead of protecting her."

Noah's spoon clanked in the ice cream bowl. "She has her own security detail. I'm not the only bodyguard in existence."

But seeing that frightened look on her face today? It was haunting him.

Even now, despite his testy response to Ginger, every cell in his body urged him to go to her house, right now. Ensure she was safe. But how was he supposed to do that if Danica wouldn't let him?

Ginger didn't want to let the subject drop. "It said in the *Vanity Fair* article that she has a lot of enemies."

Noah frowned. "Nobody gets things done in the world by only having friends."

"Defensive, are we?" She gave him a Cheshire Cat grin.

Gramps cleared his throat. "All right, enough baiting my grandson. Noah, how're those kids you were volunteering with?"

Noah perked up, grateful for the new topic. "They're doing well."

A couple times a month, he and some friends volunteered with teens who were interested in the military. Noah had started the program and funded it himself. Probably the most satisfying hours he spent on any given Saturday. Sometimes, he wondered if he could turn the project into something bigger, but wasn't sure how.

"We had a couple kids graduate this year," Noah said, "and both are heading to college on scholarships. One chose an ROTC program, and he's planning to serve as a Marine after he graduates."

"That's fantastic. You must be proud."

"I am. Definitely."

"Do you think any will become SEALs?" Gramps asked.

"I hope so."

"But would that be difficult for you?" Ginger mused. "Your grandfather said how hard it was when you were injured and had to leave the Navy."

Gramps hit his palm on the table. "Gigi, do you have to bring up *every* topic Noah doesn't like to discuss?"

Noah stood, grabbing his bowl. "On that note, I'm going to get cleaned up."

Their bickering usually ended up with Ginger in his grandfather's lap, so Noah rinsed his dish, excused himself, and went to his room.

Lucifer, Ginger's British shorthair, jumped down from his bed and wandered across the rug. She meowed in annoyance at his presence. She liked Noah's room, but not with him in it.

"Sorry, Lucy. You have to put up with me again."

Normally, he didn't spend so much time here in the hills. Yet this house was just as much "home" as his condo in downtown West Oaks.

He spent a few minutes on his phone, checking in with Tanner and his work email, staying on top of the various assignments they had going at the moment.

Then he heard something slide across the carpet. Someone had just pushed a magazine under his door. He got up and scooped it from the floor.

It was an issue of *Vanity Fair* with Danica on the cover.

He heard Ginger's slippers receding down the hallway. Such a busybody, that one.

Settling back onto the bed, Noah flipped through the pages until he found the article on Danica. More photos of her were splashed across the pages, and yeah, she did look amazing.

But he preferred the Danica he'd seen that morning. No makeup, hair pulled into a messy ponytail. Sweat dripping a trail down her chest and disappearing into the gap between her ample breasts.

He skimmed the article, then got pulled in. It described how Danica had lost her mother at eight years old to a sudden brain aneurysm. She'd wanted to carry on her mother's legacy by heading the foundation, while applying her father's business acumen.

She blew him away. She really did.

Noah had always been ambitious. But when he'd become a SEAL, he'd believed he'd found his ultimate calling. The thing he wanted to do for the rest of his days, if possible.

And the universe had laughed. His back injury had taken that dream away.

Since leaving the teams, he still hadn't put a finger on what he wanted most out of life. But Danica knew her purpose, and she hadn't let anything stop her. He respected the hell out of that.

In all the years they'd been apart, he hadn't met anyone who could compare to Danica. Her integrity and intelligence and outspokenness. That little curve in her upper lip, the clean smell of her skin.

The fire in her eyes in the rain, when she'd asked him back to her house, and he'd known she wanted him to fuck her… And he'd wanted her, too. More than he'd ever wanted a woman before that. Maybe since.

He was getting hard remembering it.

Soren's older sister. She'd used to boss them around, and honestly? Noah had liked it.

He tossed the magazine onto his dresser. Rubbing his length

through his shorts, he glanced over at his door, making sure he'd flipped the lock.

How many times had he beaten himself off thinking of Danica when he was a teenager? And later, when he was in college, even though beautiful girls had surrounded him and he'd had no shortage of willing partners, Danica had still been the ideal. Even after he'd lost her.

He lay back on the bed, closing his eyes as he pictured her. His hand slid inside his waistband and over the head of his cock.

Then his thumb dragged along the underside of his shaft as he reached down to play with his balls. In his mind, it was Danica. Her tongue moving over him. Her mouth on his sac.

He started stroking himself. His grip was loose at first, closing tighter as the need built inside him.

Noah thought about going to the bathroom for some lotion, but he decided to pause and lick his hand instead, adding that to the wetness leaking from his tip.

His fist worked over his dick as the dirty images sped through his brain.

He wanted Danica every way possible. Behind her while she braced her arms against the wall. Beneath her while she rode him.

Anything she asked for, he'd give to her.

Except his heart. He couldn't afford to make that mistake again. But anything, *anything*, else.

His balls felt tight and full. Noah moaned.

A feline yowl shocked him out of the moment. "What the *shit?*" He yanked his hand out of his shorts and almost leapt off the bed.

Lucifer looked at him from the bookcase, where she'd camped out beside his collection of military memoirs. The cat's tail swished disapprovingly. He'd forgotten she was there, and she clearly didn't appreciate it.

"I can't get a moment alone around here? Really?"

He flopped back onto the bed, grabbed a pillow, and shoved it over his face.

From the moment he'd seen Danica again, he'd wanted another chance with her. Even though he knew in his bones how dangerous it was.

She didn't even live in West Oaks. Her family hated him. Even if he—somehow—managed to win a few nights with her, she'd leave eventually, and his heart would be right back where it was twelve years ago. Crushed.

But he'd grown up since then. Now, he knew better.

If Danica got in touch, he'd be there for her. As a friend. But aside from that? He needed to let her go.

Chapter Nine

On Monday morning, Danica's driver stopped the car in front of the museum.

"Are you sure you don't want to pull around back, ma'am?" Rosie asked. "Go in that way?"

After a brief stint of calling her "Dani," the bodyguard was back to formality. Danica wasn't sure what accounted for the change, but it hardly mattered.

Her biggest concern at the moment was that knot of reporters and cameras waiting outside the natural history museum. No doubt waiting for *her*.

She took a steadying breath. "Nope, I'm all good." Tomorrow, she could slink in the back entrance. Today? She was proving to the world that she wasn't afraid.

She'd woken early that morning to go over her day's agenda, but she'd decided to skip her run. After the emotional roller coaster of the last few days, she'd needed some time to think and refocus.

Time without Noah there to distract her from work. She did want to see him again and catch up more. But maybe tomorrow, once she'd gotten back on track.

The car door opened when she pulled the handle, and she swung her legs out.

She could almost see the collective inhale go through the crowd of reporters. Like they were getting ready. Sharpening their blades.

Rosie got out of the other side and raced around to join her. Pushing her shoulders back, Danica marched up the steps.

A microphone shoved into her face. "Ms. Foster-Grant, how did it feel to almost be abducted? What do you think their intentions were?"

"Danica, what do you want to say to your would-be kidnappers?"

She dodged out of the way. "No comment." Her expression battled to remain serene, though her pulse was thrumming at her neck. The sun was bright in her eyes, forcing her to squint.

She'd almost made it to the entrance when a platinum blond in a red blazer blocked her path. "Danica, what do you have to say to claims there was no threat at all? That your kidnapping was actually a hoax?"

"*What?*"

Rosie stepped forward. "Clear the way, please."

But the blond reporter wasn't listening. "Aren't you planning a gala here in a few days? Are you using the supposed kidnapping attempt to get publicity?"

Danica looked to the side, hoping for another means of escape. If only she could make use of her pepper spray again, but macing a reporter might be frowned upon.

Then she spotted a dark shape across the street. A man in a coat.

What the hell?

Instantly, her heart rate tripled. She couldn't see his neck tattoo, but his frame, his jawline—it was all the same.

It was *him*, the man who'd been inside the museum just before the kidnapping attempt.

Danica grabbed onto her bodyguard's shoulder. "Rosie, call the police. *Now*. One of the men who tried to kidnap me is here."

She'd tried to keep her voice down, but these words set off a frenzy among the reporters. Which was only making this scene worse. People were swarming around her. Danica couldn't see the man in the dark coat anymore. Where was he?

Microphones kept being shoved at her face. Arms, reaching for her. She couldn't breathe.

Within moments, Rosie had hustled her inside the museum, across the lobby, and into the executive director's office.

Lindley Colter stood up from her desk chair. "Dani? What's going on?"

"Can you tell me exactly what you saw, ma'am?" Rosie asked.

Danica sat in a chair, struggling to keep herself calm. "Man in a dark coat," she said haltingly. "He's got a big tattoo on his neck. Just call the police, Rosie. *Please.*"

The bodyguard took out her phone and stepped out of the office.

Danica sat at the small conference table. Lindley rushed over to her. "Are you okay?"

She could hardly breathe, but still nodded. "I'm fine."

"You thought you saw that man again? The one who was visiting the museum at the same time as you last Friday?"

"Yes. Do you remember him?"

"Vaguely," Lindley said. "I don't remember a neck tattoo, though. That sounds distinctive. Anderson didn't mention it, either."

"It's a two-headed eagle symbol. But he had his collar up, and I only saw it at a certain angle. I don't know for sure he was involved in the kidnapping attempt, but I just had this gut feeling. You know?"

"Yeah. Of course." But Lindley didn't look convinced.

An idea occurred to her. "Do you have access to the museum's camera footage? I could show you how he was acting."

"A patrol officer came to download the video clips, but she ended up deleting our originals from the cloud. I think the police have their copies, though. You'd think they would've found that man by now. Or the rest of those assholes who went after you, right? If a billionaire can't get the police to deliver results, I don't know what hope the rest of us have."

Danica refused to demand special treatment in these kinds of situations. But Lindley had a point.

"Did you know there are reporters outside?" Danica asked.

Lindley grimaced. "We've been getting a lot of media inquiries. Outside, it's public property. But I could request more police presence."

"I just don't want this nonsense to scare our donors away."

"I'll make sure that doesn't happen. But nobody would blame you if you'd rather get out of West Oaks. I know the museum revamp is your baby, but…"

Danica's stomach twisted. "You think it would be better if I'm not at the gala?"

"No. Not what I'm suggesting at all. I just want you to feel comfortable." Lindley sighed, sinking into the chair beside her. "I barely slept this weekend, and those kidnappers weren't even after me. How are you not falling apart right now?"

"I'm not letting anyone scare me away from doing my job." Especially terrorists in ski masks. Or with creepy neck tattoos.

Run from West Oaks? No way. Not happening.

She was strong, and she could handle anything the world threw at her.

I am Danica Foster-Grant. My mother's daughter. I can't ever forget that.

"Do the police have any idea yet who's targeting you?" Lindley asked. "Or what they want? Could it be related to the museum, somehow?"

"Not as far as we know."

"But how did they know you'd be here on Friday at that time? Or today?"

Danica had been pondering the same thing. She'd meant to bring it up with Blake, her father's chief of security. But he'd been too busy to meet with her over the weekend.

The door opened, and Rosie stepped back into the room.

"Have they caught him?" Danica asked.

"I'm afraid not. The police station isn't far, so they sent a patrol car quickly. But we've been checking the area around the museum and haven't seen anyone matching the description you gave me."

"But you saw him, right? When I pointed him out? He was wearing a dark overcoat."

Rosie opened her mouth, but didn't speak.

Danica stood up. "Didn't you?"

"I'm sorry, ma'am. I didn't. Is it possible that you didn't, either? Maybe it was someone else entirely."

"No, that's not possible. I know what I saw."

"You sound agitated," the bodyguard said calmly. "Are you feeling all right? Would you like us to escort you home?"

Lindley and Rosie were both staring at her with concern. Danica's skin had flushed painfully.

She braced a hand on the back of the chair, then sat down again. "No, I don't. I just want to get back to work. You can wait outside."

Rosie left, and Danica regretted her sharp tone. The bodyguard wasn't to blame for failing to see a random guy across the street. With the crush of reporters, it was any wonder Danica had seen him.

But she *had* seen him. Danica trusted herself, even if Rosie didn't.

THAT AFTERNOON, Blake finally offered to update Danica on the investigation.

She went down to the wing of the house reserved for staff. Whenever William was in residence, Blake stayed here, too. The decor was more subdued. It looked like a corporate hotel, simple but comfortable.

Tori, Blake's assistant, was at her desk. She looked up as Danica approached. "Ms. Foster-Grant. Thanks for coming down. I'll let Blake know you're here." She picked up her phone.

"Thanks." Danica clasped her hands, looking up and down the hall. She felt a little awkward after having seen Tori and her father together the other night. Should she say something?

No, that would probably make Tori uncomfortable. And Danica would look like she'd been spying.

Usually, Tori barely said more than a few words to her on the phone, even when Danica had tried to make friendly conversation. Danica hadn't met Tori in person until this visit, and she'd been surprised their gruff chief of security would hire such a shy, waif-like assistant.

"I heard what happened today," Tori said. "It sounds really scary. Seeing one of the kidnappers again?"

"It was unsettling."

Blake opened his office door, beckoning Danica inside. Tori looked down at her desk.

Danica sat down in an armchair in front of his desk. "What have the police found out?"

"We're in communication with West Oaks PD. Our friends in the LA FBI office are working their angles as well, given your father's public profile. There's video surveillance footage from the museum and surrounding streets. Witness statements. A number of leads that we're pursuing."

She clenched her jaw. "That's it? Tori said a detective was here."

"I wish I had more specifics for you. As soon as I do, I will let you know."

"But what about the man with the tattoo who was visiting the museum? Who I saw again *today*? I got a good look at his face, so the cameras must have as well. Have the police run facial recognition?"

"I assume they have. But they haven't identified him, and we simply have no proof he was involved in the attempt to abduct you. As far as today, Rosie Consuelo couldn't confirm she saw the man at all."

"But *I* saw him."

"And what did you think he was going to do? Grab you in front of all those reporters? Hardly an opportune moment for another kidnapping attempt."

Danica rubbed her forehead. "Okay. Fine. Let's set that aside. There's something else that's been bothering me. How could they have known I'd be at the museum at that time on Friday? It seems likely they knew my schedule beforehand."

"Or you posted about visiting the museum on social media."

"I *didn't*. You know me better than that." At least, she'd thought he did.

Their security chief was practically part of their family. Like a gruff uncle, perhaps. Blake and her father had been friends since Danica was a baby. *Never question Blake's loyalty to this family*, her father often said. William's highest praise.

"I know you wouldn't have done it intentionally." Blake spoke in his usual authoritative yet soothing tone. Neither quiet nor loud, but infused with confidence. "It's natural to let things slip, though. Any number of people could've figured out where you'd be."

"But are you looking into the possibility that someone within our organization leaked my location?"

For a long minute, Blake just looked at her.

"You're under tremendous stress," he finally said.

"What does that have to do with anything?"

"It means you're more likely to see connections that aren't there."

Danica shrank back. "You think I'm inventing conspiracies?"

"Rosie said there were a lot of reporters at the museum today, and you insisted on approaching them instead of avoiding a confrontation. You were agitated. It must've been upsetting, and you've already been subjected to a lot."

"I don't believe this."

At first, Danica had liked her new bodyguard. But Rosie had been talking about her behind her back.

"You know that I care about you," he said. "I'm only asking

you to let me and the authorities handle this investigation. And perhaps it would be better if you work from home for the time being? To avoid reporters and crowds?"

She shot up to standing. "Absolutely not. If you think I'm going to hide in my father's house, you don't know me at all."

"Danica—"

She turned on her heel and stormed out of his office.

Both her father and Blake were trying to shut her out of this investigation. Why? She was far from fragile.

Were they just being over-protective? Or was there something more going on?

Something they didn't want her to know?

Back in her bedroom, Danica stared at the phone in her hand, wondering what she should do.

Chapter Ten

*N*oah ran a full lap around the neighborhood before he found Danica. Just like the last time, she and her bodyguard Rosie were keeping pace side by side.

He fell in next to them. "Morning, Dani. Morning, Rosie."

"Hi, Noah." Danica's eyes met his.

He got the feeling she was trying to telegraph something to him, though he couldn't imagine what.

She'd written him during the night, asking if he was going to run in the morning. He'd said yes, but then she hadn't texted further. It had been very mysterious. First thing after he'd woken, he'd dressed in his running gear and driven here from his condo.

"What's up?" Noah asked. He wondered if she was ready to discuss whatever had been bothering her the last time they'd spoken.

"Just felt like a run. I didn't get one yesterday." She glanced back at her bodyguard and frowned. Like she was worried about Rosie overhearing.

What the heck was going on?

"Dani…"

"Want to race?" Danica took off, a coy smile suddenly playing at her lips, saying, *Catch me.*

He didn't understand any of this. But he ran after her without even making a conscious decision. When a woman like her looked at him that way? It was kind of a base instinct.

They rocketed up the next hill, then slowed to a walk. She put a hand on his arm, and his heart turned over in his chest.

"I need to talk to you," she murmured. "In private."

"Yeah?" He didn't look back at Rosie, but he remained aware of the bodyguard's constant presence.

"It's sensitive. I might need your help."

Now, he was all business. "Why? What happened?"

"In private," she whispered, lips barely moving.

He had an idea. They kept walking. His hands fidgeted as if he were nervous.

"Dani, I need to tell you something." Noah had raised his voice so Rosie wouldn't miss it. "I just have to put this out there."

"Oh…kay."

"I still have feelings for you."

Danica turned sharply to look at him, eyes bugging. "*What?*"

He lifted one eyebrow slightly. *Play along.*

"Oh. *Oh.* Wow."

"Can you put a guy out of his misery? Have I got any chance?"

"I don't know. It's really sudden."

Noah held back an eye roll. She wasn't making this easy.

"Can we at least talk about it before you shoot me down?" he asked.

Her lips screwed up thoughtfully. "Sure. Let's talk. Tell me about these *feelings* of yours." She was coming awfully close to sarcasm.

"What I need to say is pretty personal. About to open my heart, here."

Danica sighed. "Rosie, could I get a minute with Noah? In private?"

Rosie's eyes darted around. "I'm not supposed to let you out of my sight line when we're outside the house."

"It'll just be for a minute," Noah said. "This way." He

grabbed Danica's hand. As soon as a narrow dirt path appeared, branching away from the road, he tugged her onto it. Trees and bushes hemmed them in.

"Remember this?" he asked.

"Yeah. Aren't we trespassing?"

"Technically. I'm sure the Larsons will forgive us."

It was a shortcut kids in the neighborhood had used back in the day. Noah assumed it was still active because the path was fairly clear and not totally overgrown. But the Larsons were only in West Oaks one month out of the year, anyway. Their house was empty the rest of the time, so they weren't around to complain.

A twig snapped. Rosie had followed them, but she was staying back to give them privacy.

They reached a small clearing. Danica spun around to face him.

"What was that all about?" she whispered.

"You said you wanted to talk in private. That was the fastest way. Though you could've been slightly more enthusiastic. Can't even pretend to like me?"

"I didn't want it to be completely obvious that I was bull-shitting."

Ouch. But he could tell from her slight smile she was teasing him. "Now that you've declared *your* feelings, why don't you tell me what's going on?"

She leaned back against a tree trunk. "Something happened yesterday. I saw one of the men who I think tried to kidnap me."

"*What?* Where?"

Danica put a finger to his mouth, shushing him. Her eyes were turned up to him. She was so close he saw the tiny beads of sweat above her eyebrows, on her upper lip. "Outside the museum. But my bodyguard and my security chief are suddenly acting like I'm crazy. I want to investigate the kidnapping attempt on my own."

"You don't trust Blake?" Noah hadn't minded the man when

they met. He was surprised Blake—or anyone—would be dismissive of her.

"I don't know. Blake has been loyal to my family for years. The real problem is, he's acting like he doesn't trust *me*. Same with my father."

"And Rosie?"

"She'll report it back to Blake. And I...I have this feeling. Like there's something they aren't telling me."

"Based on what?"

"The people who tried to kidnap me knew my schedule. The more I think about it, the less likely it seems that someone outside my inner circle would know when I'd be at the museum on Friday. If I hadn't shown up early? Those assholes might've been successful in snatching me."

"You're saying someone leaked your schedule?"

"Maybe?" Her teeth pressed into her lower lip. "It sounds paranoid. I hope I'm wrong. But I want to find out, and I need someone in my corner. I thought of you."

"I asked you to tell me what I can do, and I meant it. Whatever you need." His fingers itched to touch her, and he decided to give in to the urge. Noah's brushed her hair from her forehead, and the plaintiveness in her gray eyes tore at his heart.

Bad idea, he told himself. *Be her friend. Don't go imagining that you'll ever be more.*

Danica was breathing hard, like she found their closeness as distracting as he did. Her breasts rounded at the top of her sports bra. "You don't know what a relief it is to have someone listen to me."

"I've got work today, but I'll clear my schedule." He'd call Tanner and figure something out. "Let's head to my family's house, and we'll talk it through. Everything you're concerned about."

She exhaled. "Okay. Good. I'll skip going in to the museum this morning, too."

Noah looked over his shoulder at Rosie, who was waiting

patiently with her hands behind her back, gaze averted. "Your bodyguard will think we're going to my place to hook up."

Danica's mouth opened as she laughed. "Hardly. I'll tell her I needed to let you down easy."

Behind them, Rosie coughed. "Um, Ms. Foster-Grant? I'm getting questions about our route. They can see we've been… stopped a while. From my location."

Danica stifled a grin. "We're almost done."

"But I was asked not to deviate from your usual path."

Danica's smile turned wooden. "Who asked you that? Blake?"

"No, your father."

"Why would my dad care about my run?"

"It was one of the security protocols he put in place."

Danica's eyes met Noah's. She looked pissed. "Let's go," she said tightly.

They backtracked along the path to the road. Noah jogged next to her, Rosie bringing up the rear.

"Rosie, I'm going to Noah's for a bit," Danica said.

"That wasn't on your schedule for today."

"Then I'll put it on my schedule," she snapped, cheeks reddening. "Am I a prisoner suddenly?"

She sprinted ahead.

"Dani, wait." Noah pushed off his back foot, arms and legs pumping. Rosie picked up the pace behind him to catch up.

Trees flashed past. The road curved, snug against the cliff-side. Waves roared into the rocks far below.

Noah heard an engine. A white paneled van barreled down-hill along the road, only its roof visible from his vantage point.

They'd seen a white work van when they'd been running on Sunday. Hadn't they? Was it the same one?

Danica had rounded the curve. He couldn't see her anymore.

This felt wrong. *Bad, bad, bad*, his pulse pounded.

Every instinct screamed. Shit was about to go down.

He raced around the curve. Danica had stopped on the side of the road. She'd seen the van now, too.

Noah sprinted toward her. The vehicle had almost reached her.

It sped up. Like it was racing him.

Fuck.

The van screeched to a stop beside her.

He was only seconds away. But everything seemed to be moving in slow motion.

A gloved hand reached from the van's open side door, followed by a set of bulky shoulders. A ski mask.

No.

Danica's arm shot out to block the attacker's attempt to grab her. She ducked and twisted away, her foot kicking out. The man fell back into the van.

Danica threw herself into the brush at the far side of the road just as Noah reached the van. Through the vehicle's open door, he caught a quick glimpse of the barrel of a pistol.

"Gun," he shouted. He leaped back toward Rosie, and the both of them dove for the asphalt. The same moment, a shot rang out.

The engine roared, tires peeling. He and Rosie both scrambled upright. The bodyguard drew her weapon and fired at the retreating vehicle. The rear glass spidered, but the van didn't slow.

Noah searched the brush frantically for Danica.

Then she screamed, and he saw her further down the slope below.

She was rolling down the steep hillside, heading straight for the drop-off into the ocean.

Chapter Eleven

*T*he world spun as Danica careened down the slope. Branches and rocks scratched her skin. She tried to grasp for something to hold on to, but she was moving too fast. Everything was a blur.

Her ankle caught and twisted painfully. She grabbed a thick tree root, ignoring the sting as something sharp scraped her forearm.

Danica pushed onto her hands and knees, gasping for breath.

"Don't move." Noah was half running, half sliding down the hillside toward her. "The drop-off is right behind you."

Carefully, she looked downhill. Just a couple of yards beyond, the slope ended in an outcropping of smooth rock, and then fell away. Seagulls circled in the air, and waves crashed against the base of the cliff far below.

Shit. That had been really close.

Noah reached her and knelt. "Are you okay?"

"Just some scratches. Where's Rosie? I heard a gunshot—"

"She's okay. Probably calling the rest of your security detail. You reacted fast."

Danica was trembling. "At first I couldn't see them well, but the side door of the van started to open, and I knew it couldn't be good. It all happened in a split second. I didn't mean to nearly throw myself off a cliff."

"As far as escape routes, that might've been overkill." Noah reached for her to help her up.

"Do you think they'll come back around?"

"Let's not wait to find out. But I think they decided to abort. If your security team knows what the hell they're doing, they'll stop the van before it leaves the neighborhood."

She wanted to know who was responsible for this. A second kidnapping attempt in a few days?

And once again, it was like the assholes had known just where to find her.

Danica was officially *done* with this shit.

Noah helped her stand. She hissed at a sharp bolt of pain. "I might've twisted my ankle." She really didn't need this right now.

"I've got you. Climb onto my back."

She looped her arms around his neck, resting her weight against him. Noah stood, grabbing hold of her thighs. His back was solid, the muscles prominent under his shirt, right up against her breasts. The fabric of his tee was slightly damp, but she wasn't complaining. No man should've smelled so good when he was sweaty.

Noah hiked them back up the hill. When they reached the road, he set her down, but he kept an arm around her to support her weight.

Rosie ran toward them, her phone in her hand. Her gun was in her other fist, but she tucked it back into the shoulder holster she always wore. "I radioed to the team to intercept the vehicle. Blake is sending another car to meet us."

"Dani needs to get to safety *now*," Noah said. "We don't know who else might be coming for her, and your team was already supposed to have secured the neighborhood."

Rosie's expression hardened. "My orders are to keep her here until—"

"Negative. Those are *your* orders. Not mine." Noah turned his head to look at Danica. "I'd rather take you to my house immediately. We're not far. We'll cut through some of the neighbors' properties. That okay with you?"

Rosie frowned at them. "Ms. Foster-Grant, I advise that we—"

"I'm going with Noah." Right now, he was the only thing Danica was sure of.

❧

THEY EMERGED through a dense patch of trees, and the back part of Noah's house came into view.

Noah was carrying her in his arms now, cradled against his torso. Despite the danger, at least some of the adrenaline in her veins was purely a response to him.

She couldn't stop looking up at him. When they were younger, Noah had kept his face closely shaved. But today, an early-morning shadow darkened his chin. His hair was messy from the run.

Danica couldn't help herself. She touched her nose to his jawline. His skin was warm. Smooth and rough at the same time.

At first, when he'd mentioned still having feelings for her, she'd thought he was serious. And she'd had no idea how to respond.

Thank goodness he hadn't meant it. Noah was very attractive, but feelings? No. She couldn't deal with that on top of everything else.

Noah glanced down at her, Adam's apple bobbing as he swallowed. "Don't worry. I'll get you fixed up."

"I'm okay."

Her ankle was throbbing, and the scratches on her skin stung. But it was really hard to focus on her discomfort with so much of him touching her, his scent in her nose.

Noah turned the handle on the back door. It wasn't locked. They strode into the kitchen.

Danica looked past his shoulder and saw Rosie trudge in after them.

"Ginger?" he called out. "Could you give me a hand?"

Footsteps came from upstairs, then a voice. "Noah? Is that you?" An older woman swept into the kitchen. "Oh, my. If I'd expected so many guests, I would've changed." She was wearing a silky robe and curlers in her hair.

Danica assumed this was the step-grandmother he'd mentioned. "Sorry to invade your home like this. I'm—"

Ginger's surprised expression slid into a smile. "Danica Foster-Grant, I presume. And look at you, poor thing. Those scratches. I'll get some antiseptic."

"And bandages," Noah said.

He set Danica on the kitchen counter. As Rosie looked on, he got an ice pack from the freezer and wrapped it in a tea towel. "Here, for your ankle."

"Thanks." The joint was red and swelling, though she couldn't tell how bad the damage was yet.

Rosie spoke into her phone, then lowered it. "Blake and the others are on their way. Couple minutes."

Danica's phone buzzed again. She pulled it out to check the notifications. Blake, as she'd expected.

Instead of responding, she sent off a message to her father, assuring William she was all right. She'd have to figure out what else to tell him.

"I'd recommend you stay here at least until they locate the van," Noah said.

Rosie was shaking her head. "Blake wants her back at the Foster-Grant residence."

Noah glanced sharply over his shoulder. "All due respect, it's safer for Dani to remain in place than going back out in the open."

"I don't need *either* of you to speak for me." Danica's tone had come out harsher than she'd intended. "I'm staying here until they locate the van." Which was exactly what he'd said. But she'd wanted it to be her decision.

Noah's mouth curled up at the corner. "Excellent idea."

Danica's eyes locked with his. "Rosie, could Noah and I have a moment alone, please?"

Rosie glanced between them. She wasn't liking this. But she clearly could tell she wasn't going to win here. "Yes, ma'am. I'll check the perimeter of the house, but I'll stay close. Just speak up if you need anything." She left the room.

Once the bodyguard's steps had receded, Danica said, "I need you to let me handle this. Blake won't be happy about me defying him, and I don't want him pissed at you, too."

Their chief of security might claim to care about her, but he didn't like having his authority questioned unless it was her father doing it.

"I don't care about offending Blake. But I get it. I'll back off."

Noah switched on the hot water, fetched another tea towel and wet it under the faucet.

The fabric dabbed gently at the scrapes on Danica's arms and legs.

"I could probably do that myself," she said.

"Probably." But he didn't stop. He brought the damp towel to her neck, his mouth just inches from hers. "I don't mind taking care of you. If you still want my help?"

"I do."

His green eyes studied hers.

Ginger bustled back into the room, carrying several bottles and boxes. "I'm sorry, I couldn't seem to find anything, and then suddenly I couldn't carry it all." She dumped the items on the counter beside Danica. "Good, Noah is getting you cleaned up. What on earth happened?"

"Fell while we were running."

"And Noah didn't catch you? How unchivalrous of him."

"Hey, I tried. Dani was sprinting ahead of me."

Behind his back, Ginger rolled her eyes.

Danica laughed weakly. "It definitely wasn't Noah's fault. Someone, um, tried to kidnap me. Again." She suppressed a shudder. Danica didn't like turning their conversation so serious, but she wanted Ginger to know. She hated to think she could be bringing danger here.

"Like last week?" Ginger asked. "What they were talking about on the news?"

"Seems that way."

Ginger crossed her arms over her robe. "Just *awful*. I'm thankful you're safe and sound. Noah, I'd better text your grandfather to let him know to stay put until the drama's over."

"Where is he?" Noah asked.

"Oh, where else? His morning tee time with his friends."

Noah dabbed antiseptic ointment onto the cuts on her legs. The long strokes of his fingers soothed her, and she felt the fear and tension begin to evaporate.

"There." Ginger set down her phone. "He'll wait for the all clear. More time on the green, which I'm sure he's just *furious* about."

"I hope I'm not disrupting your plans for the day," Danica said.

"Not at all. I was just watching Netflix when you arrived with such fanfare. I *do* have a show to get ready for later on."

"A show?"

Ginger moved her hands in a flourish. "Darling, I'm the headliner tonight at the Pacific Burlesque Theater near Santa Barbara."

Danica felt herself grin. "Really?"

"Every Tuesday and Wednesday, and the occasional Saturday in summers. You're welcome to a front row ticket anytime you'd like to check out my act. You'll have to invite another young man to take you, though. Noah's always declined. We wouldn't want to offend his delicate sensibilities."

He grumbled, opening a bandage. "You're married to my grandpa. Some things I don't need to see."

Ginger opened the dishwasher and started unloading the dishes, most of which appeared to be wine glasses. "Back in my day," she whispered, "Navy men weren't so prudish."

Danica snorted.

"Laughing at me again?" Noah's head was down, but he was looking at her through his eyelashes.

"Hope your ego's not too fragile."

"Nah. Whatever you've got, I can take it. But you're supposed to be letting me down easy." His tone was low. Unmistakably flirty. "You've got a cut here, too." Noah's thumb brushed her cheek as he smoothed antiseptic over it.

His irises were each a different shade of green. The one on the right was slightly darker. She'd noticed when they were talking beneath the tree. How could she have forgotten that for so many years?

But the freckle just above his upper lip, visible through the stubble. *That* she remembered.

"You're staring at my mouth," he said.

"No, I wasn't."

Ginger closed a cabinet door and looked over. "Pretty sure you were, dear."

Smirking, Noah threaded the cap onto the tube of antiseptic. "You're all patched up. How's the ankle feeling?"

She wiggled the joint. "Not bad."

He lifted the ice pack and prodded her skin with gentle fingers. "This hurt?"

"No." But with his hands on her, she was starting to overheat, even with the ice.

"I don't think it's sprained too badly," he said. "I can be your crutch, if you need one."

He was being so sweet. An overpowering sense of attraction filled her belly with warmth. She wanted him to pull her into his arms again, hold her close.

Her nose burned. Oh, no.

She was going to cry.

"Dani?" Noah asked. "You okay?"

She wished he'd stop asking her that.

In the side pocket of her shorts, Danica's phone started to buzz. It was probably Blake. He could wait. For the moment, she switched off her phone.

What she needed, right now, was a chance to calm down. So she didn't start bawling in the Vandermeers' kitchen.

Chapter Twelve

"Is there someplace I could lie down?" Danica asked. "I need to regroup."

Protectiveness filled Noah with energy like a shot of caffeine on an empty stomach.

Noah turned and found Rosie had returned. She was watching them intently.

"I'm going to take Danica upstairs," he said. "Feel free to grab something to eat or drink here." In other words, no need to follow us.

Rosie frowned. "That what you'd prefer, Ms. Foster-Grant?"

"Yeah," Dani said wearily. "I need some rest."

"But Blake said—"

"I'm safe here. *Please*, Rosie. Just tell Blake to wait."

Noah held out his arms to carry her, but she slid off the counter, testing her foot. "It hurts. But I can make it." She limped along beside him.

Noah led her up the stairs to one of the guestrooms on the second floor.

He stopped in the doorway, leaning against the frame. "Take all the time you need."

"I assumed we were going to *your* room."

"You want that?"

"Your room would be nice." Her expression was more open than she usually seemed. Vulnerable.

He nodded his head. "It's down the hall."

When Danica walked inside, a gray shape leaped off Noah's bed and streaked across the room.

"That's Lucifer," he said. "She likes my bed. Especially when I'm not in it."

"I didn't mean to displace her."

"Ginger indulges her too much. That cat eats better than most humans I know. Sashimi and caviar."

Danica went to the bed and curled up on top of the covers. Noah shut the door most of the way, leaving it open just a crack.

He'd updated his bedroom over the years and kept enough belongings here that he didn't need to transfer anything back and forth. One of the walls was exposed red brick, and the others were painted dark gray. He'd chosen oversized furniture in warm wood tones. Photos he'd taken overseas decorated the space above his bed: snowy-peaked mountains in Pakistan, sunsets over the Indian Ocean.

He sank onto the couch by the bay window. "This okay?"

"Yeah. Just…stay there? Don't go?" She was lying on her side, looking at him.

"Not planning on it."

The whole world had distilled down to the woman in front of him. It felt like that moment before a mission when everything was quiet, and he knew in his bones he'd do whatever was necessary to complete his task.

Noah wanted to get Blake Halston on the phone and demand to know what the guy was doing to fix this situation. Surely Blake had someone at the gate to the neighborhood, checking on whoever came in and out. How had they allowed that van to get so close to Danica? It was inexcusable.

But her chief of security would probably refuse to explain. Noah had no standing in this situation. He wasn't her bodyguard. Just her neighbor. Her friend.

And Danica? She'd asked him not to speak for her. So he had to keep his opinions to himself. For now.

A ball of gray fur leaped onto the bed. "Lucy," Noah said, starting to get up, but Danica waved him away.

"It's okay. She's cute."

"She's a demon."

The cat curled up against Danica's side. "See? Look at that. She's so sweet."

"Maybe she doesn't hate everyone, then. Just me." Noah sat back down. The cat was purring.

Danica laughed. "I think Lucy and I have a lot in common."

He sputtered. "You both hate me?"

"No." Danica closed her eyes, smiling. "We might seem a little prickly sometimes, but...we find your bed very comfortable."

Danica rested for a while, and Noah watched over her. She was so beautiful it hurt.

She'd never been here in his bedroom, not even during the weeks they'd spent together before his sophomore year of college. He hadn't gone to her room that summer, either. Probably because, up until that last day, they'd both been trying not to give in to their attraction.

It was way too easy to imagine her under the blankets, pressed up against his skin. Like it was still that summer years ago, and they'd spent those weeks in each other's arms while they'd had the chance.

But that would've made the hurt so much worse when he'd lost her. Because he would've known just how good it could be.

Her eyes fluttered open. "I remember when you were shorter than I was."

So she was thinking of the past, too.

"I doubt that ever happened."

"It's true." She was speaking just above a whisper. Lucy was fast asleep at her side. "You were my annoying brother's annoying friend. Then... something else."

His heart was pounding as fast as his sneakers had pounded

the asphalt earlier. Wanting to touch her. Kiss her. Tell her all the things he should've said long ago. Even though it was impossible to go back in time.

"And then you were gone," she said.

"What am I now?"

Her smile was languid. "Slightly taller. Less annoying. A little."

"Glad I'm improving."

"There's something I've been wondering. Why did you leave the SEALs?"

Noah figured they were talking about these things because she needed space from her current problems. He was happy to oblige.

"A back injury. It was becoming a whole thing." The pain had been irrelevant. He'd ignored it for the rest of that mission, and would've kept on ignoring it. But when he'd finally had to get a medical evaluation, the doc said he'd fractured several vertebrae. Surgery was the only solution. They'd stuck metal rods in his back to hold him together. Even though he'd healed, Noah's back would never be quite the same.

So? No more jumping out of airplanes or hauling hundreds of pounds of equipment through war zones. No more being a SEAL. He could've stayed in the military in a different capacity, but he'd chosen to move on and pursue new challenges. Because being so close to the job he loved, but not being able to do it? That would've been harder to take.

"Is it exciting to be a bodyguard?" Danica asked. "I'd think it would be boring, following people like me around. Recent kidnapping attempts notwithstanding."

"I don't just follow around billionaire heiresses all day." His back didn't allow him to serve his country as an elite operator anymore, but he could still do plenty. He'd turned down far more lucrative security jobs that would've taken him all over the world. Military contractor work. Private security for big corporations overseas. That didn't interest him. He didn't want to be a mercenary, and he didn't see the point of amassing more and more money for its sake alone.

"But it doesn't sound like the adrenaline rush you must've had in the military. Do you miss it?"

She'd always seen past the bullshit to the heart of things.

"Yeah. I do. But I get my fix in other ways."

"An endless parade of sexy women?"

He laughed. "This is quite the interrogation."

"Answer the question."

There'd been women. Not a parade. But in the back of his mind, he'd always thought of Danica as the one who got away. The one he'd wished he could forget.

He wasn't wishing that right now.

"I bought a Ducati Diavel. Hugs all the curves of the Pacific Coast Highway."

"I'm sure your mother loves that."

"For Christmas a couple years ago, she bought me a fancy SUV in the hopes that I'd drive that instead. And I do, most of the time. I keep the bike here. More room in the garage."

Mischievousness gleamed in her eyes. "Can I see it?"

Chapter Thirteen

*B*efore Noah could answer, a knock at the door interrupted them. It was Rosie. "Ma'am, Blake sent a car for you. It's outside."

Danica sighed. "Thanks, Rosie. I'll be down in a little while."

"What do you want to do?" Noah asked.

She wanted to check out his Ducati. Maybe take it for a spin. Aside from that, she had no idea.

But going back to her father's house? That was absolutely not happening yet.

"I guess I'd better stop avoiding Blake." Until she spoke to him, he'd just keep bothering her. At least her pulse had finally slowed enough that she could function.

She sat up on Noah's bed, crossing her legs, and switched her phone back on.

Immediately, it rang in her hand.

She answered. "Blake?"

"We're ready to transfer you back to your home." He'd practically barked at her. No doubt he was furious at her lack of responsiveness so far.

But Danica was pissed, too. His anger only fed hers.

"I want to know what's going on. For the second time since

I've gotten to town, men in ski masks have come after me. This time it was in my own neighborhood. After you told me yesterday to mind my own business."

"Those were certainly not my words, Danica. I'm communicating with the police on the situation."

"That's not good enough. Has anyone stopped that van? Have those men been arrested?"

"The police are trying to locate them."

"Then I'm not going anywhere. When you've figured out who's been coming after me, let me know. Until then? I'm not interested in your opinions. If my father wants to convince me otherwise, he's welcome to try."

She ended the call.

Her voice had sounded confident, but inside, she was a mess again. Danica hung her head and closed her eyes.

The fear was creeping in. Deep down, she knew she'd barely begun to process what had happened on that hillside.

And Noah was right here, watching her. Probably seeing the uncertainty radiating from her being.

"What do you need?" he asked softly.

Danica rubbed her forehead. *Get it together*, she thought. "Um, I have to let my museum director know I won't be in today at all. Lindley. We have so much work to do."

"I have to think she can spare you for a few hours."

"Probably. Yeah." She started typing on her phone.

They exchanged texts. Of course, Lindley promised to handle everything on their agenda while Danica sorted this out.

A few hours. She couldn't remember the last time she'd had a few hours to kill, with no plan, no work, no meetings to prep for.

"Could I see your motorcycle now?" she asked.

His dimple sank into his cheek. "Whatever you want."

～

IN THE GARAGE, Noah switched on the light. It was huge, climate controlled, with a row of vintage Ferraris taking up most of the slots.

"Are those yours?" Danica asked.

"My dad's. He's a sucker for a V12 engine."

Danica remembered that his father had invented some computer connector back in the 90s, and the patent had sold for a fortune. "But your dad's not living here."

"No, he retired to his island with his new wife. I try to take the cars out, but it's been a month or two."

Funny how a month could seem like a long time, but over a decade could feel like nothing.

Noah swept the dustcover off his motorcycle. Gleaming black metal, a curvy black and red seat. Sleek, elegant, powerful.

A little like Noah, actually.

"It's gorgeous." Danica dragged her fingers over the leather seat. "Can I?"

"Go for it."

Noah put a hand down to steady the bike as she climbed on. She swung her leg over the seat. Her knees stretched wide over the body of the motorcycle, and the sexual overtones of this position weren't lost on her.

Danica closed her eyes, resting her hands on the bars. "I can just imagine it rumbling underneath me. Does it feel like flying?"

"In a way."

"Aren't you going to join me?"

She wanted to be close to him again, which wasn't the same as feelings. They were just enjoying each other's company.

And *he'd* started the flirting, not her.

Noah straddled the seat behind her. He'd left a few inches between them. "You gonna take me somewhere?"

"Where to?"

"Anywhere with no stoplights."

She ran her fingers over the handlebars. "Sometimes, I imagine just taking off, driving out of town into the sunset. Getting away from all my responsibilities."

"Really? The woman who hates changing her schedule?"

"I know. I don't want to let anybody down, but a few days of freedom? Where nobody knows me or my name? That's the kind of thing I fantasize about. Boring."

"Not boring at all. I like your fantasy. You could make it come true."

"Maybe someday." Danica looked over her shoulder at him. "What do you fantasize about?"

His eyebrows lifted. "What do I fantasize about in general? Or the past couple days?" He had a naughty gleam in his eyes.

"You pick."

"World peace. And a magical solution to global warming."

She tutted. "Such a boy scout."

Her heart rate was picking up again, but in a far more pleasant way. She could almost pretend it was that summer back when they were still in school. That her world wasn't twisting into frightening shapes around her.

He must've seen the chill move through her.

"You sure you're all right?" he asked.

"Trying to be. You'd think I'd be used to this kind of crap by now."

"I hope you never get used to it."

But they both knew the threats weren't over. For a person in her position, there'd always be more.

She rested her back against him, and he leaned into her in response. His muscular chest pushed into her back.

"Noah," she whispered. "I'm scared."

This wasn't easy for her to admit. But she couldn't keep it in. Not with him.

"That's okay. I'm here. I can hold you if you want."

She did want him to hold her. So much. But earlier, Noah had asked what she *needed*.

The answer was starting to become clear.

Just an hour ago, she'd worried she was being paranoid by asking Noah to help her with a secret investigation.

But now? Somebody out there was determined to make her

life hell, and they were doing a bang-up job of it. She couldn't just assume Blake and the police would sort this out for her.

No matter what, Blake and his precious Valoris Security team had failed. What was the point of listening to the man's instructions if he couldn't even keep the streets around the house secure? This was the West Oaks hills, not Manhattan.

"I want to hire you. Not just to investigate. As my bodyguard."

"Hire me?"

"And the company you work for. I don't know who's behind this, and I don't know when they'll come after me next. I thought I was safe at home, but I might not be. I need someone who I know is one hundred percent on my side."

She'd worried he might not agree. Might even dismiss her concerns. But Noah didn't hesitate.

"Then we're hired. I'll make sure you have whatever you need. The full resources of Bennett Security."

Slowly, she exhaled. Having an extra line of defense would help her to sleep better at night.

Hopefully, without any more nightmares.

"Thanks. I want to keep this confidential." At least until she could figure out what was really going on. She didn't need to hear her father's or Blake's opinions about her security situation. Nor did she want to get Rosie fired.

"I need to make sure you know what you're asking, though," he said. "If I'm your bodyguard, I'll be with you all the time. Unless I have a teammate from Bennett Security to discreetly replace me—if it's essential—I'm not going to leave you."

She looked back at him. "All the time? Even at night?"

"If we're keeping it a secret, then yeah. Sleeping in the same room, staying with you all day. Which sounds a lot like being your boyfriend."

"I don't usually move that fast."

He shrugged, and she felt the movement against her back. "I didn't think you did. People might not believe it. Especially not your family."

Crap. Those were good points. "Do you have a better idea?"

"We just need a good cover story. Basically, it's the same thing we let Rosie think earlier, but you don't turn me down."

"I fall into your arms?"

Noah pressed even closer to her, and his large hands moved to her knees. She felt the scratch of his chin by her ear.

This was the most physical contact they'd had in twelve years. So many memories were overwhelming the fear and the uncertainty, even if they were bittersweet.

Danica rested her head back against his collarbone. "And how would we make this convincing?"

"If we were going to get together that fast—in this hypothetical world in which I'm suddenly your boyfriend—here's how it would happen. It all starts with the fact that I've wanted you since you were just my friend's older sister. But you were out of my league. Unattainable. Even though I drove myself crazy with wanting you, I never got to have you. Hypothetically."

His voice had dropped to a rumbly murmur. Her own breaths were moving faster.

"And?" she asked.

"Now that we're older, and I'm not some twenty-year-old kid anymore, I know exactly what to do to win you over. How to make you feel safe and cared for." His hands squeezed her knees, and Danica felt goosebumps rise on her skin. He probably felt them, too.

"Then what?"

"When you're at my house after nearly getting kidnapped a second time?" Noah shifted, and his lips brushed her temple. A shiver passed through her. "I kiss you."

"Do you?" Her voice was hoarse. "That's forward."

"I kiss you because I know you want me to. And then I pick you up and take you to my bed. Because you want that, too."

Danica breathed out, making a tiny sound. Part surprise, part longing. His lips trailed back to her ear.

"What then?"

"I undress you."

"And?"

"Touch you. In any way you ask me to."

Shivers ran through her, straight down to her core.

He kept going. "And once we're naked together? We can't get enough. Maybe we'll burn out hot and fast. But while you're in town, you're mine."

She could feel his heart beating against her back. *Boom, boom, boom.* Danica's mouth was slightly open, her chest moving as she gasped for air.

"What do you think?" he asked. "Will anyone believe it?"

There was a knock behind them. Danica startled away from him, turning around.

"Dears? I hate to interrupt." Ginger was grinning at them. "The doorbell just rang, and I assumed you didn't hear. There's a police detective at the door. Danica, she's asking to speak with you."

Chapter Fourteen

They headed back upstairs. Noah let Danica and Ginger go ahead first. After their conversation on his motorcycle—and the view of Danica's round ass just inches from his crotch—he'd needed to make some adjustments. His dick had been thickening up as he'd told that story.

Once we're naked together? We can't get enough.

He'd actually said that to her. Noah liked to flirt, but that had been overt even for him.

It had been mostly wishful thinking, combined with some truth. But she'd asked what he fantasized about. Now, she knew.

Of course, it couldn't happen. Starting something with Danica had been a long shot before. Now that he was her bodyguard, she was off limits. It was too bad. But her safety was far more important than any of his fantasies about finally having her.

When they reached the front of the house, they found a plainclothes detective waiting there, along with a patrol officer in uniform. Rosie looked on, impassive as usual, hands behind her back.

"Ms. Foster-Grant. I'm Detective Angela Murphy. West Oaks

PD." Her cornrows were pulled into a bun, and she wore a pantsuit with a slim-cut blazer.

They shook, and Detective Murphy turned to Noah. "And you must be Mr. Vandermeer. Pleasure to meet you. I'm sorry you both had so much trouble this morning."

"Trouble is an understatement," Danica said.

The detective cringed, though Noah thought she'd overdone the gesture. Like she was going out of her way to seem sympathetic. "True. But I have some very encouraging news. Units responded within minutes after your security team notified us of the attempt. We blocked their escape route and arrested three individuals inside the vehicle. They were posing as contractors, and that's how they got access to the neighborhood. At this moment, they're back at the station awaiting questioning."

Noah had been hoping for this exact scenario to play out. Yet hearing it now, he was surprised it had all gone so smoothly.

"Do you know yet who they are?" Danica asked. "What they want?"

"We'll find out. In the meantime, I'd like to get your statement. Is there somewhere we could speak alone? The patrol officer here can speak to Mr. Vandermeer separately."

Noah opened his mouth to protest, but Danica beat him to it. "Noah and I can speak to you together. We were both there at the same time, and...I'd like him to stay with me."

Detective Murphy inclined her head. "If that's what you'd prefer, Ms. Foster-Grant. The officer can talk to Ms. Consuelo, your bodyguard. I believe she was also present this morning?"

Rosie and the patrol officer stepped away.

"Shall we sit?" The detective gestured at the living room. Noah and Danica sat on the couch, while the detective took the chair across from them.

She pointed to the small square device attached to her blazer, which Noah recognized as a body cam. "All right if I record this? Saves the need to write up your statements, and it's standard procedure."

"I remember from my last interview," Danica said. "Go ahead."

The detective switched on the camera.

Danica proceeded to recount what had happened that morning. How they'd been out for a run and the men inside the van had tried to grab her.

Noah felt her tensing up beside him, and he put his hand over hers.

Noah added what he'd seen: three men inside the van, all wearing ski masks. One shot fired before they fled.

"Thank you," the detective said, switching off the camera on her jacket. "Ms. Foster-Grant, I understand from your chief of security that you've been eager for updates on the investigation, and I apologize that's taken so long."

Danica laughed without humor. "I feel like I've been shut out almost entirely."

"I assure you, that's not the case. Even before these latest developments, I planned to meet with you today to share what we've found. If I may?"

The detective reached into a messenger bag and brought out a laptop. She opened it and typed in a password. When she'd pulled up the window she wanted, she turned the computer to face them.

Noah leaned forward to study the screen. It showed images of two white SUVs, obviously taken from street traffic cameras.

"Last Friday, two vehicles were involved in the attempt to kidnap you from outside the museum. The driver of the first SUV crashed into your security detail's car. The second vehicle approached you and, we believe, intended to complete the abduction. Two suspects inside."

The detective hit a key, and more images appeared. Three men in ski masks, exiting the vehicles in an isolated industrial area. It was hard to tell if they were the same three Noah had seen that morning.

"We were able to find this footage of them abandoning the vehicles outside of town. Unfortunately, their trail ran cold there.

Of course, this morning's events changed everything. As frightening as today must've been? This is a huge advance in the case. I hope you feel some relief, knowing that we've now apprehended them."

Danica didn't respond immediately. Noah felt her indecision. It was great news that the investigation had suddenly made so many leaps forward.

But it just felt…easy.

"Are you saying the men you arrested today are *definitely* the same ones who tried to kidnap Danica at the museum?" Noah asked.

"Just what I was wondering," Danica said.

Murphy inclined her head. "It's early to be definite. But I believe so, yes. Their heights and builds match the three in our video footage. And their method matches as well."

"Not exactly," Noah pointed out. "One vehicle versus two. And they didn't go after her bodyguard like the first time. Unless you count the shot they fired, but that was sloppy. Didn't come close to hitting me or Rosie."

"What about the man inside the museum with the tattoo?" Danica asked.

"Tattoo?" Detective Murphy looked confused.

Danica heaved an exasperated sigh. "The man I mentioned in my first interview. Dark coat, cap, staring at me. I saw him again yesterday? Outside the museum?"

"Ah. Right." The detective nodded. "We've had no luck identifying him yet, but we're working on that. He's not one of the suspects we apprehended today. We can't even say he *is* a suspect at this juncture."

Noah could tell Danica didn't like that answer.

"Do you have the surveillance footage of him from inside the museum?"

"We do, but there are no clear shots of his face."

"I want to see the footage."

"Any particular reason?" the detective asked.

Danica stared at her, eyes narrowing. "Because that man may

have been involved, and I want to see exactly what he was doing."

The detective shrugged. "Of course. I don't have it on this device, but as soon as I return to the station, I'll have someone send a copy to you. Could I get your email?"

Danica recited it. Detective Murphy jotted down the address.

"As soon as we've finished interrogating the suspects and know more, I'll have an update for you."

"Will I have to face another kidnapping attempt to hear from you?" Danica's sarcasm was clear.

The detective smiled serenely. "I'll make sure you don't."

Chapter Fifteen

*A*fter Detective Murphy left, Danica asked to use the guestroom shower. Between the run and rolling down that hillside, she felt sticky and gross. And a few minutes away from Noah didn't hurt, either. Just to get her head on straight.

Sitting on Noah's motorcycle, feeling him behind her, all she'd wanted was to run away with him for a little while. Steal a few moments that would belong only to them. She'd been tempted to make that story of his a reality instead of just a cover.

It was a good thing she'd honed her willpower to precision levels as William Foster-Grant's daughter.

She was going to keep this completely platonic. They had enough to deal with already.

Danica turned the water to cold, bowing her head as the spray thundered against her neck.

She didn't know what to think about the arrests. It was fantastic news, of course. But Detective Murphy had seemed eager to pin the entire kidnapping plot on the three men they'd captured today—not the man with the tattoo.

The tattoo Murphy hadn't even remembered.

After she was clean, she got dressed. Ginger had given her a soft pair of pajama pants and a T-shirt that said *60 is the new 20*.

Danica checked her phone. Her father had written, asking for updates. She let him know what Detective Murphy had said, and that she was staying at Noah's house for the time being. Her father wasn't going to be happy about it, but at least he did her the courtesy of not arguing with her.

Then the phone chimed with a new email. Detective Murphy had written.

Danica knocked on Noah's bedroom door. He'd left it cracked open. "Come in."

"I got the email with the surveillance videos." When she walked inside, she didn't see him at first. But then she spotted him through the open doorway to his bathroom. Noah was standing in front of the mirror, running a comb through his damp hair.

"Hey. I'll be right there."

She was trying not to think of him in the shower. The salt and sweat washing away from his skin. Beads of water dripping over his lips, like that day in the rain...

Nope. Not thinking about that.

Noah had a cozy sitting area by a bay window. She curled up on the sofa and opened the detective's email on her phone.

"So the detective followed through?" he asked.

"Yeah. There's a bunch of clips." They'd have to sort through them one by one.

Noah lowered himself to the cushion beside her. He'd changed into jeans and a light green polo shirt, the same preppy look he'd always favored, and he smelled like peppermint shampoo. But she was glad he hadn't shaved. She liked a little edge to him.

"Want to watch them now?" he asked.

She nodded, opening the first file and waiting for it to load. Noah leaned in, his arm pressing into hers as they looked at her phone screen.

The video was in color and had a timestamp running at the bottom. It showed the lobby of the museum. At just after five o'clock, the man in the dark overcoat pushed through the entrance doors and approached the ticketing desk.

Danica pointed at the screen. "That's him." Her heart thrummed like a bird trying to escape its cage.

The man had his collar popped up, just as she'd remembered, so his neck wasn't visible. The black ball cap obscured his face.

He approached the desk, and Anderson appeared to greet him. There was no sound, but they saw Anderson take cash from the man and hand him a printout from the computer.

"This was before you arrived?" Noah asked.

"Yes. Around fifteen minutes, I think." She'd been on her way to the museum in the Range Rover at five o'clock. They would've been pulling off the freeway into West Oaks after the long car ride from the airport.

Danica clicked on the next video in the detective's email. This one showed the man in the overcoat walking through the museum's hall of evolution. He seemed to be examining the displays and reading the informational signs. He was keeping his head down, the bill of his cap still blocking his face from the cameras.

Danica clenched her jaw. If the camera hadn't actually caught his face, it was no wonder facial recognition hadn't identified the man.

But there were still a lot of video clips in the detective's message.

In the next clip, the timestamp had skipped forward to around 5:30. That was when Danica had arrived at the museum. This clip showed the man in the overcoat looking at his phone and typing on his screen.

Come on, she thought that. *Look up. Give us something.*

She increased the playback speed, and the video moved rapidly forward. Then Noah touched her hand.

"That's you, isn't it?"

She played the video at regular speed. She saw herself and Anderson walk past the camera, chatting.

The man in the overcoat glanced over, then looked at her again. She could see the change in the way he was holding his body. The moment before, he'd been relaxed. But as soon as he'd spotted Danica, he'd seemed to go rigid. It was obvious even with that bulky coat.

It reminded her of the way her martial arts teachers held their bodies right before they demonstrated a move.

"You see that?" she asked. "How he's holding himself?"

"I'd bet he's got training of some kind. Maybe even ex-military."

Without thinking about it, Danica put her hand on Noah's knee, seeking out his solid form to steady herself. She didn't like thinking about this mystery man having the kind of training and experience that someone like Noah had.

"He definitely recognized you."

She was relieved to hear him say it. Danica felt confident about what she'd observed, but you could only take so many people doubting you before you started to wonder.

She cued up the next clip.

The camera angle had switched back to the lobby, where the man was speaking into his phone. This had been just shortly before he left the building. Danica remembered the unease she'd felt as she watched him. The conviction that he'd been studying her and listening to what she and Lindley had been saying.

The man turned and headed for the exit, the front of his coat flaring open as his body moved.

Danica leaned forward, staring at his neck, ready to point out the tattoo so Noah could see it. So she could *finally* show him what she'd been talking about all this time.

But the video seemed to jump forward a split second. The man pushed out of the doors and was gone.

She'd missed it somehow. That was the only thing that made sense.

"Hold on. I'll slow it down. I'm pretty sure he was facing the camera for a moment there, but it's really fast."

Noah didn't say anything. He was staring at the screen in concentration.

She moved the video clip back by a few seconds. She hit play again, but this time ran the playback at a lower speed. The video was now moving in slow motion.

And as she watched, nausea threaded through her stomach and up into her esophagus.

This wasn't possible.

"I don't understand," she said. "He had a tattoo. It should be right there."

But as the man's body turned, the video cut forward. One moment, his coat was about to flare open. The next, he'd already turned, and the front of his neck wasn't visible.

But that brief moment in the middle was missing. When the man should've been facing the camera directly.

Danica's chest was starting to tighten. Every breath of air took more effort.

Noah took her phone and moved the timestamp back yet again. "Let's just be sure."

But nothing changed. His coat was about to flare open, and then he'd already turned.

Noah rubbed a hand over the stubble on his chin. "Are you sure the tattoo was on the front of his neck? Maybe you saw it when he was at a different angle."

She was trying not to panic, but frustration snuck into her voice. "It was at the *front* of his neck. And it was huge. A black two-headed eagle. Like this."

Danica closed the video and pulled up her photos instead. She'd taken a picture of the drawing she'd made last night.

As Noah studied it, Danica touched her own throat, where the man's tattoo had been.

Noah handed back her phone. "Let's call Detective Murphy. It looks like a technical glitch."

She nodded, grateful. That had to be it. "Okay. Yeah. I'll call her."

Danica pulled up Detective Murphy's number and held her phone to her ear, trying to stay calm.

Noah was right. There was an explanation for this.

"Are you sure this is the original footage?" Danica asked.

"Of course," the detective said. "Is there a problem?"

"Maybe. There was a distinguishing mark on the man's neck. A tattoo. I mentioned it earlier?"

"Oh, right. I wasn't sure what you were referring to."

She bit her cheek in exasperation. "I definitely saw it. But it's not in these video clips. Even though it *should* be."

"Unfortunately, the camera didn't catch it."

"Is there anything else? Another clip?"

"This is everything. Maybe the tattoo just wasn't visible at these camera angles."

"That's not it. There's a moment that the man should be facing the camera, but then it skips forward. Isn't that strange? Could it have been tampered with?"

The detective sighed. "Cameras skip. Glitches happen. Ms. Foster-Grant, I think our departmental resources are better spent questioning the men we caught today, not chasing far-fetched theories."

Danica lowered her phone.

"No luck?" Noah asked.

She shook her head. Her initial frustration had turned into numbness.

What was happening right now?

"I should ask Lindley." But even as she called the executive director, Danica was already remembering that Lindley hadn't noticed the tattoo. Anderson hadn't mentioned it either.

Still, she double-checked with the museum employees. Their answers didn't waver.

No one except Danica remembered the tattoo.

Noah was staring at her with a wrinkle between his eyebrows. She could see him from her peripheral vision.

"You still think there's an explanation?" she asked.

"Maybe just one."

"I swear, Noah, if you say I'm confused or reading too much into this or just imagining it…"

"That's not what I'm thinking. At all. *Hey.*" His fingertips touched her chin, gently turning her head so she faced him. His gaze was tender, but completely confident. "What do you think happened?"

Her breath skipped in her chest. She'd been afraid he would say she'd lost it. Danica felt like the heroine of some old black-and-white Hitchcock movie who saw conspiracies everywhere she looked.

But in those movies, the conspiracies were real, weren't they?

"I think someone altered the surveillance footage," she said, "so that man couldn't be identified. At least, not as easily." It just didn't make sense that the camera skipped at the single moment the tattoo would've been visible. Not when the rest of the videos looked crystal clear.

"You realize what that would mean," Noah said. "That the person who altered it is involved in the plot to kidnap you. And so is the guy with the neck tattoo."

"Yes. Do you believe me?"

Please, she thought. If Noah didn't believe her, then she'd have nowhere to turn.

Chapter Sixteen

"*O*f course I do."

Noah had never seen Danica like this. She was one of the most confident, assured women he'd ever known. But right now, redness rimmed her eyes. Her face was drawn, her skin pale. Her hands were shaking.

"Someone altered the footage," he repeated. "Now, we're going to find out who. And we're going to track down each and every person who's responsible for going after you."

She exhaled, nodding. Her fingers swiped at her eyes, though not a single tear had fallen.

"Let's talk through this," Noah said. "Who would've had access to the video footage? Detective Murphy, we already know. And West Oaks PD."

Danica bent her knees, wrapping her arms around her legs. "The people who work at the museum, I would assume."

"What about your security team?"

"Well…yeah. It's possible. Blake has been working closely with the detectives from the beginning." But she couldn't imagine him doing something like that. More importantly, *why*?

"Do you know exactly who got the camera footage from the

museum? Was it a police officer, or was it someone working for Blake?"

"I don't know. Lindley said something about the police coming and downloading the videos, deleting the originals. But if the *police* are involved in the kidnapping attempts? Or *Blake*? That's… That's…" She was shrinking into herself, and Noah could almost see her mind going to a dark, desperate place.

"I don't think I can trust anyone." Her eyes lifted. "Except you."

Back when they were younger, Noah had looked up to her. But now, he wanted to take care of her. Prove to her that nothing would happen so long as he was around.

"You can trust me. We're going to find who's doing this. And I'm going to protect you." Noah rested a hand on her shoulder. But Danica got up from the couch. Like she had restless energy and needed to move.

Immediately, he started running through logistics in his head. "We'll have to get you to a safe house as soon as possible. I'll talk to my co-captain, figure out the best location, and assign a team of bodyguards to be there around the clock while we investigate the kidnapping plot. It'll be tough to get it all into place, but—"

"Whoa. Wait a second. A *safe house*? You mean, going into hiding?" Danica had stopped her pacing. She looked incredulous.

"That's the best way to make sure these people can't find you."

"No. *No.*" She was shaking her head like she couldn't believe he'd suggested it. "That's not going to work. The museum gala is on Thursday night. I have to be there. Absolutely no exceptions."

He got up from the sofa, matching her posture. Arms crossed, head back. "It's a fundraising event. Compared to your safety? It doesn't even rank."

"But it does to me. You don't get to decide what's important, Noah. I'm not going to run away and hide and let these people control me. And if it's someone within the police? A safe house might not be enough."

"All the more reason to make their job harder."

"But I'm not giving up my freedom. That's final."

Damn it. She was making this difficult.

But he could improvise.

"Okay, then we stay here," Noah said.

"And we tell *no one* about me hiring you. The plan hasn't changed. Whoever's doing this, I want to catch them by surprise."

"That'll leave you more exposed."

They held one another's gaze, neither backing down.

Then Noah dropped his hands to his hips, taking a step back. He had to deescalate this conversation. If this was going to work, they had to be on the same page.

"Dani, I'm serious. You said you trust me."

Her eyelids shifted down, lashes heavy. "I do."

"I get that you're used to taking charge. But during this assignment, you'll need to let me take the lead and make the decisions that'll affect your safety."

"I'm not so good at taking orders."

He respected her for that. But this wasn't the typical situation. "A hierarchy of decision-making is essential to be effective. In *any* team. You know that."

She rolled her eyes. "Yes. I know."

He could tell they might clash later on about that subject. But for now, he moved on. "There's something else we should talk about. We can't *actually* get involved. Putting on a show for whoever's watching is one thing. But we can't really end up in bed together."

For a long moment, she just stared at him, eyebrows slowly raising. "You're making a lot of assumptions."

"Just being up front." Really, he was saying this to remind himself. But her cheeks were turning red. It wasn't easy to make her blush.

"You're the one who's been flirting constantly."

"A little. But you've been staring at my mouth. And at the rest of me."

"In your dreams."

"Straddling my motorcycle? How much more metaphorical can you get?"

"I can assure you, I won't be flirting with you anytime soon. Can you promise the same?"

"Yes. I can be completely professional."

"So glad that's settled. Can we keep working on the investigation now? I want to get this rolling."

"You got it, boss. Whatever you say."

Chapter Seventeen

"We should start by writing down everything we know." The pen in Noah's hand clicked, his thumb on the end. "Two kidnapping attempts. One at the natural history museum, one during your run this morning. Four days apart. At least three people involved, possibly the same people in each."

"Plus the man with the neck tattoo," she said. "Who I saw across the street from the museum yesterday. Like he was watching me again."

"Right. And, we know someone altered the surveillance video of him. So he's likely at the center of it." The ballpoint went still as Noah thought. "We don't know how many people are behind this. But they've clearly got funding. They've got connections that would allow them to tamper with evidence."

"And somehow," she said, "they were able to figure out when I'd be at the natural history museum and where I'd be on my run."

"Who could've known about your appointment at the museum?"

She thought. The list was disconcertingly small. "Lindley and

Anderson, because I was supposed to meet with them. My personal assistant in New York."

"Who else?"

"I gave Blake and his assistant Tori access to my scheduling app so they could arrange security while I'm in West Oaks."

"So your first bodyguard team knew your schedule? The ones who took you to the museum?"

"Well, no. I don't think Blake told them. They asked me where to go when they picked me up at the airport."

Noah jotted this down. "What about your running routine? Who would've known you'd be out this morning?"

"That might've been easier to guess. I've taken morning runs in Central Park for years. Sometimes Soren runs with me."

The pen scratched over the paper. Danica leaned over. "Your handwriting is terrible. How can you even read that?"

"I hate taking notes on my phone. Writing it out by hand helps me memorize what I need to know, and usually I never look at the paper anyway." He shrugged, his shoulder sliding against hers like a caress. "Or I shred it if it's sensitive."

His eyes went distant, like his mind had gone somewhere else.

"What is it?" she asked.

"Just thinking about notes. Records... You mentioned a scheduling app you use. Who has access to it?"

"Like I said, my assistant, plus Blake and Tori for this visit. And my father. He uses the same app, and we usually share our schedules. It allows our assistants to make plans for us if we're in the same city. Otherwise, we can be like ships passing in the night."

Noah wrote the names in a separate list. Her stomach burned to think of these people as suspects.

"Your brother?"

"Not Soren. Wait, I did share access to the app with his assistant previously, so we could work out a scheduling conflict over the holidays. But his assistants seem to change all the time." Then she had a concerning thought. "Could someone else have gotten unauthorized access to the app?"

"It's possible. Anything digitized could be hacked if it's connected to the Internet."

In a way, this made Danica feel better. Because some outsider could still be responsible. But the thought of a stranger going through her personal information made her ill.

"I want one of our computer experts to check your devices," Noah said. "Laptop, phone. If there's any kind of spyware on there, some way these people could've hacked into your schedule, we need to know."

"We have IT people who manage cybersecurity for both the foundation and my dad's company. They've set up anti-virus software and firewalls that're supposed to keep us secure. But...god." Her eyes blinked closed. If she truly started contemplating the people that could've betrayed her, who could be selling her out, it would become paralyzing.

Noah's hand reached for her, fingertips about to brush her skin. Danica inched away from him. The last thing she needed was to fall into his arms for real—because that was *exactly* what she wanted. To wish all this away. Make the rest of the world disappear.

Noah was helping her, and she could trust him. But she couldn't turn over full responsibility for this situation to anyone. Not even him.

"If these people know your schedule," Noah said, "then you'll have to stop doing what they expect."

"Wait." Danica turned sharply to face him. "Are you suggesting I give up *my schedule*?" She'd done that today. But for the rest of the week? Even longer?

"Change it," Noah said. "Rearrange it. You didn't mind getting to the museum early on Friday, right?"

"But that was a half hour change, and the kidnappers still almost got to me."

"Just shows you need to shift things more. Keep them guessing."

She grumbled. But he was onto something.

Crap.

Give up her schedule. Just the thought made her want to break out in hives. But if she was unpredictable, it would be that much harder for the kidnappers—if they were still after her—to find her.

She made a decision.

"I'll cancel as many meetings as I can. And I'll cancel my flight back to New York on Friday. If we're really going to track down who's responsible, then I should stay in West Oaks until it's done."

"Agreed. I'll let Bennett Security know we'll be protecting you until this is over. However long that takes."

Danica nodded, her nerves starting to calm again. In a way, this was a new plan. And when she had a plan, she felt secure.

"What's going to happen next?" she asked. "How is this investigation going to work?"

"While you were showering earlier, I called in to the office to let them know what's going on. I had to keep it brief, but my co-captain has the general contours. Next, I'll be sending them all the info we've put together so far, and they'll get started on research. Our computer experts will need your devices, as well as those video clips the detective sent you. I also know someone we can trust in West Oaks PD. A friend of a friend. We can ask him to poke around, see who might've had access to the surveillance video to alter it."

"But how can we do all of that without anyone else finding out? Especially if you're also going to stay with me as my body-guard. If anything, Blake is going to *expect* me to investigate on my own. I'm troublesome like that."

She'd been demanding more involvement for days. If she suddenly went quiet and was inseparable from Noah, who happened to be a bodyguard with Bennett Security?

If she didn't know whom in her inner circle to trust, that meant she couldn't trust *any* of them.

"That's why you're supposed to be unpredictable," Noah said. "What's the last thing Danica Foster-Grant would normally do at a time like this?"

"Um…host a raging kegger?"

Noah's grin widened. "Exactly what I was thinking."

Chapter Eighteen

"Your keg's here," Gramps said. "Where do you want it?"

"Patio," Noah called. "There's a good spot near the grill."

A couple of his bodyguard teammates came through the kitchen, wheeling the beer. Noah gave out fist bumps and hugs.

Gramps was right behind them. He clapped a hand on Noah's shoulder. "You kids have fun. I'd better go. If I miss Ginger's act I'll never hear the end of it."

Danica was unloading the grocery order that had just arrived. Burgers, buns, potato salad—everything they'd need for an impromptu get-together with his friends.

This party was going to be the safest place in all of West Oaks.

Noah spotted Rosie hovering by the sliding glass doors to the patio, arms crossed. For part of the afternoon, another Valoris guard had replaced her so she could get changed out of her running clothes. Now, she had on a pair of black pants and a black button-down, her shoulder holster placed over the top.

Noah grabbed a can of sparkling water. "Rosie, are you thirsty?"

She accepted the drink, nodding with a tight smile. "Thanks, Mr. Vandermeer."

"If you need anything else, grab it. Make yourself at home."

Rosie gave every indication of being a well-trained professional who kept her personal opinions to herself. But Danica had said before that Rosie didn't take her concerns seriously.

Noah hadn't made his mind up about the woman yet.

Whether they could trust Rosie or not, she'd definitely report back to Blake and Danica's father. It made him furious to think someone in Danica's inner orbit had betrayed her.

But this "party," right now—they were taking a big step toward making Danica safe again. Even if they had to put on an elaborate ruse to do it.

That afternoon, Danica had spoken to his boss Max on the phone, and she'd e-signed the contract formally hiring them. Max had no problem with the secrecy, just as Noah had expected. Like any guy who'd spent time in special ops, Max was an unconventional thinker. Anything to get the job done.

By the end of this evening, Bennett Security's investigation would be well under way.

Noah went back to where Danica was standing in the kitchen. She wore a pair of cut-off shorts and a silky, sleeveless top. She'd asked the staff back at her father's house to send over a bag with fresh clothes and some other items she needed, which they'd delivered earlier.

Noah wrapped his arms around her waist and planted a kiss at the bend of her neck. "You don't have to do all that, babe. I'll set up the rest."

"That's all right, *sweetheart*, I don't mind." She looked over her shoulder at him, a sarcastic look in her eyes. "Laying it on a little thick, aren't you?" she whispered. "We've been back together a single day, not married for five years."

"But you really do deserve to relax." He brought his hands to her shoulders, feeling the tightness in her muscles. His thumbs gently rubbed at the knots. This entire evening was for show, but he genuinely wanted her to enjoy herself.

At least half a dozen of the guys here tonight would be keeping an eye on her. They were here to work, not to drink or kick back. That meant Danica didn't have to worry.

But clearly, she was having trouble letting go of the day's events. He couldn't blame her for that. Now that he was her bodyguard, he considered it his job to give her peace of mind, not just physical security.

More people kept streaming in, waving hello, exchanging hugs.

Music started up on the speaker system. It was an upbeat pop song, the kind of thing Danica usually loved. But she wasn't dancing.

Noah grabbed Danica's hand and spun her around, right there in the kitchen. She had to set down the hot dog buns she was holding.

"You're making me dizzy." But she was laughing.

"It's a party." He pulled her in closer, swaying side to side and bringing his mouth to her ear. "If you're not having any fun, this won't be believable."

"Shouldn't we be working on the investigation?" she murmured against his neck.

"The party just started. Is this not fancy enough for you, Ms. Foster-Grant? Because it's not a thousand-dollar-a-plate dinner?"

"I'd much rather be at a party like this, trust me."

"Not sure I buy that. But don't worry, if you get desperate, I could break out some caviar for the potato chips." Which was delicious, especially with crème fraîche.

"But that would be expected, right? I thought I was supposed to be unpredictable."

"Then you should be getting wild. Dancing on the dining room table." He wanted to see that.

She barked a laugh. "I would need a lot more than club soda to get me up on the table."

"I guess we'll just have to keep dancing right here." Noah put his forehead against hers.

"Oh, aren't you two adorable?"

They both looked over. Aurora Bennett, Max's younger sister, was walking into the kitchen with Devon in tow. Tanner was right behind them with his girlfriend Faith.

Noah waved. "Hey, you made it."

Danica turned around, and Noah introduced everyone, keeping his arm around her shoulders. He felt the stupidly big grin on his face as she met some of his closest friends.

"I've seen you on TV," Aurora gushed. "Your skin is even more amazing in person."

Danica laughed. "Oh. Thanks."

Aurora's eyebrows drew down. "I'm really curious. What were the flower arrangements like at the Oscars after party this year?"

"I'm afraid I don't remember."

"Aurora's an event planner," Noah said.

"*Really.*" Danica touched Aurora's arm. "I'm always looking for event planners. We should talk."

"How did you and Noah meet?" Faith asked. "I bet you have a cute story, and I want to hear every detail."

Danica turned to smile at him. "We were in high school. He was my younger brother's friend. And he was about…" She held up her hand to her shoulder. "This tall? With braces."

"I only had braces for a year," he protested.

Faith clapped her hands. "Pictures! We need to see pictures."

Noah frowned. "No pictures."

The others all laughed.

Devon and Tanner knew this was a job. That Noah and Danica weren't really together. But Aurora and Faith didn't. Noah never liked lying, even when it was necessary. The girls would probably be disappointed when they found out, which he regretted.

But this bantering with Danica and his friends didn't feel forced. If anything, it was far too easy. Like she really belonged here in his life.

Danica lifted her chin, nodding at the stairs. "There's a whole wall of photos devoted to Noah on the second floor, in typical only-child fashion. Want to see?"

He groaned. "Dani, can you not…"

"But I'm supposed to be having fun, aren't I? I've had *such* a stressful day." Her eyes were round and innocent.

The three women dashed off toward the staircase. Devon went to follow them. "I gotta see this shrine to you," he said.

"Yeah, and next time I see your mom and sister, I'm asking for your baby pictures," Noah warned.

Devon held out his arms, walking backward. "You want a war, Vandermeer? Bring it. Ranger versus SEAL."

All their teammates milling around in the near vicinity hollered at this challenge.

Noah chuckled as Devon ran after the women.

They'd already planned this out. Devon would take point on Danica's protection so Noah and Tanner could meet with a potential source.

And just as Noah had predicted, Rosie trailed Danica and the others upstairs.

"Is Chase here?" Noah asked Tanner, leaning over and keeping his voice down.

"Yep. Devon brought him like you asked. He's in the backyard, waiting to talk to you. 'Cause you insisted on being all mysterious about it."

"A lot's happened today, way more than I could explain on the phone. Let's grab some beers to pretend to drink, and we'll go have a chat."

~

OFFICER CHASE COLLINS of the West Oaks PD stood in the backyard sipping an IPA, a hand tucked casually into the pocket of his board shorts.

Noah and Tanner strode across the grass toward him. The air smelled of cooking meat, and the sun beat down on them from the aqua blue sky.

Noah held out his hand. "Chase, good to see you."

Chase was one of Devon's closest friends, and the other bodyguards had gotten to know him. Like Devon, Chase was in his twenties. He'd helped Devon save Aurora's life a while back, and Noah knew he could trust Chase just as much as his teammates.

"So what's this really about?" Chase took a small sip of his beer, which Noah noticed was almost entirely full. "The message Dev passed on from you was very cloak and dagger. This is way more excitement than I usually get lately when I'm off duty."

"We have to be discreet. The client is well known, and we think someone close to her could be leaking information."

Chase nodded. "I think I can guess who you're talking about. A certain neighbor of yours? Who's almost been kidnapped twice now? Everyone at the station has been going on about it."

"That's exactly why we want to talk to you. How well do you know Detective Angela Murphy?"

"She's new. She's got a good reputation with patrol so far. Tough but effective."

Noah told Chase about their conversation with the detective that morning, catching up Tanner at the same time.

Given Danica's profile and the danger involved, Bennett Security had cleared the decks as much as possible for this assignment. Tanner was going to be handling all logistics of this operation from the outside, since Noah would be occupied as Danica's personal bodyguard. Tanner would also be taking Danica's laptop and phone to their computer experts for analysis.

But Tanner had been a SEAL with him, and they both knew that a mission was only as strong as the intelligence behind it.

"Detective Murphy sent us the surveillance footage we requested," Noah said. "When we watched the video clips, it seemed like one had been altered."

"*Altered?*"

"To make it harder to identify the suspect. He had a distinctive tattoo, but in the video, that frame is missing. I want to know exactly who had access to that video, and when this alteration might've happened."

"Shit," Tanner said. "That's messed up."

Chase was tapping his beer bottle against his lips. "Yeah, I can definitely look into it. Without anyone else realizing, obviously. But if it's really somebody in West Oaks PD…"

"Yeah, it's bad."

"I haven't worked with Detective Murphy much. But I can find out more about her, too."

"Sounds good. Thanks, Chase."

Tanner scratched at his beard. "What about this tattoo? What's it look like?"

"A two-headed eagle, mostly black, the size of a hand. Front of the guy's neck. Heard of anything like that?"

Tanner had tattoo sleeves on his arms, plus more ink on his chest and back. "I've heard of things that're similar. I could ask my artist in LA. But I'm wondering if it could have a gang connection. You should send the description to Sean Holt."

"Who's he?" Chase asked.

"LAPD Gang and Narcotics Division," Noah supplied. "Former jarhead, like you." Though Sean was older than Chase, and Noah couldn't imagine they'd crossed paths in the Marines.

Chase nodded. "Then he must be a stand-up guy."

"I'll see what Sean makes of it," Noah said. "Whoever's doing this, they have the resources to hire thugs for the kidnapping and pay people—maybe in the police department—to help them not get caught. They aren't messing around, and if they find out the client hired us? I'm not sure what they'll do."

Chase patted his arm. "I get it. I'll be careful."

They heard laughter over on the patio. Danica, Faith and Aurora had just come outside. Devon and another of their teammates were serving up burgers, both beef and veggie.

For a moment, Noah's breath stopped, watching her. The easy way she smiled. The way she already seemed at home here.

Faith waved at them, beckoning them over.

"Looks like the chow's on," Tanner said. He started to cross the lawn.

Noah went to follow, but then Chase spoke up. "Hey, Noah. One more thing."

"Yeah?"

"I hope this isn't overstepping, but I consider you a friend." Chase looked down at his nearly full beer. "How well do you know...the client?"

"We used to be close a long time ago." Noah didn't see any point in denying it. "My cover is that we're hot and heavy after reuniting."

"But she's not staying permanently in West Oaks, right?"

"No. She's not." Danica would stay put until she was out of danger. In the long term, though? Home was back in New York.

Chase nodded. "I have some advice. If you're willing to hear it? From a fellow lovesick fool?"

Noah laughed. "Shit. It's that obvious?"

"Don't fall for a woman who's not in the right place to love you back. It sucks."

"Sounds like you're speaking from experience."

Chase pushed out a half-hearted laugh. "I wish I wasn't."

"I appreciate the wise words. I'll do my best to listen." Noah flashed his most disarming grin. "Let's get something to eat."

But as they walked across the grass, Noah's heart was drumming out a beat with every step. *Danica.* Anticipating the time they'd be spending together. The way he'd get to touch her, pretending they were more than they'd ever be.

Fuck. Chase was right. He was in so much trouble.

Chapter Nineteen

*D*anica walked onto the patio. Noah was out on the lawn, talking to Tanner and another man. She wanted to go over there and find out what they were saying about the investigation. But she also knew that Noah was capable of handling this, far more than her.

She hated giving up control, though. Type-A ran in her family, and she didn't apologize for it.

Faith nudged Danica with her elbow, noticing where she was focusing her attention.

"I'm sure you already realize this, but Noah's an incredible guy," Faith said quietly in her faint Texan drawl. "He helped Tanner and me get together when we were both being total idiots." Her laugh had a musical lilt to it. "And Noah's been such a good friend to Tanner, including through some tough times. We all want to see Noah happy."

"He's not usually happy?" Danica asked.

Faith pushed her blond braid over her shoulder. "I mean, he smiles all the time, and he's always ready to have fun. He would do anything for his friends, just like Tanner. But to me, Noah seems like he wants more out of life, and he hasn't found it yet. Maybe...he has now." She held up her hands, shrugging. "I'm just keeping my fingers crossed. That's all I'm saying."

Noah appeared at Danica's side. He wrapped his arm around her, that dimple sinking into his cheek. "Why's Faith keeping her fingers crossed?"

Instantly, the blond woman's face turned bright red. "We were having some girl talk. It's none of your concern."

Tanner edged into their circle, holding two plates of food. He gave one to Faith. "Uh oh, girl talk? That's code for comparing notes on *you*, Noah."

Faith poked Tanner in the side. "Shush. Not another word." They took their food and found a place to sit.

Once they were out of ear shot, Danica turned to Noah.

"What was Tanner talking about? Comparing notes?"

He dragged out an exasperated sigh. "I took Faith on a date once. *Half* a date. I hadn't realized she and Tanner were practically in love with each other. And apparently, neither had they, until that night."

"Oh." Danica was surprised at the twinge of jealousy in her chest.

Noah kissed her on the forehead, just another of the small intimacies he'd been showing her all night. And she knew it wasn't real. Even this party wasn't real.

But it still felt...*good*. After the terror she'd experienced the last few days, including that morning, she actually felt relaxed. She'd had fun chatting with Aurora and Faith. Enjoyed the music and laughter and casual banter this group shared.

And she liked Noah's arm around her. Liked it so much more than she should.

"So," she said. "You and Faith?"

"There was never any 'me and Faith.'"

"It's fine. I don't care either way."

His expression said he suspected this was bullshit.

"But she's way too nice for you, anyhow," Danica said.

"Too *nice*? I don't deserve nice?"

"You don't *want* nice." She remembered their interactions

from that long-ago summer. The heat in his gaze whenever she bossed him around or challenged him.

And earlier that afternoon? When they'd been arguing over the terms of this assignment? Pure chemistry, even though he'd tried to brush it off.

"I don't know what you're talking about," he said.

"Oh, really?" Danica was annoyed that he was denying it.

And she was feeling just a tiny bit possessive. She wanted to prove her point, and prove to everyone else in this room that Noah was hers.

Not *really* hers, of course, but…supposedly hers.

She grabbed the collar of his polo, pulled him down, and kissed him.

Noah reacted immediately. He made a sexy hum, like this was just the thing he'd been craving. His hand touched her hip, the other sifting into her hair.

His mouth opened as hers did, their tongues meeting and sliding over each other.

Arousal sped through her like a shot of tequila, lighting her veins on fire.

This was *a lot* more PDA than she usually went for at a party. But she didn't want to pull away.

Noah tasted too good. The heat of his mouth and the firm grip of his hands were making her knees weak.

Her teeth bit into his lower lip, and Noah moaned, his fingers traveling along her hip toward her ass.

"Damn, Vandermeer," someone shouted, "get a room."

They broke apart, their eyes wide. Then Noah grinned. "I guess you're right," he murmured. "Whatever that was, it wasn't nice. But I liked it."

"Let's get some dinner." Her skin was still burning. That had gotten way out of hand.

But had she enjoyed it?

Yes. God, yes.

After she ate, Danica took plates of food around to Rosie and the other Valoris bodyguards. Rosie accepted the offering. "Thanks. This looks great."

"I'm going to stay here tonight," Danica said. "Just FYI."

Rosie didn't blink. "Of course, Ms. Foster-Grant. I had assumed as much. One of my colleagues will take over when I go off duty."

"I haven't heard from Blake since this morning. I hope he's not still mad at me?" Danica was fishing here. But Rosie didn't bite, even though she'd been over to the house that afternoon and must've seen the chief of security.

"Not that I know of, ma'am. If you need anything else, be sure to let one of us know."

"Thanks. I will."

Danica had wondered if Rosie might argue on behalf of Blake. But she hadn't. Did that mean Rosie was trustworthy?

What about her dad's chief of security?

It was bizarre for Danica to think that *anyone* close to her could be plotting against her.

She really hoped she'd been wrong. Yet Danica also had far too much confidence in herself to believe that was the case.

BY ELEVEN, Danica was sitting on the living room couch, eyelids heavy. Noah was saying goodbye to the last of his guests.

Rosie's replacement, another bodyguard from Valoris, had taken up a post by the front door.

It seemed like the party had been successful. They'd gotten Danica's laptop and phone into Tanner's hands, with the promise that they'd quickly be returned.

Now, Danica was exhausted. And still unsettled. Too many thoughts and questions were swirling in her head.

And she was really trying not to think about that kiss on the patio. It had served a purpose—cementing their story that they were sleeping together. Childhood crushes thrown together by a stressful situation, finally reunited and unable to keep their hands off each other.

But they couldn't repeat it. Even if she really wanted to.

Ginger swept into the living room with Noah's grandfather behind her. "Don't tell me the party's already over?"

"It's my fault," Danica said. "I needed to call it a night early."

A giant wool shawl draped around Ginger's shoulders like a cape. "Oh, of course. I'm being thoughtless, after the day you've had. But you'll at least have a nightcap, won't you?" She turned to her husband. "Dearest, would you find Noah and bring us the Sauternes and some glasses?"

Ginger threw off her shawl and sat down next to Danica, tucking her legs beneath her. Ginger was as trim as she was, with defined muscle on her willowy arms. "I trust Noah's been taking good care of you?"

"He has. This day actually hasn't been so bad, considering how it started. Thanks for letting me take over your house today. I promise I'll get out of your way tomorrow."

She wasn't sure where she'd go, but she couldn't put Noah's family in danger by sticking around here too long.

"It hasn't been the slightest bit of trouble." Ginger leaned over and whispered, "Noah thinks he's being top secret, but he can't fool me. I know he's protecting you, and I thoroughly approve. I want you to stay here as long as you need." She squeezed Danica's wrist.

Danica was relieved she knew the truth. "But people are trying to kidnap me," she murmured back. "The police caught some, but I don't know if that was all of them."

"You obviously won't let anyone intimidate you. Well darling, I'm the same. When a friend of mine is in need, I don't scurry off with my tail between my legs. Besides, the more people who are around you, the safer you'll be. No?"

Danica had to admit, that made some sense.

Ginger patted her hand reassuringly. "But next time you visit, we'll plan something nice and relaxing. I'm thinking a dinner party. No more than thirty or forty people. Catered with wine pairings."

"You and I have different ideas about what's relaxing. But I'd like that."

Noah and his grandpa returned, carrying a bottle of golden-colored dessert wine and glasses. Noah held a plate of something, and he presented it to Danica.

Potato chips, each with a tiny dollop of caviar.

"Madame?" He had one hand tucked behind his back, his body leaned forward like he was a waiter. She took a chip and slipped it into her mouth, trying not to laugh as she chewed.

"I looked for brown-butter chocolate cookies," he said, "but Ginger's out."

So he'd remembered. Danica had a sweet tooth, especially when she felt anxious. "That's okay. This is just what I needed. Thank you."

After their late-night snack and a few sips of wine, Noah and Danica excused themselves to head upstairs.

Noah started toward his bedroom. "You coming?" he asked, when he saw her standing in place.

"I was thinking we'd stay in a guestroom. The one with the blue curtains, where I showered earlier? If someone's after me, they'll expect me to be in your bedroom. Right?"

Actually, after the day they'd had, she felt like his bed was a little more intimacy than she could handle. Too tempting.

Not thinking about that kiss.

"Yeah. No problem. I'll get changed and meet you there."

Danica's bag was already in the guestroom. She followed her nighttime routine, washing her face and brushing her teeth. When she came out of the bathroom, she found Lucifer the cat sitting on the bed.

She sat down, and Lucy stretched toward her. Danica's mind worked as she scratched the cat's soft head.

This was the first time in as long as she could remember that she had no idea what was going to happen. Apart from the gala, her schedule was completely up in the air.

But she actually didn't mind it.

Uncertainty also meant *freedom*, and she hadn't experienced that in so long. Nearly getting kidnapped twice was a sad excuse for a vacation. But taking some time off could be a good thing. A reset.

Eventually, of course, she'd return to her regular life, with all its benefits and drawbacks.

Which would also mean saying goodbye to Noah.

The door opened, and Noah stepped into the room. He wore only a pair of pajama pants. Dark hair lightly dusted his broad chest and ran down between his abs.

Danica averted her gaze before she could start to stare. "*Really?* You couldn't find a shirt?"

"I usually sleep naked. This is already a concession. You'll just have to keep your eyes to yourself."

"Don't worry, I will." The man could be so infuriating. She grabbed a pillow from the bed and threw it at him. "I assume you're sleeping on the floor? Since we're keeping this professional."

"The cat's claimed the other half of the mattress, so I don't have much choice. I got voted off the island." He selected one of the extra blankets that was folded at the end of the bed.

Noah arranged the pillow and blanket on the floor, taking the side of the bed closest to the door. It was hard to imagine someone coming after her tonight in his family's house. But she doubted she would've been able to sleep alone.

If she really started thinking about who might've betrayed her, she wasn't going to be able to sleep, *period*. Not even with Noah right here.

Danica slid beneath the covers and turned so she could see him. "Did you talk to that West Oaks PD officer you mentioned?"

Noah put his arm above his head, looking up at her. "Yeah. Chase Collins." He told her what they'd discussed, and that Chase was going to make discreet inquiries. "I have a friend in the LAPD, too. We can send him your drawing of the eagle tattoo and see if he can connect it to known gangs in the region."

"Thank you." Noah sounded confident they'd find a lead, and that shored up her confidence, too. "I want to be part of every step of the investigation going forward. I need to know what's going on."

"You will be." Then he added, "As much as possible."

"You had to qualify that statement?"

"I can't predict every eventuality."

She lay on her back, staring at the ceiling. "You realize you'll have to be my date for the museum gala on Thursday, right? I hope you have a tux."

He scoffed. "I have more than one. I get a lot of assignments where I'm the guy in a monkey suit and sunglasses at a fancy event."

"Except this time, you're supposed to be my…boyfriend. Is that what we decided?" She felt silly saying it.

"I've been told I'm a good boyfriend."

"I can't promise I'm a good girlfriend." She hadn't had that many relationships, actually. The men in her past had complained she was too unavailable. They'd wanted her to fawn over them, lose herself in their lives and interests, which Danica would never do.

"And I don't usually move this fast," she reminded him.

"So you need to be wooed? A dozen roses and a diamond tennis bracelet?"

"Hardly. More like *lots* of persistence." *And caviar and potato chips*, she added silently.

"You don't think I'm persistent?"

"It's only been a couple of days. Hardly impressive."

"But combined with my extreme levels of sexiness?"

Danica grabbed another pillow and threw it at him. The jerk caught it easily and tucked it beneath his head. She couldn't help laughing.

But somehow, that laughter stuck in her chest, turning softer and more tender as she looked down at him.

"Thank you for doing this. Helping me. If it wasn't for you, I'm not sure where I'd turn." Damn, her eyes were stinging again.

She'd hired Bennett Security, and she was paying for their aid. But she felt she owed Noah and his family so much more. That wasn't a comfortable feeling for her. She'd have to find a way to pay them back.

Noah held out his hand, palm up. Danica reached down, and his fingers clasped around hers. "Dani, you're not alone. Even if it wasn't my job, I'd do whatever I could to make sure you're safe."

"I know. You've been saying that."

"And I'll keep saying it until you believe it."

Chapter Twenty

The next day, Noah gave Danica his spare laptop, and she holed up in the guestroom for most of the day. She only came out briefly to grab lunch, and she ate it upstairs.

A courier pouch arrived with her phone, which had received a clean bill of health from Bennett Security. No trackers or spyware. When he knocked, Danica snatched the phone from his hand and shut the door again.

Last night, he'd lain awake, listening to her breathing while she slept. She'd tossed and turned, moaning like she was having a nightmare, but he'd stayed put on the floor. Even though all he'd wanted in the world was to crawl into that bed with her and hold her.

Every moment he spent with Danica was filled with temptation. Like that kiss on the patio. He'd nearly popped a boner in front of his teammates. But really, could they have blamed him? When she'd bitten his lip... Jeez. Way too hot. And the fact that he hadn't expected it had just heightened the experience.

That woman was dangerous. In more ways than one.

Part of him wished they could just drop the "romance" subterfuge altogether. He'd miss having that excuse to touch her, but it would be a lot easier to focus on his job. This wouldn't be such a damned test of his willpower if they weren't playing this game.

Acting like he wanted her wasn't difficult. The real fiction was pretending she *didn't* fire up every part of him with need.

Noah opened his encrypted messenger app and checked in with Tanner and Chase, neither of whom had any updates for him. Then he contacted his friend Sean, the detective with the LAPD. He sent along the photo of Danica's eagle tattoo sketch.

Sean replied quickly. He thought the design looked familiar, but he wanted to check up on a few things before stating any opinions.

That left Noah to sit back and ponder what they should do next. Even though he already had a strong hunch.

So far, Danica had scrapped virtually all of her plans for her visit to West Oaks. All except the museum gala, which would be tomorrow night.

Which meant that, if the kidnappers wanted to make another attempt, they'd probably do it at the museum.

Noah planned to add bodyguards from his own team to the guest list, and Danica had promised to discreetly arrange it with her museum contacts. But at the event tomorrow, it wasn't going to be easy to keep his teammates placed in key positions. They also wouldn't be allowed to carry weapons through the metal detectors.

He decided on two people—Tanner and Rex. Noah trusted Tanner completely. As for Rex, he was quiet and serious, always reliable. Both had extensive skill with hand-to-hand combat, which would make up for their lack of defensive firepower. And unlike Devon, neither had gone to the initial meeting with William Foster-Grant, so their employment with Bennett Security would be less obvious.

Danica had also provided him with the layouts for the museum, showing all the entrances and exits. Tomorrow, Noah's team would be as ready as they could be.

Finally, Noah got tired of waiting for Danica to emerge. He knocked on the guestroom door again, then went inside.

Danica was sitting at the small desk in the corner.

"Are you finished stalling?" he asked.

"What are you talking about? I've been trying to reschedule meetings and deal with the absolute mess that all this chaos has created. Not to mention the fact that I don't have my own computer back. I'm not...stalling."

"Pretty sure you are. You said you didn't want to hide, but you haven't left this room in hours. You haven't left this *house* since you arrived. And as much as I like having you here, it makes me think you're avoiding something."

She glared.

"Dani, if you want to get out of town and head to a safe house instead, we can do it. Right this second. That would be my first choice. But you vetoed that idea."

"And my decision is the same. I'm not running away."

"Then you know where we have to go."

She sighed, rubbing her forehead. "My father's house."

"Exactly." If someone close to Danica had betrayed her, it was very likely that the individual was in the Foster-Grant residence right now. The longer Danica stayed away, the more obvious her suspicions would become.

And there was always the possibility they'd turn up new clues while they were there.

"It's not like me to avoid *anything*," she said. "Especially things like confrontation. But this... I still can't get my head around the idea that someone I trust could be trying to hurt me."

"I know." He crossed the room and put his hands on her shoulders. "Anything I can do to make this easier?"

"Except for just being there with me?"

"That goes without saying. But how will your family react when you tell them we're together?"

She glanced away. "I'll handle them."

"Just give me some advance warning if Soren decides to duel me with a poison-tipped sword."

"A bodyguard who makes Shakespeare references? How do women ever resist you?" Then a grin slowly snuck onto her face.

"This is going to be hard no matter what. But I have an idea that could make it slightly more fun."

Noah hoped so. Otherwise, this was going to be one of the most awkward "meet your girlfriend's father" moments he'd ever participated in.

THE ENGINE of Noah's Ducati rumbled as he pulled into the Foster-Grants' driveway. Danica's arms were tight around his waist. They hadn't gotten to ride very long or very fast, but she was right.

It had been fun.

He stopped the bike in front of the house.

Danica got off first, pulling her helmet from her head. She'd worn a backpack carrying her own bag from yesterday, plus a few items of his that he'd added. They weren't sure if they'd stay overnight. That depended on their reception. But Noah wanted to be ready for anything.

He tugged off his helmet and carried it under his arm. Rosie had parked behind them in her sedan, and she followed.

They walked toward the front entrance to the house, where Blake Halston was waiting on the steps.

"Is there a reason for this stunt?" Blake barked.

Noah figured it was best if he not answer. In fact, this seemed like a time that the less he said, the better.

"You wanted me to come back to the house, didn't you?" Danica said, gesturing with her hands. "Here I am."

Blake's hard gaze moved over to Noah, accusations in his eyes.

But before Blake could speak, William Foster-Grant emerged from the shadows of the open doorway.

Unlike Noah's own dad, who looked every bit the mechanical engineer he was, William could've been an aging billionaire straight from central casting. He had thick brown hair that had gone silver at the temples. A slim but strong build. Expensive, yet understated business casual clothes.

"Danica. It's a relief to see you back. You have no idea how worried we've all been." William hugged his daughter.

"Noah was looking out for me," Danica said.

"So you've been telling me." William's scrutinizing gaze slid over to Noah. "It's been a long time. This is not the way I would've imagined us meeting again."

"No, sir. I guess not."

William grasped his hand in a vise-like grip. Noah squeezed back.

He'd chosen to avoid the man the other day, but not because he was intimidated. Noah didn't actually give a fuck whether William Foster-Grant liked him. Not unless it caused problems for the people he cared about.

But this was the man's house, and Noah had been raised to be polite.

"Give my regards to your mother and father?" William asked. "I understand they've moved out of West Oaks. It's been years since I've seen them."

"Yes, sir." He assumed William didn't actually want details on the Vandermeer family, and Noah didn't feel like giving them.

"Are we going to stand around out here, or can we go in?" Danica asked.

William waved for them to follow. Danica grabbed Noah's hand.

Blake brought up the rear, and Noah felt the man staring into his back.

Suddenly, he wondered if this was such a good idea. He felt an urge to sweep Danica into his arms, get back onto his bike, and speed away as fast as he could.

But it was too late now. They were inside, and a security guard shut the door.

"If you all don't mind," William said, his voice suddenly a deeper pitch, "I'd like to speak with my daughter. Alone."

Noah took an involuntary step toward her. She glanced at

him, giving him an almost imperceptible shake of her head, then walked away with her father.

They disappeared down a hallway, going toward a different wing of the house. It was the first time Danica had been completely out of his near vicinity in more than twenty-four hours.

Chapter Twenty-One

*H*er father's office was paneled in rich wood, with thick velvet drapes and antique furniture. An engagement portrait of Danica's parents dominated the wall behind his desk.

William settled into his leather chair. He hadn't said anything yet. But this was one of his favorite negotiating tactics. Silence, until the other side caved and rushed to fill it. Usually making an admission.

She never fell for it.

Danica resisted the urge to rub her eyes. She was exhausted after not sleeping well. She'd had nightmares again, and had used up much of her remaining energy today holding herself together.

If she'd fallen apart, Noah would've reassured her, but Danica had shown enough vulnerability in front of him already.

The more time she spent in Noah's arms, the harder it would be to say goodbye.

William blinked first. "You didn't notify Blake that you were ready to come home. He would've sent a car."

"It didn't seem necessary. It was easier for Noah to take me."

Seeing her father's tense interaction with Noah outside hadn't helped her mood. Somehow, she'd imagined William could set aside old grudges for her benefit. But she'd been wrong.

William crossed his legs. "I was surprised that you spent so long with Noah Vandermeer. I assumed you were simply upset after your brush with those kidnappers. But now, it's clear this connection between you and Noah is something more."

"So what if it is? I haven't made any comments about *your* liaisons."

"I don't have the faintest idea what you're referring to."

"Tori? I saw her here, in your office, just the other night. I don't have a problem with it." She sighed when he didn't react. "Dad, I want to see you happy. It doesn't have to be a secret."

He paused, his expression carefully neutral. "That is not a subject I wish to discuss with my daughter."

"But you feel a need to discuss *my* love life?"

"Danica, please don't throw around the word 'love.' I happen to believe that word means something. But you just showed up on the back of the man's motorcycle. You wanted to get my attention, and you've got it. Is this a response to the stress you've been under? A belated rebellion, since you didn't have one as a teenager?"

A defiant part of her was glad she'd irked her father. "Why would I need to rebel? I'm in charge of my own life, as far as I know. And Noah isn't some neighbor boy in a leather jacket."

She couldn't bring herself to call him her "boyfriend." The word seemed both too serious and too frivolous for this moment.

She didn't actually believe her father had anything to do with those kidnapping attempts. But was he hiding things? Absolutely. She was sick of looking the other way.

Sick of secrets.

"No, you're right," her dad said. "Noah is a man with a history with this family. That's what concerns me."

"Noah did nothing wrong."

Her dad grunted. "The scandal was Soren's fault. I have no doubt of that. He brought shame to our family and to himself.

But Noah should've come to *me*. I would have dealt with the issue quietly instead of in public."

"So he failed some test of loyalty? Noah would never have agreed to cover up Soren's mistakes."

William spread his hands. "Exactly my point. It's his character that's the issue. I admire Noah's accomplishments and his service. But we can't trust his discretion."

"*We?* Who I decide to date isn't a group decision."

"I beg to differ. In a family like ours, many things become a group decision. Especially when the acts of one threaten the many."

"You're talking like we have something to hide."

"Doesn't everyone?"

A drop of ice ran down her spine.

What else are you keeping from me? she wanted to demand.

But she'd never felt so wary of her own father.

He stood, rounded the desk, and pulled her into another hug.

Her dad was thinner than Danica had remembered. It had been a while since they'd embraced like this, especially twice in one day.

"I hate when we argue," he said.

"So do I."

"Do your father a favor. Stay home where I know you're safe."

"Fine, I'll stay tonight. But Noah stays, too."

He gave her a disappointed frown. At one time in her life, she'd have done anything to avoid that look.

"All right," he said, "if you're so infatuated. Get him out of your system. But I hope you'll be careful, and that you'll think of the Foster-Grant name, not just yourself."

Chapter Twenty-Two

"Vandermeer? I'd like a word as well." Blake crossed his arms, making the fabric of his suit jacket pull taut.

"Sure." Noah faced him. They were still in the front entryway of the house, with guards stationed by the door. Noah didn't see Rosie, and he wondered where she'd gone. "What can I do for you?"

"I'd like to know your intentions regarding Danica."

"Isn't that a question her father should be asking me?"

Noah smiled, but Blake didn't react to the joke. "I'd like an answer."

"I care about her," Noah said. "She's a very special woman."

"Yes. And she credits you with saving her yesterday from the kidnappers."

"Pretty sure she saved herself. I just helped out afterward."

"Don't give me that false modesty. I know your type. You're the kind of cocky asshole who waltzes into a situation assuming he belongs there."

"*Excuse* me?"

The other day, Blake had seemed like a nice enough guy. Someone the Bennett Security team could work with. Now, Noah was seeing the man's other side.

"I don't think you misheard. I spoke clearly enough, didn't I?"

"I'm here because Danica *wants me* here."

"I was under the impression you had a job. With Bennett Security?"

"I called in some vacation time."

Blake closed in on him, doing his best to be intimidating. Noah's pulse didn't change its steady beat. But he was surprised Blake had chosen outright confrontation.

"I didn't recognize you when you arrived with Max Bennett at the office a few days ago," Blake said. "But I know your name. I'm familiar with your history with Danica's brother."

Noah tucked his hands casually into his jeans. "What does that have to do with anything?"

"Thanks to you, Soren nearly ended up in prison. Since then, you haven't communicated with Danica—or anyone in this family. But suddenly, you've insinuated yourself into a place of trust and access. Just a few days after William chose not to hire the company you work for."

"I was just there when she needed me."

"You saw an opportunity to impress Danica by playing her knight in shining armor? Is that it?"

Shit, had the guy seen through their ruse? Blake had realized Danica had hired him?

"You make it sound like an insidious strategy," Noah said.

"Plenty of people want to get close to the Foster-Grants for their own ends. Social climbers always want to climb higher."

Noah's smile was vicious. He should've been pleased that Blake was so far off base. But his annoyance won out. "I'm not after her money or her status, if that's what you're implying." It was true that the Vandermeer family had nowhere close to the fortune the Foster-Grants did. But social climbers? Hardly.

"Then maybe it's some kind of vengeance you're after? You didn't do enough damage to her brother before?"

"I feel nothing toward Soren. He's irrelevant to me. But Dani and I have known each other a long time. We lost touch because of factors outside our control, and in the last few days—when her father invited Bennett Security to his office—we reconnected. It's as simple as that. Our relationship is none of your business."

He felt Blake scrutinizing him. The moment dragged out before the man finally spoke.

"I'm going to be frank. If Danica wants you in her bed? That's her issue. But don't go thinking that gives you a voice around here. I don't care if you were a SEAL. I don't care if you're James-fucking-Bond. If you get in the way of my ability to do my job, I'll deal with you as I see fit. I protect this family from *all* possible threats. No matter where they come from."

Chapter Twenty-Three

When Danica stepped out of her father's office, she found Noah waiting down the hall. She'd left the motorcycle helmet on a table, so she grabbed it as she passed, along with the backpack.

Noah raised his eyebrows, asking a silent question.

"My room," she said. "Upstairs."

Once they'd reached her bedroom, Danica shut the door. "Well that was—" she began, but Noah held up a finger to his lips.

What? she mouthed.

Noah slid the straps of the backpack from her shoulders. He set the pack on the floor, unzipped it, and dug around inside. When his hand came out, he was holding a black plastic device.

He walked around the room with it.

Danica realized what he must be doing. She waited for him to finish.

"You're clean," he said. "No listening devices in this room."

She breathed out. She wished she could say he was being ridiculous to think her room could be bugged. But, considering recent events?

Danica sat on her bed and fell backward, covering her eyes. The mattress compressed as Noah sat next to her.

"How'd it go with your father?"

"Could've been better."

"He's not happy I'm here?"

"Happy? No. Not so much."

"I don't expect him to like me. How could he, after what happened with Soren? But then I showed up here today with you on my motorcycle." Noah chuckled. "Not the smartest idea, in hindsight."

"It was *my* not-smart idea. But I was trying to get a reaction."

"Was it the reaction you expected?"

"Unfortunately? Yes." William had acted like a man who didn't trust his daughter, no matter how much she'd done to earn it.

"I'm sure he'll be relieved when he finds out we're not really together."

Her jaw tightened. "No doubt."

"While you were with your dad, Blake gave me a talking-to."

Danica sat up. "What did he say?"

"He warned me away from you. He thinks I'm sleeping with you for your money and social status. Either that, or I have some everlasting vendetta against Soren, and taking you to bed is my latest tactic."

She tipped her head back, cackling. She'd needed a laugh.

"Here's my question," Noah said. "Do you think your father and Blake are on the list of potential suspects?"

Her laughter died in her throat. Nausea had replaced it. "For hiring those men who came after me? Plotting my kidnapping?"

In her dad's office a few minutes ago, she'd been thinking that was impossible. If the kidnappers wanted ransom, they'd expect her dad to pay it.

But really? She wasn't sure of anything anymore.

Her father and Blake had known her schedule. They'd had the means and opportunity to set her up, though their motives were unfathomable.

"I guess it's possible they're involved," she finished. "Though I hate even thinking it."

Noah put his hand over hers. "Our computer analysts could find out you were hacked. In that case, the plot would've come from the outside, and your family's probably got nothing to do with it."

"God, I hope so." And if she could stop the hack and change her schedule, then the kidnappers would have nothing left to go on. No way to find her without starting all over.

If that happened, Bennett Security would still have to find the man with the eagle tattoo and whomever had altered the video footage. But at least she'd know her family wasn't behind it.

ONCE AGAIN, Noah set up a pillow and blanket on the floor, and Danica took the bed. She switched out the light, but she still felt his presence. She could hear him breathing. Smell his soapy, manly scent.

"Noah? Can I tell you something?"

"Always."

"It happened last year. But I don't think that this has anything to do with the kidnapping attempts." At least, she really didn't want to think there could be a connection.

But at the moment, she was questioning everything.

"Okay," he said. "What is it?"

Her father had said, *We can't trust his discretion.* But she trusted Noah with anything. He'd proven himself to her, over and over.

Danica wanted to trust him with this, too.

"Last fall, someone tried to blackmail me."

The message had appeared a month after her profile in *Vanity Fair.* She remembered the day being crisp and clear, all the leaves changing to fiery colors in Central Park.

She'd sat down at her computer, checking her inbox first thing as she usually did. The email had come in to her foundation address.

I have information about your father that you won't want publicized. Contact me and we can talk.

She hadn't responded, of course, dismissing the message as meaningless. Just some internet troll attempting to squeeze a few dollars out of her.

But a week later, another message had arrived.

You're not taking me seriously. But I have a question for you. What was your father doing January 17th, exactly twenty-eight years ago? If you value your father's legacy, you'll get in touch. I have proof of certain things, and if you aren't interested, the media will be.

This time, the message had unnerved her enough for her to forward it to their security chief.

"You never heard if Blake found this person?" Noah asked.

"He said it was just a prank. That the trail led nowhere." But the incident still bothered her. That message had been so specific.

"Did you look into this date they mentioned?"

"I tried. I asked my father about it, and he said he had no idea." Danica and Soren had been little kids then. Her mom had still been alive.

"You told your dad about the message?"

"Of course. At the same time that I'd sent it on to Blake. After their investigation didn't go anywhere, my father and I didn't speak about it again."

"There are two options," Noah said. "Either Blake was telling the truth, and this person was just blowing smoke. Or…"

"Or Blake paid the person off," she finished for him. She'd been thinking the same thing. "I feel like I don't have a clue what's really going on in my family."

"Do you want me to look into it? I could ask our research team to see what might've happened in your father's life twenty-eight years ago on January 17th."

"Not yet. Let's wait to hear back about my computer, whether it was hacked. I'm not even sure I should've told you."

Her father would be furious. He'd see it as a worse betrayal than she'd ever committed. Especially if he truly had something to hide, which she now believed.

"Then why did you?"

Because she'd never told anyone apart from Blake and her dad about the blackmail message. Not even Soren.

"Because I knew you'd listen," she said.

Danica closed her eyes and tried to sleep.

Chapter Twenty-Four

*N*oah woke in the dark. Danica was crying. Thrashing around on the bed.

Instantly, he was on his feet. The blinds on her window were closed, but enough moonlight shone through that Noah could see her. Danica's eyes were squeezed shut, the sheets pushed down below her legs.

She was having a nightmare again, like last night. But this one must've been worse. Tears were leaking from her eyes.

He'd never seen her cry before. Not once.

"*Please,*" she murmured. "*Don't.*"

Noah put a hand on her arm. "Dani?"

"*No.*"

"Dani." He couldn't stand seeing her like this. He knelt over her on the mattress and held each of her arms, trying to nudge her awake.

Danica's eyes flew open. She gasped.

Her leg hooked around his knee, and she threw her weight toward him. Suddenly they'd flipped, switching places. But instead of landing on the mattress, Noah fell completely off the bed.

He thudded onto the floor with Danica on top of him.

"*Oof.*" He was feeling those metal rods in his back. Damn.

"Noah? What happened? What're you doing?"

"Trying to wake you. It worked."

"But…" Her knees were on either side of his stomach. She glanced up at the bed, then down at him, like she was tracing the chain of events. "Did I hurt you?"

"Nah." Even if the strain in his voice suggested otherwise. "Your self defense skills are impressive, though."

"I'm sorry."

"It was my fault. Are you all right? I thought you were having a nightmare."

"I might have been. It's no big deal." She wiped her face.

"You were crying."

Her palms pressed onto his bare chest, fingers splaying. She wasn't getting up. Instead, she was staring down at him, eyes now defiant. "I don't cry."

"Sure about that?"

Her eyes narrowed, and her hair fell around her face. "I *wasn't* crying. I think you might be, though. Are your eyes watering? Are you sure *you're* all right?"

His blood pumped faster, enjoying this more every second. Especially now that she seemed annoyed at him instead of upset.

Danica had on leggings and a loose top, and he was working very hard not to sneak a peek down the front.

"Okay, fine, you don't cry." Noah brought his hand up to tuck her hair behind her ear. "But if you ever do, you don't have to worry." He was murmuring softly. "I won't tell anyone."

"Noah, I…"

"Yeah?" He knew he was staring at her mouth, but he couldn't help himself.

"I really am sorry for attacking you."

"Don't be. You can flip me around any time you want."

She smirked. "Can I?"

"In fact, it was kinda sexy." He hated that she'd been afraid, but the way she'd handled him had been hot.

"You shouldn't say things like that," she whispered. But she didn't seem all that disapproving.

"Just being honest."

"Maybe I should shut you up."

A new burst of heat flooded his veins. Whatever was happening right now, he liked it. "You could try."

Before he knew what was happening, her mouth crashed onto his.

Yes.

The last couple of days with her had been nonstop temptation. She'd kissed him at the party, and he'd managed to set that aside. To go back to good behavior.

But he'd been wondering when he'd reach the limits of his willpower, and this was it. Danica straddling him, the scent of jasmine filling his nose, her tongue licking at the seam of his lips.

The word "no" was no longer in his vocabulary.

His mouth opened to her, and their tongues slid against one another. Noah's cock jumped at the sensation.

She brought her hands up to either side of his face, pushing her tongue even deeper. Taking from him. Demanding.

Noah reached up to wind his fingers into her hair, tugging at the strands. Her shirt had inched up, the smooth skin of her stomach meeting his torso.

A fist pounded against her bedroom door. "Ms. Foster-Grant? The hall cameras registered a loud noise. Do you need assistance?" It was a male voice, one of the bodyguards who subbed in for Rosie.

Shit.

They both froze, and Noah figured this was it. Danica would realize what a stupid idea this was. Or get embarrassed at the interruption.

But she just shouted, "I'm fine. Go away."

And then she went right back to kissing him.

All his good behavior and "do the right thing" were officially forgotten. Noah's dick was tenting his pajama pants, and his body was on fire, and he'd needed her too badly and for too fucking long to listen to any voice except hers.

Anything Danica wanted. That was all that mattered.

But she was too busy sucking on his tongue for either of them to breathe, much less speak.

She was ravaging his mouth like she owned him.

Noah reached beneath her shirt. His palm met her breast, its round fullness swaying, the nipple jutting out. His thumb flicked over it, and she panted.

He wanted his mouth on her naked breasts. He wanted his mouth *everywhere*.

Noah hooked her around the waist and flipped them over. He cushioned her fall, making sure she hit his pillow and blanket.

This was actually Danica underneath him. The girl he'd been aching for since he was a kid. Now that it was really happening, he knew he should slow down. Turn on the lights. Kiss and touch and appreciate every part of her so he'd never forget this night.

But he also worried, deep down, that it wouldn't really happen. Someone else would knock on the door and refuse to be ignored. A natural disaster would hit. The universe would laugh.

But he wanted this so fucking bad. He'd never felt this kind of desire. So intense it could break him.

So he wasn't going to slow down, wasn't going to stop, unless Danica told him to. Like he was racing against all the things that might keep them apart.

"What do you want, Dani?"

"You. Everything you said when we were on the motorcycle."

"You want me to touch you? Fuck you?"

One of his hands pushed up her shirt. He brought his mouth over her nipple and sucked.

He dipped into her pajama shorts and stroked between her folds, seeking out her opening. Already soaking wet. Damn, she *really* wanted this.

Danica moaned. "*Yes.*"

Noah pushed his fingers inside her, coating them with her liquid, then withdrew. His tongue flicked out to taste her on his hand. So good. Pussy was like nothing else, and Danica's was an elixir, making him drunk with lust.

Noah rubbed his hand over his face, wanting to mark himself with Danica's heady scent. His cock thickened even more in response, balls already full and heavy.

He wanted to suck her clit until she came in his mouth, so he could drink in every drop.

Chapter Twenty-Five

*W*hen Danica had kissed him, she hadn't been thinking. In fact, she'd been making her best effort *not* to think.

Not think about that nightmare of men chasing her, faceless and relentless.

Not think about the secrets and lies and people out there who wanted to hurt her... The things that threatened to make her cry.

Not thinking was working just fine.

She and Noah had wasted so much of their time together resisting. Both when they were younger, and now. Wasn't it better just to let go? To give in?

The jolts of pleasure roaring through her body were screaming, *Yes. Please.*

But giving in was intense. It was vulnerable. And some part of her was still holding back. *Needed* to hold back in order to protect herself.

Suddenly, Noah sat back on his heels. "I need my tongue in you." He reached for her pajama shorts and yanked them past her hips and off.

Shit. The thought of his mouth between her legs, of opening herself up to Noah in such an intimate way, was a little more than she could handle right now. Even with long-term boyfriends, she'd rarely let them go down on her.

Danica needed to retake control.

When Noah dropped forward again, she grabbed his arm, wrapping her legs around his hips. She had him in closed guard. Danica used a scissor sweep to knock Noah off balance and onto his back.

Now she was straddling his chest, pushing his shoulders down into the floor. This was better. Desire crowded out the fear again.

Noah's eyes were wide, his mouth open. "That was, by far, the sexiest thing I've ever seen."

"I've never done it half naked before."

"Glad I was your first."

She crawled off of him, wriggling her shirt past her head and tossing it aside. In her suitcase, Danica dug around in the pockets.

"What're you doing?" he asked.

"Finding a condom." A few seconds later, she was back, kneeling in front of Noah.

He'd already kicked off his pants, and he was gripping his erection.

Danica swallowed. Noah was naked on her bedroom floor, dick in hand, eager and ready for her. It still felt like she was dreaming, but this was a far nicer dream than her last one.

Noah took the condom. "You're ready? I thought we'd keep going with the foreplay."

"I think twelve years is enough foreplay."

He opened the wrapper and rolled the condom on. Immediately, she swung her leg over him, thinking of the way she'd straddled his motorcycle. The power she'd felt beneath her.

His hands went to her hips, and they both gasped as she sank down, filling herself with his cock.

Noah's thick shaft was inside of her, stretching her, something she'd fantasized about a thousand times before.

And even in the dark, on the cold floor, the reality was so much better.

He squeezed her ass, then reached up to cup her breasts. Her hands landed on his pecs. Noah's hips moved as she started to rock. She was so wet, sliding against him.

"Kiss me," he whispered. But instead of waiting, Noah put a hand to her neck and pulled her to mouth to his.

She was on top, but Noah was still trying to direct this, and she actually didn't mind. She liked seeing the aggressive side of him. Just so long as she felt like she had the upper hand.

Her legs opened wider as she leaned forward, searching for just the right angle. Danica scratched her nails through his chest hair and along the ridges of his abs. She looked down at their bodies, but they were all shadows and faint lines, like a charcoal sketch.

The feeling of him inside her, though. It was bright color and heat. Vivid. She'd never felt so alive.

His hips thrust upwards, harder and faster.

She tipped her head back and let out a feral groan.

Noah's hands were everywhere. On her stomach and gripping her neck and in her hair.

She was sweating and panting and so close to tipping over the edge.

"Dani," he moaned, and that was all it took. She cried out as her body convulsed. She felt when he started to come, too, the pulsing of his cock adding to the moment and the sensation.

They rode out their orgasms together, foreheads touching, sharing each other's air.

His eyes were shining in the faint light. It was so dark she couldn't see the green of his irises, and she missed that.

"Hi," he said.

"Hi."

"I swear I usually last longer. Next time I want to worship you with my tongue. I didn't get to taste you nearly enough."

Next time.

He sat up to kiss her shoulder. "You tasted so fucking good I could bottle you and drink it."

Her skin flushed and prickled. She loved when he talked like that, and it also made her feel like she was falling down that hillside again. Careening toward something she couldn't see.

And now, the thinking was starting.

Of course, she'd been thinking enough to get a condom. Thinking enough to stay in charge. So maybe she'd known exactly what she was doing, and had figured she could still keep her heart out of it. Flirting with danger but staying just on this side of safety.

But she hadn't been thinking about *after*.

She'd wanted Noah for so long, but now what? What was she supposed to do with the ache in her chest that had, somehow, only gotten worse?

Noah lay back against the floor, resting his hands against her thighs. His teeth were pale in the low light as he smiled.

"I should probably…move," she said.

"I'm not rushing you. Except, at some point I need to take care of the condom."

"Um. Yeah, of course." She crawled off of him, feeling impossibly awkward.

Noah went to the bathroom, then came back. "You're freaking out."

"I'm not."

"You don't regret it, do you?"

"Of course I don't." Danica pushed back the covers and lay down in the bed. It seemed strange to put her pajamas back on at this point.

"Can I sleep in there with you? Or am I still relegated to the floor. Should I go down to the staff wing?"

"Stop. You can sleep here." She scooted over to make room on the mattress.

Still naked, Noah lay down next to her and pulled her to him. His skin was smooth and warm, his body firm. She wanted to spread herself over him, kissing him and caressing him until he was hard again. So they could get tangled up together for a second time, and a third, as if this never had to end.

Which was exactly the reason that tonight had been a mistake.

Chapter Twenty-Six

The next afternoon, Noah was getting ready for the gala when Danica came out of the bathroom. He whistled, taking a moment to let his gaze drag over her. She was wearing a green silk dress that hugged all her curves. It had a long slit up to one thigh. The thin straps showed off her toned shoulders and the swoop of her collar bones.

She'd styled her dark hair in loose curls, and she was wearing more makeup than usual. He preferred when she wore less, but he had to admit the silver shadow brought out the different shades of gray in her eyes.

"You look incredible," he said.

"Thanks. You look…nice yourself."

"I heard that awkward pause in the middle."

"You look great." Her teeth dug into her lip. "But after last night, I'm trying not to notice."

"So you *do* remember. I was wondering if I'd just imagined us getting naked."

She averted her eyes. Which was not a good sign.

When Noah had woken that morning, Danica had been in the shower. She'd barely glanced at him when she came out. All day, she'd been either ignoring him or peppering him with random, sarcastic comments. It had been fucking annoying, actually. Like she'd been trying to ghost him, even though they had to stay in the same space. This interaction right now was the most attention she'd paid him.

Exactly why you shouldn't have sex with a client, dumbass.

Except Danica wasn't just some client. She meant a lot more.

All the more reason that he shouldn't have done it.

She gestured at his tie, which was draped around his neck. "Can I do that for you?"

"I won't say no. But you already know that."

Her eyebrows ticked up. "Be good."

This *was* him being good. "You're the one who's insisting on touching me."

"I know," she murmured. "But I might not get many more chances."

He had to look away from her. Because damn, it hurt to hear something like that. He was pretty much screwed, as far as his feelings went.

But when he'd been a SEAL, he'd learned to embrace shitty moments like this. Life didn't always go the way you wanted. You just had to go forward and complete the mission. And make a joke or two so it all went down easier.

She tucked the end of the tie through the knot. "Any word about my laptop?"

"Tanner will be there tonight. I'll get an update."

From what he'd heard from Bennett Security, nothing suspicious had turned up on her computer. But they were being thorough.

Danica tightened the tie around his neck and adjusted his collar. He wished he could enjoy these few brief moments of being close to her without longing for more.

As soon as she was out of danger, she would be leaving West Oaks again. He'd known from the start of this assignment that was how it would end. But trying to keep his feelings out of it had been futile.

Noah put his coat on. Danica brushed lint from his lapels,

then took a step back from him. "I was thinking that we'd skip the red carpet tonight. I don't want to deal with reporters. And it would just bring unnecessary attention to you."

"Don't want all the gossip columns writing about your new boyfriend?"

"Trust me, you'd rather avoid that. It's tedious as hell."

He would've braved just about anything for her. But her plan made sense. Otherwise, they'd have to deal with answering questions about their sudden breakup later on. "Then are you planning for us to sneak in the back?"

She nodded. "I was thinking about what you said the other day. How I need to be unpredictable. If we take your motorcycle, no one will see me coming."

"You can get on the bike in that dress?" He looked skeptically down toward her feet.

"Just wait and see."

"The helmet's going to mess up your hair and makeup."

"I'll survive."

"But you've been planning this night for months. You've been looking forward to it, and it's important to you."

"*Noah.*" She grabbed his lapels. "I'm okay. I promise." Danica kissed his cheek, lingering a beat too long. His heart thumped in his chest. "You're supposed to protect me, not fuss over me."

"I'm a multi-tasker."

Smiling sadly, she brushed a thumb across his lips, and he couldn't stop himself from kissing it.

A crack had opened up in the middle of his chest.

The mission, he told himself. *Focus on the mission.*

THEY LEFT their motorcycle helmets at a security checkpoint as they walked inside.

Noah had never been to the West Oaks Natural History Museum before. One wall of the atrium was open, and music and lights spilled out onto the patio.

Rosie and another Valoris bodyguard followed in their wake. They'd driven in an SUV behind the Ducati from the Foster-Grant house.

Noah's eyes scanned the crowd, instinctively ignoring the regular partygoers and searching out the bodyguards. He spotted half a dozen that belonged to Valoris, like Rosie. They were providing the official security for the event.

He saw his teammates—Tanner and Rex. They'd each taken up posts on different sides of the atrium.

"There you are, Cap," Rex said in his ear. "Had to sneak in the back entrance?"

"They wouldn't let him in the front," Tanner quipped. "Thought he was one of the caterers."

Hilarious. Noah didn't answer, but he pursed his lips.

His teammates wore tiny earpieces identical to his, and they'd be able to hear anything he said tonight, and vice versa.

"Quit that," Danica whispered to him.

"What?"

"Acting like a bodyguard. You're frowning and glaring at everyone."

Noah rested his hand on her lower back, the corner of his mouth inching up. "Force of habit. I spend a lot more time on bodyguard duty than as a boyfriend."

"And it shows," Tanner muttered in Noah's earpiece.

Noah scratched his forehead with his middle finger.

"Oh, very subtle," Rex said.

Danica couldn't hear any of this juvenile exchange, which was for the best.

She reached up to touch his face, fingers sliding along his freshly shaven chin. After avoiding him for so much of day, she was suddenly all about the physical contact. First the neck tie, now this. She'd been holding him awfully tight on their ride over here.

Maybe she was trying to make their cover story convincing. Or maybe she was torturing him.

"I look okay?" Noah asked.

She patted his cheek. "You'll do."

"Danica!" A redhead in sequins and stilettos dashed over. "What a gorgeous dress. And who is this?"

"Lindley, this is Noah. My…boyfriend. Noah, this is Lindley Colter. The executive director for the museum."

Lindley's eyes were curious. "I didn't know you had a boyfriend."

"I've been chasing her for a while," Noah said, "and she finally gave me a shot."

"Sounds like a good story."

Danica's head swiveled toward him. "It really is. Why don't you tell it, Noah?"

"Maybe later. I'll get us some drinks."

She squeezed his arm. "Of course, *sweetie*. Hurry back."

He blew her a kiss as he walked toward the bar. Tanner was a few yards away, watching with amusement. Behind Noah's friend, a string quartet played classical arrangements of modern pop songs.

Noah asked for a glass of soda from the bar, then wandered over to the bar-height table where Tanner was casually leaning his elbow.

"Fancy meeting you here." Noah clinked his glass against Tanner's.

"Looks like the assignment is going well?" Like Noah, Tanner was wearing a tux, though he'd opted for a bowtie. Tanner's unruly hair was slicked back with gel.

"The assignment's great. Her father despises me. Her brother wishes I'd drop dead. Her chief of security thinks I'm an asshole. And I fucked up and slept with the client. Aside from that, no problems."

Tanner choked on his drink. "Shit. You pulled a Devon?"

"Is that what we're calling it now?" Everyone knew Devon and Aurora had gotten together when he'd been her bodyguard. But they'd wrangled a happy ending out of it.

Noah shouldn't have been saying any of this stuff. But his nerves were too frayed from holding his battered heart together.

It took a few seconds for Tanner to stop coughing.

"Do you have news?" Noah asked.

"Some. Sylvie just finished analyzing Danica's laptop."

Sylvie was their lead computer expert. "And?"

"Totally clean. Not compromised in any way, as far as Sylvie can tell. Including the scheduling app you were concerned about."

"I was afraid of that." Noah glanced around the room, mind working.

"Isn't it good news?"

"In a way, yeah. But not for Danica. It definitely means the person behind the kidnapping is someone close enough to know her schedule. That's a very small group."

Tanner ran a hand over his beard. "We can narrow the investigation, though."

"I'll get you the list tonight. We'll need full background on each one of them. Whatever we can dig up. Which includes her father."

Tanner nodded. "That'll be sensitive. I see the issue."

Noah glanced toward Rex's position over near the patio. "Anything, Rex?"

"Negative. All quiet here. Valoris has a decent perimeter around the patio, actually. They don't suck as hard as I'd expected."

That was good. But Noah intended to be vigilant tonight all the same. "There's one other thing I'd like to investigate, since we're doing background on her father anyway." He told them about the blackmail message and its reference to January 17th.

She'd asked him not to look into it, but as far as Noah was concerned, the news about her laptop made the blackmail fair game. They needed to know absolutely everything that William Foster-Grant—and everyone else close to Danica—could be keeping secret.

As he and Tanner spoke, Noah kept an eye on her. Partygoers kept coming up to her, their expressions brightening as she spoke to them. She *glowed*, and that glow rubbed off on anyone who came near her.

Every time Danica smiled and touched someone, giving them the gift of her notice, Noah felt an unreasonable surge of envy.

He would never try to hold her back from anything she loved. And she would never let him do it, either.

But he wanted her for himself all the same.

Her body and her affection. Even her criticism. He wanted it all.

He wanted to be the thing she loved most.

I am so fucked.

He had to get it together. Stop these possessive thoughts. Remember his job.

Someone she'd trusted had betrayed her. Noah was going to make sure they didn't get away with it.

Chapter Twenty-Seven

*D*anica greeted the donors, making sure they felt welcomed. She and Lindley talked up their plans for the museum renovation. But from the corner of her eye, she was watching Noah.

Of all the people in this room, all the people in the world, she most wanted to be right next to him.

It had nothing to do with the fact that he was her bodyguard. She just wanted to see his dimple when he smiled. To tease him. Kiss him.

Make love with him, like they had last night.

When she looked at Noah, she kept hearing that epic swell of soundtrack music. The signal in a cheesy movie that the two romantic leads would never let the other go.

And that depth of feeling, welling up from within her, was really starting to scare her.

Danica wanted things that just *weren't possible*. Not because of her family—she hardly cared what they thought—but because of the life she and Noah had each chosen. She traveled all the time, and he stayed put. Her home base was the East Coast, and he was on the West.

She was so close to falling for him. And that would only guarantee she'd get her heart broken.

Yet she couldn't bear to stay away from him, either.

Noah finished his conversation with Tanner and returned, sliding his arm around her waist. She introduced him to the donor she'd been chatting with.

"I'm her boyfriend," Noah said, the lie flowing so easily from his lips. Lying for her.

Noah had been the one to point out that they couldn't end up in bed together. But he'd been willing to break that rule as well.

I won't say no, he'd said. Yeah. No kidding.

She had to be the strong one when it came to their attraction. But her heart was getting whiplash from the mixed signals she'd been giving it. Pushing him away, only to pull him close again.

Right at this moment, Noah's arm around her waist was excruciating, even though it would've torn her apart to see that arm around anyone else.

Her chest tightened. She struggled to get enough air.

Damn it. This wasn't like her. She didn't let men distract her from her job and her responsibilities. But when it came to Noah, she was an absolute mess.

"Would you excuse me?" she asked, interrupting what the donor had been saying. She hadn't been paying attention anyway. "I'm so sorry, but I need to dash away. Grab another drink, and I'll catch up with you later?"

The donor nodded politely, walking toward the open bar.

Noah looked over at her with concern. "Everything okay?"

He was probably thinking she was worried about the kidnappers. And she was, at the back of her mind. But the museum was crawling with security, both Valoris and Bennett. If anything, she felt *too* surrounded.

Noah was too close, and also much too far away, and she had to get her head on straight.

"I just need to stop by the ladies' room. Stay here, keep being charming with the donors for me. I'll be right back."

As she crossed the room, Danica nodded at Rosie, who

followed her. Rosie had been sticking fairly close to her all evening, as Blake had no doubt instructed.

She wondered if Rosie's colleague had mentioned last night. At least the Valoris team would believe their romance cover story. Though hopefully, they hadn't heard *too* much. She and Noah hadn't exactly been trying to stay quiet.

Her skin flushed as she remembered how he'd felt inside of her. How he'd moaned her name. How he'd wanted to fuck her with his tongue, and god she wanted that too, even though it would mean letting down her barriers completely.

Danica was washing her hands at the bathroom sink when Lindley came inside. A partygoer left at the same time, and Danica and Lindley were the only ones there.

"Everything's going perfectly, don't you think?" Lindley asked. "The food, the music. The donors seem really impressed with the renovation plans."

Danica nodded. "Thank you for all the work you've put in. Especially with me being unavailable a lot of this week."

"Are you kidding? It was my pleasure. None of this would've happened without you." Lindley gave her a fond smile in the mirror. "Oh, I almost forgot. I got the strangest text a little while ago. Do you know someone named Tori Peterson?"

"Tori? She works for my father's chief of security."

Why on earth would Tori be texting Lindley?

"See for yourself." The museum director took out her phone and showed Danica the message.

My name is Tori Peterson, and this message is for Danica Foster-Grant. I need to speak with her urgently. But please keep this request private. It's a sensitive matter.

Anxiety flooded Danica's stomach. "I don't get it. Tori didn't say anything to me." She checked her own phone, but saw no message. She wondered how Tori had even gotten Lindley's number.

A sensitive matter. Could it have something to do with Danica's father?

"What're you going to do?" Lindley asked.

"Talk to her. I have to. It could be important." Why else would Tori go to the trouble of speaking to a third party like Lindley?

Was Tori afraid of the message being intercepted?

If the "sensitive matter" was about her dad, Danica had to know.

She sent off a quick text to Tori, asking if this was a good time to call. "I need to see if she calls back," Danica said. "Could you go back out with the donors? One of us should be there."

"Yeah. Of course." Lindley's expression was bewildered, but she did as Danica asked.

Dani paced in front of the sinks, waiting for a response. With each second that passed, the more her anxiety grew. What did Tori need to tell her?

A couple of donors came into the bathroom, smiling at Danica. She chatted with them when they spoke to her.

Finally, a text came in. Tori had asked her to call.

Danica pushed out of the bathroom. Rosie caught her eye and joined her. She must've seen the look of uncertainty on Danica's face. "Anything I can do for you, ma'am?"

Danica glanced at the entrance to the exhibits. "I just need a moment for a phone call. Someplace private. The exhibits are secured, right?"

"Yes, ma'am. We made sure those spaces were cleared and blocked off as you requested."

Danica and Lindley had wanted to focus the donors' attention on their new plans tonight, rather than the old exhibits that might soon change.

"Good. I'll just be a few minutes."

A velvet rope blocked the walkway, and she unhooked it to go past. Rosie waited just on the other side.

Danica walked into the hall of evolution, then turned a corner, entering the maze-like exhibit rooms.

The lights were dimmed, and her heels clicked against the hard floor. Her sore ankle twinged, but she'd been wrapping it with a sports bandage. It was nothing compared to the rest of the stress she was under.

Arrows showed the path for guests to follow. Danica ventured further in. If she was going to talk to Tori, she didn't want this overheard.

The noise of the party faded away. Danica stopped in front of a huge fossil of a tyrannosaurus footprint.

She pulled up Tori's contact and called her.

The phone rang and rang. The shrill noise was loud in her ear, but the exhibit around her seemed like it was frozen in time. Fossilized skeletons cast strange shadows across the floor, and brightly colored illustrations of Mesozoic plant life created an uncanny backdrop.

The ringing stopped.

"Hello? Danica?" Tori was speaking quietly. Almost a whisper.

"Hi. I got your message. What's going on?"

"I was hoping we could meet."

"Now? I'm at the gala. At the museum."

"I know. I'm nearby. Can I meet you there?"

"Well, I guess. I can let security know to allow you inside."

"Where will you be?"

"I'm in the exhibit halls. But—"

The phone made a noise. The call had ended. She couldn't tell if Tori had hung up, or if the connection had dropped.

Danica tried calling back, but it didn't go through.

Her phone said *No Service*.

Suddenly, despite Rosie's assurances, Danica didn't feel so secure. She was thinking of the other day. How her phone had showed *No Service* shortly before the first kidnapping attempt.

I need to get back to Noah.

She started back toward the lobby. But the maze of rooms seemed like it had tripled in length. The path kept extending, and she started to run, tracing the arrows backward as they took her from one space to the next.

Had she already come through here? Had she taken a wrong turn?

She entered a new room, and Danica's heart jumped into her throat.

Someone was standing there in the shadows.

"Hello?"

Then she realized it was just her reflection. A glass case was acting like a dark mirror, and Danica was seeing herself.

She exhaled. That had really scared her.

But as she stepped forward, a different shape emerged in the reflection.

The shape of a man, standing right behind her.

Danica screamed just as a hand closed over her mouth.

Chapter Twenty-Eight

*N*oah watched as Lindley went into the bathroom. Danica was still inside.

He was trying not to get overly concerned by her sudden change in mood. She'd been under a tremendous amount of pressure and had been trying not to show it. That was just Danica's way, but he understood the impulse.

For someone who didn't know her well, she might even seem unfeeling. But Noah could tell how much it all had been getting to her.

He wished she'd told him what was wrong. Let him comfort her. But even that, it seemed, was more than she wanted from him.

Noah went to the bar for a glass of seltzer with lime. The bubbles popped on his tongue as he both kept an eye on the bathroom door and studied the room. The donors continued to chat and enjoy themselves.

But Noah's attention caught on a newcomer. Someone he hadn't noticed before.

This guy was walking along the edge of the lobby, carrying a glass of champagne. But he wasn't drinking it. He wasn't talking to anyone, either. Instead, he was staring into the distance with a focused expression. He had on thick-framed glasses, but somehow they seemed wrong for his face. Like they were borrowed from someone else.

He wore a tux, but he didn't move like one of Danica's rich donors. He moved with purpose, like a man who knew just how dangerous he was. It was a look Noah had seen plenty of times before.

Noah held the glass in front of his mouth as he spoke. "Tanner? Do you see the guy on my ten o'clock? Blue bowtie. I'm not liking the looks of him."

His friend's voice came through the earpiece. "Yeah, I had my eye on him as well. He just walked in. I didn't see where he came from, but I don't think he was here before. Rex?"

"Didn't come in from the patio area."

Noah looked back toward the bathroom. He'd only been distracted a minute, maybe two. He still didn't see Danica.

But he noticed that Rosie wasn't outside the bathroom anymore. And Lindley was back in the atrium, chatting with the partygoers.

"Tanner, keep an eye on blue bowtie," he said. "I need to check on Danica."

"Copy that."

Noah went over to Lindley. She smiled as she saw him approaching.

"The boyfriend. What can I do for you?"

"Do you know where Danica is? I thought she was in the bathroom, but her bodyguard isn't outside anymore. Did they go somewhere else?"

Lindley shrugged. "Last I knew, Danica was in there. She was waiting for a phone call."

"A phone call? From whom?"

She hesitated. "I really don't know what it was about. You'll have to ask her."

"I get that you're trying to respect her privacy." To her, Noah was just Danica's boyfriend. Not her bodyguard. "But Danica could be in danger. I need to know where she is."

Lindley relented. "How about I go over and check the bathroom. See if she's still there. Maybe Rosie went in with her."

Noah followed her. But after a few seconds in the ladies' room, she came back out, looking worried. "They're not here. I really have no idea where Danica could be."

Shit. This felt wrong. Especially with the appearance of that guy just a few minutes before. "Thanks," he said. "I'm going to look for her."

"Do you really think she's in trouble? With all this security everywhere?" Lindley sounded like she was starting to panic, which wasn't going to help.

"I'm sure it's fine. But if you see her, tell her to stay in the main lobby area. Don't let her go anywhere else."

"Yeah. I will."

He spun, heading down the hallway.

"Do you want us to help look?" Tanner asked in the earpiece.

"Negative. Stay in the atrium with blue bowtie and watch for Danica there. I'm going to check the exhibits. Rex, you check the museum's front offices. Make some excuse if security tries to stop you."

"Got it, Cap," Rex said.

Noah's shoes echoed as he strode down the hallway into the exhibit area. His chest loosened slightly when he saw Rosie. She looked over at the sound of his footsteps.

"Where's Danica?" he asked.

Rosie pointed her thumb into the exhibits, which were on the other side of a velvet rope. "She asked for privacy."

"And you left her *alone*? Are you kidding me?"

She bristled at his strident tone. "This area is secure."

From deeper inside the exhibit halls, there was a scream. Immediately, it cut short.

Every cell in Noah's body surged with fury in response.

The metal stand holding the rope clattered to the floor as he pushed past. Noah started running.

He had to get to Danica. *Now.*

Chapter Twenty-Nine

The man clamped his hand over Danica's mouth.

She jammed her elbow into his muscled side. He grunted, but hardly budged. His other arm cinched around her waist, lifting her up.

He was dragging her backward. Deeper into the exhibits.

No. *Stop him*, her instincts screamed. *Fight*.

She dropped her weight down so he couldn't carry her. At the same time, she hooked his arm and twisted her body to face him.

Danica now had his arm bent backward. The man grunted again, but this time in pain. She kicked him square in the crotch, a seam in her dress ripping. He stumbled back, and she got a good look.

It was *him*. The man with the two-headed eagle tattoo.

His teeth were bared in a snarl. "You're going to be sorry for that," he wheezed.

He dipped into his pocket and came out with a gun. Immediately, she kicked at his hand. The gun went skittering across the smooth floor.

But he just pulled out a long knife instead, and he held his body at an angle. She wasn't going to surprise him again.

Danica turned and ran.

At the next doorway, she almost barreled into Noah. She didn't even have a chance to speak.

Noah shoved her behind him just as the other man attacked. He lunged at Noah with the knife.

The metal came away red with blood, and Danica screamed.

Rosie appeared and took hold of Danica's wrist. She had her gun drawn. "You have to get out of here."

"No. Not without Noah. Help him."

Rosie tried to aim the gun, but she shook her head. "I can't get a clear shot."

Noah had grabbed the man's arm. There was a hideous crack as Noah slammed his free hand into the guy's elbow, breaking it.

The knife went flying. But the man with the eagle tattoo didn't make a sound except a muffled grunt. And he wasn't done yet.

His leg swept forward, knocking Noah off his feet. Noah landed on his back with the other man on top of him.

Oh, god. A splotch of red was spreading from beneath Noah's shirt.

Rosie was just standing there, gun in hand, indecision on her face.

Danica ran and picked up the knife.

Noah was grappling on the ground with his opponent. Despite that destroyed elbow, the man with the eagle tattoo fought back viciously. Like he knew this was his last chance.

His good arm barred over Noah's neck, pressing down. Choking him.

Do something, she thought.

Danica raised the knife in both hands and drove it into the man's side near his armpit.

He roared, arching his spine, arms flailing.

Noah's next movements were so fast, Danica could barely follow them.

He yanked the knife from the man's side and plunged the blade into the center of the eagle tattoo.

Danica turned away from the spurt of blood.

This was too horrible. She could hardly believe any of it was happening. That it wasn't some nightmare.

And it wasn't over.

A gunshot rang out, and the glass case behind them shattered.

"Get down!" Rosie cried, spinning and aiming her gun to return fire.

From somewhere else in the building, Danica heard screams.

"Dani, come on." Noah was at her side, pulling her down behind another display case.

The gunshots continued. Rosie fired. Crouched. Fired again. Noah was shouting something to his teammates through his earpiece.

Abruptly, the shooting stopped.

Noah put his arm around Danica, standing her up. "Tanner just took out the gunman who was shooting at us, but we don't know what else is coming. I'm getting you out of here."

"You're bleeding."

"I'm fine. There's an emergency exit this way."

"What if that's how they got in? What if they're waiting?"

"Rex is already seeing to that."

"Wait!" Rosie shouted. "Ms. Foster-Grant, I'm in communication with the rest of the security team. You need to—"

"Don't tell me to stay here."

Rosie was cursing, but she didn't try to stop them.

They dashed through the exhibit rooms. "Rex, are we clear?" Noah asked. He must've gotten an affirmative answer, because he pushed open a door marked *Exit*. Danica waited for an alarm to sound, but nothing happened.

Noah glanced around, then pulled her outside. They were at the back of the building.

Danica heard sirens, shouts, screams. Chaos, everywhere.

Noah's friend—the guy named Rex—was in the parking lot a few feet from Noah's Ducati. He held a Glock, and Danica wondered where he'd gotten it. Only the Valoris bodyguards were supposed to have guns. Yet the man with the eagle tattoo had had a gun, too.

What a disaster, she thought. The gala... The donors...

"Phones," Rex said, holding out his hand. "In case someone can track you." Noah handed his over, but Danica couldn't find hers. She must've dropped it somewhere in the exhibits.

"I lost mine."

"Then don't worry about it. We'll find it later. You two get moving." Rex nodded at them as Noah jumped onto the bike, firing up the engine.

"Dani, let's go!"

She climbed on behind him, thinking vaguely of helmets, but they obviously didn't have time to go back for those.

The engine growled as Noah raced out of the parking lot and onto the road.

Her arms were tight around him, her cheek pressed to his back.

They sped onto Ocean Lane, the main thoroughfare closest to the beach. Danica noticed a silver SUV pull out of another lot, its tires screeching as it accelerated. Its windows were tinted.

Shit.

It was a different make and model from the one that had come after her before. But she felt the danger in her bones.

"Noah, someone's following us."

"I know. Hold on."

They leaned side to side as Noah wove through the evening traffic. He took a sudden left and darted off the main road.

Wind tossed Danica's hair. The fabric of her dress whipped against her legs.

She glanced back. The SUV had turned onto the road. Still following them.

The motorcycle roared through an intersection just as the

light turned red. Noah made another hairpin turn, taking the entrance onto the freeway. She held on. The engine and the wind were so loud she couldn't hear anything else, though she felt her heartbeat pounding in her ears.

Another glance back showed the SUV was still there.

Another car suddenly cut across their path, and Noah pumped the brakes. The momentum pushed Danica hard against him.

The silver SUV caught up, drawing alongside. She could see through the driver's side window.

A man in a ski mask was behind the wheel.

He edged closer. He was trying to force them onto the shoulder.

Noah accelerated, steering the bike into a diagonal course across the lanes. They darted around a semi, barely missing running into it. Horns blared. Danica screamed. She could barely hold on.

Headlights and tail lights blurred into a haze of reddish-orange.

Oh god oh god oh god

They kept going. Mile markers flipped past.

She had no idea where they were or how far they'd traveled. Every moment was endlessly slow, and yet it also felt like they were going so fast they'd spin right off the earth.

But it seemed like they'd lost their tail.

Then Danica's heart plummeted as she saw the silver SUV again, coming up on their side.

No.

What kind of engine did that freaking thing have? How was it keeping up?

Noah leaned the motorcycle into a death-defying turn, nearly brushing the silver SUV's fender as he squeezed onto the next exit at the right side of the freeway.

Danica heard brakes squealing as the SUV tried to stop. But she and Noah were already hurtling onto the exit ramp.

He turned at the next intersection, blowing past the stop sign.

She saw trees. Wilderness.

They zoomed down a dark, two-lane road. The freeway faded into the distance behind them.

She buried her face against the smooth fabric of Noah's tux jacket, and she didn't let go.

Chapter Thirty

_N_oah steered along the gentle curves of the road as they wound deeper into the woods. He was pretty sure he remembered the route, but everything was different in the dark.

He hadn't been here in over a year, not since Max bought the place and fitted it out with supplies.

As far as Noah was aware, Bennett Security hadn't made use of this cabin yet. But he hadn't been able to think of anywhere else to go. That SUV could've easily followed them to the West Oaks safe house. And the Los Angeles ones were too far, too exposed.

He still had no idea what other threats could be coming, or who was really behind this. Right now, the safest thing would be for them to disappear.

Noah spotted a familiar landmark and exhaled. He really hadn't wanted to pull over and tell Danica they were lost.

The bike roared into the next turn.

A few miles later, they pulled up to a gate. He entered a code at the keypad, and the heavy steel slid open.

Trees hemmed them in on either side of the narrow driveway.

He pulled up in front of the cabin and cut the engine. Instantly, silence fell. All except for Danica's rapid, shallow breathing.

She still had her arms cinched around him, which was mildly uncomfortable given the knife wound in his side. Not to mention the soreness in his back after getting tossed around multiple times the past few days. Made him feel old.

"Hey," he said. "It's okay now. You can let go."

He put the kickstand into place, then turned around to pick her up from the seat and set her on her feet.

"Can you stand?"

"Yeah. I…think so. Where are we?" Danica's hair was a wild tumble around her face. Her green dress was ripped so the slit opened to the top of her leg, where he caught a glimpse of creamy lace. Her whole body was trembling.

"Los Padres National Forest. This is a safe house."

"How is that possible? Isn't this public land?"

He smiled at her. "Really? After everything that just happened, you're asking real estate law questions?"

He put his arm around her and walked her to the front door. There, Noah entered another code into a keypad, and he heard the electronic lock disengage.

"I'd like to know how safe this place really is," she said. "Do we have a right to be here, or is this some illegal hideout?"

"This is an inholding. It was private land before this was national forest, so it was grandfathered in. Max bought it and turned it into a safe house, the most remote one we've got."

Special contractors took care of the building periodically and kept it stocked. But now that the keypads had been activated, no one would approach without prior authorization.

They walked inside the small cabin, and Noah locked the door behind them.

Blood continued to seep from the wound in his side and soak his clothes, which was a minor concern. Something he might want to take a look at eventually.

Too bad about his Armani tux. It was never going to be the same.

"First thing we need to do is call in." He found the light switch and flipped it on. The cabin was rustic, filled with cozy furniture.

Noah opened a closet near the front door. Inside were shelves with essential supplies. That included a laptop and smartphone, both with satellite uplinks.

He looked over at Danica. Her eyes were glassy, her expression glazed. She was hugging herself around the elbows.

"Why don't you sit down?" He nodded toward the kitchen table. The cabin was just one room, apart from the bathroom, with a king-size bed beyond the small sitting area.

"I don't want to sit. I want to know what's going on."

Noah placed the laptop on the table and opened it. It still had some battery power, so he didn't bother yet to plug it in.

Here, they were mostly off the grid. This place had solar panels and a generator, but the back up battery would only last so long. The more they could conserve electricity, the better.

He logged on with his personal access codes. A messenger window popped up.

Noah typed in a message, which would go to their team back at the office. Someone was always manning a desk, twenty-four hours a day, for emergency situations. Though usually, it was a false alarm from one of their clients and not a gun battle and car chase.

The phone began to ring.

Noah answered it, putting it on speaker.

"Code, please," the voice said.

He gave his access code again, and then said, "Ms. Foster-Grant is here with me on speaker."

"Do you need emergency medical attention?" their dispatcher asked.

Danica was leaning in next to him. "Yes, he does," she answered.

"Negative on the medical." He continued to ignore the

uncomfortable burning sensation at his side. "You need to contact the police about a BOLO. Silver SUV." He gave the make, model and plate.

"I've got it. Entering that info now."

"Have Tanner and Rex checked in?"

"Yes, sir. They're safe. Glad to hear you are as well. I've been instructed to tell you to remain where you are, and we'll contact you as there are updates."

"Trust me, we're not going anywhere."

Noah set down the phone.

Danica was digging around in the supply closet. She came out with the first aid kit.

"That's it?" she asked. "They can't tell us more?"

"Not yet. I'm guessing the police are crawling all over the museum. And probably responding to reports about our car chase. But there's nothing you or I can do about it right now."

"I guess not." Danica set the medical supplies on the table. "Do you want me to take off your jacket? Or can you do it?"

He sighed. "It isn't that bad." But he carefully took off his blazer and tossed it over the back of a chair.

Danica sucked in a breath. "Jesus, Noah."

Okay, it looked bad. There would be no saving this shirt, even setting aside the fact that there was a long slash through the fabric.

Danica pulled at the knot in his tie, removing it, then went after the buttons on his shirt, slipping them quickly through the buttonholes. He'd been about to pull his arms through the sleeves, but Danica just opened the sides of the shirt and grabbed a pair of scissors from the medical kit.

She sliced his undershirt straight up the middle, peeling the T-shirt fabric away from his side.

"It looks worse than it is." Noah was pissed at himself for letting the guy make contact at all. But the man had been well trained.

"Well, it looks terrible. Do you need stitches?"

"Nah, not real ones." Noah grabbed a pack of gauze that

contained a blood clotting agent. He opened it and pressed it to the wound. "That'll stop the bleeding. Then I'll use an adhesive to close it up. Could you get me a damp cloth?"

She went to the sink and wet one of the towels there. While he held the clotting agent to the damaged skin, she gently wiped the drying blood.

"Thanks for helping me at the museum," Noah said. He'd been getting a little worried when the guy had him on the ground, arm over his throat. Noah would've gotten out of it eventually. But Danica had made it a lot quicker and less painful.

"He's dead, isn't he?" she asked quietly. "That man with the eagle tattoo."

"Most likely." He was 99% sure the man was dead. Noah didn't see how anyone could survive a knife to the throat or that much blood loss.

She grimaced. "I don't even know his name."

Noah put his free hand on her arm. "Dani. Look at me."

Her large gray eyes lifted to meet his.

"His name isn't important. You already know everything you need to about that guy. I don't know the names of most of the men I've killed."

Neither of them had wanted anyone to die. But Noah would kill if it was necessary—if it meant saving someone he had a duty to protect. Saving her.

But her expression was still conflicted.

"You should be proud," Noah said. "He tried to hurt you, and you wouldn't let him."

"When I picked up that knife, I only wanted to stop him from hurting *you*."

His heart squeezed.

Noah blotted the wound dry and sprayed on antiseptic. He applied the medical adhesive, holding the lacerated edges of skin together until it dried. "See? Good as new." Though it would be a new scar for his collection.

Danica got up, rinsed out the towel, then brought it over again. She tugged the ruined dress shirt from his shoulders. She did the same with the remains of his undershirt, piling the clothes on the ground.

The towel swiped around the wound, avoiding the liquid stitches.

"I could do that myself," he murmured.

"I don't mind taking care of you."

Then she bent forward and gently kissed his bare shoulder.

Tingles of pleasure spread across his skin, battling against the stinging pain of the knife wound.

"Dani."

The damp towel kept moving in careful strokes.

And now, he couldn't hide how his body was responding to her attention.

Despite the pain, Noah was riding high on adrenaline. He was still primed to fight or to flee. SEAL training had taught him to ignore pain, exhaustion, fear. To push himself beyond normal human limits.

But all that energy could just as easily translate into fucking.

Ugh, he shouldn't have thought the word "fucking." His dick was perking up even more.

Danica's fingers reached for his belt. Slowly, she undid the buckle.

"What're you doing?" he asked.

"These are ruined, too."

She went for the button of his pants. Noah stopped her hands.

"*Dani*," he said sharply.

She looked up, her expression hard to read.

"I'm very turned on right now. In case you hadn't noticed."

"I noticed."

Her voice was low. Husky.

Oh, boy.

"You shouldn't start something you don't intend to finish."

"Shut up, Noah," she whispered. "Let me take off your pants."

Slowly, he stood. Danica unzipped his fly and pushed his

pants down partway, exposing his black boxer briefs and the very prominent erection inside them.

For a moment, she just looked. Then Danica picked up the towel again.

Noah was holding his breath.

Her fingertip slid into the waistband of his underwear and tugged them down by a couple inches. She wiped the traces of blood. The dampness was cold against his overheating skin.

Then she tossed the towel onto the table, and it was her fingers tracing over his exposed skin instead. Her thumb dragged along his happy trail, stopping at his waistband.

A needy moan escaped from his chest, even though she still hadn't touched the unmissable bulge inside the fabric.

Danica's eyes flicked up to his, as if the sound had surprised her.

He waited to see what she would do, even though it took all his willpower to remain motionless.

Her hand went behind her back. There was the sound of a zipper opening. She wiggled out of her dress and let it fall to the floor.

Her bra and panties were matching, a pale cream color. The fabric was translucent, revealing her dark pink nipples and a strip of pubic hair.

She didn't even look real, she was so beautiful. And he could see her so much better than last night.

Noah reached for her. The motion was utterly involuntary. He couldn't have stopped himself if he'd tried.

He felt her soft, smooth skin under his palms. Then the gentle friction of silky lace as his hands moved down along her hips.

The adrenaline and the heat in his veins crested inside of him, turning into something savage. It refused to be held back.

He pulled her closer and crashed their mouths together.

Danica moaned, her hands going to his chest.

His tongue slid into the gap between her lips. She sucked on it. Her hand curved around his erection and squeezed.

Oh, fuck yes.

Noah felt a primal need to claim her. To prove that nobody could touch her. Nobody except him.

Now, *right now*, he was going to have her.

This wasn't like last night, when he'd been on the floor, and Danica had been in control. Noah was way too worked up for that. He'd pulled his motorcycle into death-defying stunts on the freeway for her. He'd *killed* for her. And he'd do it again in a heartbeat and ask nothing in return.

But years ago, he'd given Danica up for the "right" reasons, all of which seemed like meaningless bullshit to him at this moment. He didn't care anymore if he was her bodyguard. It didn't matter who wouldn't approve or who hated him, any more than that stuff had mattered last night. All he could think about was her.

And she was standing in front of him in nothing but her bra and panties, kissing him like they were both on fire, and this was the only way to put it out.

Danica was strong and fierce and stubborn. Somehow, her strength only made him want to possess her more—because he knew it was impossible to make her do anything she didn't want to do.

Noah backed her up toward the bed.

When she was almost there, Danica spun him around. He sat on the edge of the mattress, bouncing against it, and she straddled his lap. She was still wearing her strappy black heels.

Her tongue thrust eagerly into his mouth, like she intended to claim him instead.

Their kisses were searing. His hands rounded over the cups of her bra. He pinched and tugged at her beaded nipples through the lace.

Next his fingers dug into her ass, sneaking beneath the edges of her panties and into the warm, wet heat between her legs. His teeth nipped at her lower lip.

Danica broke away from his mouth. She trailed soft kisses

and kitten licks down the side of his neck, then switching to sucking at his skin. It felt incredible.

When she reached the curve where his neck and shoulder met, she bit into the thick muscle. Not hard enough to break the skin, but not gentle, either. A thunderbolt of heat shot down his spine and into his balls.

"Oh, Dani. That's...*fuck.*" Noah tipped his head back, and she ran her tongue over his Adam's apple. His cock strained his boxer briefs, leaking all over the fabric. "You play dirty."

"Do I?" She sucked hard at the bite mark on his shoulder.

Danica had been right. He didn't want nice. He wanted her to be rough with him, push him, and he intended to push right back. He loved that battle, that tension between them.

She stood up and yanked her panties down, kicking them off. His hand immediately pushed between her legs, and his middle finger slid inside of her. Just as wet as she'd been last night. Danica moaned and grabbed onto his arms to brace herself. His biceps flexed under her touch.

He loved knowing how much she wanted this. Wanted *him.*

Usually, he would've taken his time. When it came to sex, Noah didn't like to rush. His favorite encounters in the past had been playful and slow to build.

But overpowering need screamed inside of him, refusing to be tamped down or ignored.

He could taste and savor her later. Right now, the most savage part of him just needed to fuck. To spill himself inside of her.

"My wallet," he murmured, the words nearly incoherent, "a condom, I think I've..."

"I want to go bare with you. I trust you. Do you trust me?"

Another wave of heat flashed across his skin. He was already barely containing himself. "I'm afraid I won't last long."

"So don't. I doubt I will either."

Noah pulled his finger out of her. He shoved down the waistband of his briefs, tucking them beneath his balls. His pants were only down to his thighs, but he was in too much of a hurry to care about that, and clearly, she didn't mind either.

A pearl of precome beaded at his slit, and he swirled his thumb over it. The head of his dick was purple and glistening and aching to thrust into her.

Danica crawled onto him, lining up her opening, letting his swollen tip tease her. So good. The feeling made his head swim. His hands grabbed her hips.

"I want you, Noah." She nuzzled her nose against his temple. "Take what's yours."

Mine.

If only she truly meant that. Noah wanted so much more of Danica than he'd ever be able to get. But having her on his cock right now was a decent consolation.

He pulled her down onto him. His shaft buried inside her, and they both gasped.

Chapter Thirty-One

The pressure of Noah's cock inside her was indulgent. But she loved the simple pleasure of kissing him, too. The slight scratch of stubble made her shiver. He smelled like soap and sweat and a spiciness that was just him.

No other man had ever kissed her as aggressively as he did. Like he was constantly struggling to contain his own need.

Danica was having all sorts of urges herself. She was so turned on, and wrung out by other emotions she didn't want to deal with, that she felt delirious.

She rode him hard and fast. The heat inside her kept building until she felt feverish with it.

Seeing that wound in Noah's side, how much he'd bled—it had awoken a fiercely protective part of Danica. But it wasn't because she was selfless. In her job, she liked to think she was making a difference in people's lives. Helping those who needed a voice, who couldn't help themselves.

But with Noah, it wasn't like that at all. She wanted to defend him and take care of him, make him *hers*, because seeing him hurt had carved out her heart.

She had been trying and failing to push him away because she was afraid of getting her heart broken when they eventually had to say goodbye. But now, Danica understood that it was already too late. Her heart was going to break regardless.

Last night had been nowhere near enough to slake her need for this man. So what was the damned point of holding back? Why shouldn't she have everything she wanted if it was all going to end the same anyway?

Noah. She repeated his name in her head, like a mantra. *Noah. My Noah.*

Danica grabbed his face in her hands, wanting to keep eye contact. He was watching her with such intensity, a look of wonder in his expression.

She never wanted this to stop, but she also needed it to. Because who could stand to feel this much and not get burned by it?

Danica arched her spine and cried out as her orgasm hit her.

She felt herself squeezing around his cock, convulsing in shock waves. The feeling kept growing instead of fading. Higher and higher. The release pushed away every rational thought, leaving her trembling and reeling. Out of control in the best possible way.

Noah held her by the waist and pumped lazily into her, smiling wickedly. "You don't know how long I've wanted to see that," he said. "You, coming on my cock."

"You saw it last night."

"It was dark then. With the lights on, it's much more of a show."

Danica leaned over to lick and kiss the bite mark she'd left. "Your turn."

Noah stood up, still inside her, cradling her against him. He took a few steps and pushed her into the wall, one of his hands bracing beside her head. His hips thrust forward, and Danica's legs wrapped around him.

His cock drove into her, knocking her breath away for a second.

It was incredible to see him like this. Muscles flexing as he fucked her, so masculine and dominant.

She still wished they'd had the chance to be together when they were younger. But it wouldn't have been as hot as this. Now, he had the strength to take her any way that he wanted. The kind of strength that had come from hard-won experience. Noah knew exactly what he was doing and he knew what he liked, and he finally didn't have to hold himself back from having it.

Danica loved giving that to him.

She felt the tensing of his body, saw the change in his expression as he started to come undone. "Yes," she murmured, breathless. "I want it all."

"Dani. Holy shit." He clenched his teeth together and let out an animalistic growl, and it was the sexiest noise she'd ever heard. Noah dropped his forehead against hers.

His dick spasmed again and again inside of her. Marking her. She loved that there was no barrier between them. That she was getting all he had to give.

When he was done, he held her in place, panting to catch his breath. They both quieted as the intensity of the previous moments ebbed away.

Danica kissed his cheek, which led to Noah kissing her mouth. But the fire between them had dimmed to a gentle glow. Warm and comforting instead of overpowering.

Their lips met a few more times, and then he looked at her. The smile he gave her was tender and sweet.

"That's nice." She really needed nice at the moment.

"See? I like nice sometimes." Noah carried her over to the bed and set her down. "Why am I still wearing pants?"

She giggled. "I was supposed to take them off you. But that would've taken too long." Danica looked up at the ceiling. "Jeez, I hope there are no cameras in here."

"No, just outside." He toed off his shoes and socks, then shoved his pants and boxer briefs off the rest of the way. Danica just lay there watching him, though her vision was going blurry.

Every ounce of energy had left her body. She felt hollow. Wrecked by the horrible things that had happened at the museum. Yet also strangely content. With Noah, she knew she was safe. And she had no regrets.

He reached for her feet and slid off her heels. "I'll be right back to clean you up."

Noah grabbed another towel, wet it under the faucet, and brought it back. He wiped the towel over the cum that had spilled down her inner thighs. She still had on her bra, but she decided she didn't care.

A trickle of red ran down his torso.

Danica sat up, her mind flashing back to alertness. "You're bleeding." The knife wound had opened up again.

"Oh. Crap." He folded over the towel and pressed a clean corner to the injury. "You shouldn't have been so rough with me."

"Like it was my fault."

"You're dangerous." He went back over to the table and reapplied the liquid bandage. Danica curled on her side so she could see him. Exhaustion was pulling her under again.

And other things, too. Dark thoughts. Even darker images. Her eyes and nose stung as she tried to hold them back. There were far too many, and if she let them in, they'd take over her mind completely.

"Noah," she whispered, feeling the tears just behind her eyes. Pressing.

"I'll be right there." He turned off the lights and returned to the bed. The sheets and blankets pulled up and over her, his warm skin against hers.

He covered her face with kisses. "What do you need?" he asked.

"Just you. You'll stay? Right here?"

"Of course I will. As long as you want me."

She cuddled into him. Her eyelids fluttered closed, and sleep dragged her beneath the surface. She hoped the nightmares weren't waiting.

Chapter Thirty-Two

*S*unlight streamed around the curtains. Noah sat up carefully. He looked around at their clothes strewn all over the room. At Danica, lying sound asleep on her stomach beside him, wearing nothing but her lacy bra. The sheet stretched up to her waist.

Images from the last two nights drifted through his mind. Danica in his arms, legs spread. Giving herself to him, taking what she wanted, too.

And his body was raring for it to happen again. His dick was standing at attention, and he didn't want his morning wood to be the first thing Danica saw.

She'd been through a lot last night. She might not be interested in a repeat just yet. Judging from her behavior yesterday morning, Danica would probably feel conflicted about this second hookup.

He really hoped she wasn't going to freak out and pull away from him again.

But when he replayed the things she'd said, how wild she'd been... *Damn*.

Noah slid out of bed and padded over to the closet. In a

small mirror, he caught sight of the livid purple hickey at his neck.

I want to go bare with you. Take what's yours.

These thoughts were not helping calm down his dick.

He checked on the knife wound, which was holding together, and found some clothes in the closet. The safe house was well stocked for emergency getaways like theirs. He found some men's items in his size and some things that looked small enough for Danica.

It was seven a.m., which meant he'd gotten a few hours of rest. The motion sensor log showed no significant activity around the safe house perimeter, and there were no messages on the phone.

He was still hopped up on stress hormones. But if there was anything he needed to do, the home base at Bennett Security would let him know.

Next, he went into the small bathroom, which was stocked as well. Noah brushed his teeth and tried to clean himself up. The water was icy cold, which helped shrink his erection. No water heater in this place.

His hair looked like shit, and his skin was paler than usual, but all in all he actually felt pretty damn good.

When he came back to the bed, dressed in a T-shirt and shorts, Danica was blinking her eyes open.

"Hey." Noah sat on the mattress. "Sleep okay?" He hadn't seen any signs of a nightmare last night, but that didn't mean she'd slept well.

"Why do you have clothes on?" She sat up, scooted to the edge of the bed, and unhooked her bra. The undergarment got tossed aside as she headed toward the bathroom. "I'll be right back."

He got only a glimpse of sideboob before the door shut. Noah fell back against the pillows, one arm over his head.

He didn't know what was happening between him and Danica right now. But if they never left this room, if they just stayed here and pretended the rest of the world didn't exist, he was pretty sure he'd be happy.

He could send a postcard to Gramps and Ginger, who'd probably be thrilled for him.

The water ran in the bathroom. Danica emerged a few minutes later, her hair slightly less messy.

"Hi." Her hand rested against the door frame. Her body was on full display. The morning light illuminated her skin.

"Hi." His eyes roved over her, hungry for every tiny detail. The curves of her breasts and hips, stomach and thighs.

His cock was back at half salute.

Danica held a small bottle in her hand. She set it on the nightstand. "You're still dressed."

"I thought you might want to talk about what happened at the museum. Or just get some more rest." She hadn't answered his question about how she'd slept.

"What I *want* is you naked."

He suspected she might be avoiding the worst aspects of yesterday. But was he going to do the "right" thing and insist they talk about it?

Nope. Getting naked with her again would be so much better.

Noah pulled his upper body into a crunch to tug off the shirt, ignoring the painful protest of the knife wound. He wiggled out of his shorts. His erection got caught in the fabric and then sprang free, slapping into his stomach.

Danica crawled onto the mattress, her gaze going soft and unfocused. "Damn, you're hot."

He laughed. "You sound surprised."

Her hand ran between his pecs and down his abs, avoiding the wound. "Nope, not surprised. You were always cute. But now... How was I supposed to resist this?"

"I certainly don't blame you."

Danica bent over, those gorgeous tits swinging into his chest. Her hand traveled back down his body, palm ghosting over the head of his cock. But her fingers kept going and curved around his sac.

She gave his balls a hard tug, and at the same time, her lips closed on his ear cartilage and sucked. Noah gasped involuntarily.

"It's fun finding out what you like," she said.

"Who says I liked that?"

"Your cock. It jumped straight into the air."

Noah usually enjoyed being the one in control during sex. But Danica made him want to lie back and let her do whatever she wanted. She'd always made him feel that, in a way no other woman ever had.

Just so long as he got his chance to switch places. To make her gasp and moan and take whatever he gave her.

She took his erection in hand and stroked him lazily. "Your cock is very pretty."

"It is *not*. Take that back."

Danica giggled, a sound he was starting to love. His chest ached as he realized how rarely he'd ever heard it.

"But it's so straight and symmetrical. Pink down here." She gripped his shaft. "And purple up here. How is that not pretty?" Her thumb traced over his glans, then thrust into the slit at the top. Noah's hips shot off the bed. He made a noise that sounded distinctly like a needy whimper.

"You like that, don't you?"

He nodded, suddenly incapable of speech.

"You *love* it," she whispered into his ear.

Noah grumbled. "Maybe."

"You love when I'm rough with you. Are you going to beg for it?"

Heat flashed over his skin. "You're only in charge because I'm letting you be. Maybe I'll turn you over and spread you open and eat you out. Then we'll see who's begging."

"Such a naughty boy." She trailed kisses over his jaw, her chest shaking with quiet laughter. "I'll be good. You're a big, strong Navy SEAL and you don't beg for anything."

"Fuck no, I don't."

Her thumb pushed at his slit again, shocking another desperate whimper out of him, which kind of contradicted his point. But it felt too good for him to care.

Danica twisted away to reach for the bottle she'd left on the nightstand. The cap flipped open. Lotion squeezed into her palm.

When her hand returned, the lubricant slicked up and down his shaft. "Better?" she asked.

"*Ughn.*"

She kept stroking him. "That's a yes?"

Noah's arm wrapped around her and pulled her down so he could kiss her. Danica tasted like minty toothpaste. His other hand closed around hers on his erection, making her squeeze tighter and work him faster. Noah panted into her mouth.

He let go of her hand, and she kept up the same pace on his cock. He reached for her breast instead, enjoying its firm weight. His fingers clamped onto her nipple, and she made a needy sound.

They were both discovering what the other liked, and Dani was right, it was more fun than he'd had in as long as he could remember.

Pleasure zapped up and down his spine. His balls drew up against his body.

"Dani. I'm so close. *Please.*"

She leaned over to bite that same spot between his neck and shoulder.

The wave crashed over him, turning his vision fuzzy and making his head swim. His breath stalled in his chest.

Noah closed his eyes as he spurted all over her hand and his stomach. He felt jets of hot cum hit his abs. Her fist didn't let up, and he kept coming, more than he would've thought he had in him after last night.

She kept pumping him until he was empty.

When he opened his eyes, she was watching him with a wicked grin.

Noah swallowed, his throat dry. "Don't even say it."

"What?"

He could see the teasing words in her eyes. *You were begging.*

Noah grabbed her and flipped her onto her back.

"Gah," she said, "you're so *messy.*"

"Now you are, too."

He claimed her mouth with a punishing kiss. Noah was finally feeling the effects of a nonstop adrenaline rush, lack of sleep, and two monster orgasms. But he had to reclaim some of his dignity.

"Do you want to come on my tongue?" he asked between kisses. "Or my fingers?"

"Mmmm, later. I'm hungry."

"Really? Working over my cock wore you out?"

"I was already worn out." All the teasing was gone.

He didn't like to hear that. "You should've saved your energy."

"Don't turn it into something bad." She reached up to caress his cheek. "I wanted to make you feel good. To thank you for what you've done for me."

"That's why we're doing this? You feel like you owe me?"

"No, that sounded wrong." Her teeth pressed into her lower lip. "I... God, I didn't want to get into this."

"Into what?"

"The way I feel about..." Dani's eyes turned shiny, and she looked away.

Shit. Was she going to cry?

"Hey, it's okay." He lay down beside her and held her against him. "What do you feel?"

Her breathing was ragged. It took her a full minute to respond.

"Confused. And scared and overwhelmed. And like..." She buried her face against his chest. "Like I don't ever want to let you go. Even though I know I have to."

"Okay." This conversation had suddenly gone places he hadn't expected. But he wanted to be here with her, talking about this. Wanted it so much that it hurt. His heart was thumping out a response to what she'd said, filling him with a painful kind of hope. "I don't want to let you go, either. We'll figure it out. But right now, we don't have to do either one."

She nodded.

"We're safe here," he said. "All we have to do is get cleaned up and get some food and just be together. In any way you want." They'd already established that he wouldn't say no to her. With Danica, he'd never wanted to say no. Even though harsh realities—like her family—had sometimes made that impossible.

Noah kissed her forehead. "We can take care of each other and make each other feel good, and we don't have to worry about anything else."

"Yeah. I can handle that."

He didn't mention how much he felt for her, too. How an all-too-familiar panic filled him at the thought of saying goodbye.

Chase had warned him not to fall for someone who couldn't love him back. *Sorry Chase*, he thought. *It's way too late. For me, it's always been Dani.*

AROUND TEN, the phone rang. It was Noah's boss, Max.

"Is this a good time?"

"Yeah. It's fine." Noah pulled up a chair at the table.

"Is there anything you need?" Max asked.

"We're all set up, depending on how long we'll be here." He looked over at Danica. She leaned against the wall nearby, crossing her arms.

They'd both gotten cleaned up and dressed, and they'd had breakfast. The food supplies here weren't glamorous. It had been a while since Noah had eaten MREs, but he was used to them. Danica had made faces as she'd choked down the ready-to-eat sandwich.

"Both the police and Danica's family want you back here

ASAP," Max continued, "but I'm not sure that's wise yet. We're still untangling everything that went down last night."

"Hey Max," Noah said into the phone, "I'm going to put Danica on speaker with us."

"You think that's wise? I have a lot more info on the investigation that might be disturbing. Is she handling this well?"

Noah's eyes met hers again. She was handling everything better than most people would, under the circumstances.

"We're both doing great over here," Noah said. He didn't want to answer Max's question directly because Danica would just get annoyed. He pushed the speaker button on the phone and set it on the table. "Speaker's on."

"Ms. Foster-Grant, this is Max Bennett. We spoke the other day?"

She sat in the chair next to Noah. "Hi, Max. You have updates?"

"I do. But first, I'd like to hear what happened last night from both your perspectives. We're doing our own investigation and putting together a timeline of events. I'll turn it over to the police, though they want to interview you separately, of course."

Danica said she'd walked into the exhibit rooms to speak to Tori, Blake Halston's assistant, on the phone. The man with the neck tattoo had grabbed her, and she'd gotten away.

"Do you think Tori intended to lure you away from the gala?" Max asked.

"I wondered about that, but I just don't know. I'm not even sure what she wanted. I didn't get the chance to find out."

Noah filled in the details on the man with the blue bowtie he'd spotted in the atrium. According to Max, when Noah had gone to look for Danica, Tanner had continued to follow the suspicious newcomer.

Blue bowtie had gone straight to the exhibit hall. Clearly no coincidence. He'd been the one shooting at them, probably when he'd realized his friend with the eagle tattoo was under attack.

"But how could they have gotten in?" Danica asked. "The

gala was supposed to be secure. How did they bring guns through the metal detector?"

"Somehow, they disabled the alarm on the emergency exit door." Max continued recounting what Tanner and Rex had told him.

Tanner had snuck up on blue bowtie and knocked him out. At the same time, Rex had run for the rear parking lot to clear the path for Noah and Danica's escape. He'd left his Glock hidden outside for just such an eventuality. Rex hadn't run into any bad guys, but now they knew why—the SUV waiting to abduct Danica had been in the next lot over. Probably waiting for eagle tattoo's call.

"But here's the good news," Max said. "The police tracked down the silver SUV that chased you. Minor shoot-out, but they killed or arrested everyone inside, with no law enforcement casualties."

Danica rested her elbows on the table. "Thank god. Max, what about Rosie Consuelo? Is she all right? She was returning fire just before Noah and I ran for the emergency exit."

"Yes, Rosie is fine. She's been answering questions, though generally the Valoris Security team has been less than helpful. Same with your chief of security. He's refusing to talk to us."

Probably because they'd botched everything. But had it just been negligence on Valoris's part, Noah wondered? Or could someone on the Valoris team have actually helped the bad guys?

"Does Blake know Danica hired Bennett Security to protect her?" Noah asked.

"Oh, yeah. That secret's out. Everybody's pissed off and pointing fingers. But thanks to you, Rex, and Tanner, Danica got out safe. And everyone who went to the museum to kidnap her either ended up dead or arrested."

Her gaze met Noah's.

"Have the police identified the man with the two-headed eagle tattoo?" Danica asked.

"Not as far as I know. We're trying to find his identity and known associates. And don't worry, we haven't forgotten about the altered video surveillance of him, either. I've got every available body on this."

Danica exhaled, nodding. "Good."

"There's something else, though," Max continued. "The guy with the eagle tattoo had a photo of Noah in his pocket."

Chapter Thirty-Three

*D*anica gasped, her hand going to her mouth. "A picture of *Noah?*"

Next to her, Noah barely even reacted. As if these were only mildly interesting developments. But her stomach was churning, acid rising up into her chest.

"West Oaks PD didn't officially tell us about the photo," Max said. "It was Officer Collins, Devon's friend, speaking confidentially. I understand Chase has been helping us out with this?"

Noah cleared his throat. "Yeah, Chase said he'd look into the chain of custody on the museum surveillance video. But…I don't think the photo is such a surprise. A lot of people think I'm Danica's boyfriend. Eagle tattoo would've wanted me out of the way."

Danica shook her head. "You're acting like it's not a big deal. It *is.*"

Noah shrugged. "Um, this probably isn't the best time to bring this up. But Danica, I didn't have a chance to tell you last night. Tanner said our computer experts finished examining your laptop. It was clean. Which means…"

She pushed back from the table, nausea overwhelming her.

"It wasn't some outside hacker who figured out my schedule. It really was someone close to me."

And that same person could've instructed the kidnappers to go after Noah, too.

Someone in her family.

Only Soren could possibly hate Noah that much. But he wasn't even in California.

"You can see why I'd rather you both stay put until we know more," Max said. "But Danica, you might want to call your father. He's got a lawyer after us, threatening to sue if we don't reveal your location. I have no plans to comply. But if you could calm him down, our phones here might be a little quieter."

"Yeah," she said, her throat thick. "I'll try."

Though she wasn't sure how she'd manage to speak to her father without screaming.

Max said goodbye, and Noah set the phone aside.

Danica hugged herself, closing her eyes. *Stay calm. Don't freak out. Don't fall apart.*

When she opened her eyes again, Noah was watching her with tender concern. He held out his arms. "Come here. It'll be okay."

"I don't want you to comfort me." If he did, she was sure she'd cry. "It was bad enough these people tried to kidnap me. But they could've been planning to kill you. That asshole didn't have a picture of Rosie, even though she was supposed to be my bodyguard. They wanted to go after *you*."

"I'm used to it. A lot of people have tried to kill me, and it hasn't worked yet."

"Don't turn this into a joke, Noah."

"You're grumpy at me? Isn't that blaming the victim? A little bit?"

He tried his most charming grin, the one that showed off his dimple. Usually, it worked on her. But she wasn't in the mood. "Stop trying to be cute."

Danica came over to grab the phone and then stormed over to the cabin's exterior door. She unlocked it and went outside.

The cabin stood in a clearing surrounded by lush trees, and mountains stretched in the distance. She couldn't remember the last time she'd gone away to a peaceful, beautiful place like this on vacation. Maybe the Catskills in New York with some of her girlfriends. But usually, her work schedule didn't allow for it.

If only this were just a vacation.

She looked down at the phone in her hand. Better to get this over with.

Danica called her father's cell. He'd had the same number for many years, so she had it memorized.

"This is William." Her father's voice sounded frayed and exhausted.

"Dad, it's Danica."

"Finally. My god. Where are you?"

"I can't tell you that."

"Why on earth not? You need to come home."

Danica walked further from the house. "I can't come home. I'm in a safe place. With Noah."

"So his employer told me. You hired him as your bodyguard? Hired Bennett Security?"

"It's a good thing I did. Noah saved my life. He was nearly killed protecting me."

"Then I'm grateful to him. But you lied to me, Danica. Defied me outright."

"Like you've never lied to me, Dad."

"What are you talking about?"

She rubbed the skin between her eyes. "I'm talking about your relationship with Tori. I'm talking about those blackmail messages I got, about some secret of yours. You're keeping things from me, and it's insulting that you keep on insisting that I'm imagining it."

There was silence on the line. "There's no reason we have to deal with those issues now."

"But why not? I'm tired of people telling me that I don't see the things I see. You and Blake wouldn't listen to me about the man I saw at the museum, and the exact same person came after me last night. I want my family to listen, and I want you to be *honest* with me."

Her father sighed. "I can explain certain things. But only when you come home. Noah Vandermeer has nothing to do with any of this, and you endanger more than you know by inviting someone like him into our circle."

She couldn't take anymore. "I didn't tell you Noah was my bodyguard, but I was honest when I told you I want him in my life. I care about him. We're seeing each other."

Even this wasn't totally true. She didn't know what she and Noah were. And technically, they hadn't been together at all the last time she'd spoken to her father.

But her feelings for Noah hadn't changed. She was starting to realize that she'd felt the same way about him for a long time. Maybe even before he'd come back into her life.

She still didn't see how things could work out between them. But she didn't want her father to be the reason.

"You're being very foolish," her father said.

"Maybe so. But—"

"You swear you're safe?"

"Completely."

"Then we'll deal with the rest later. When you come home. But no sooner."

DANICA HEARD the cabin door open. She was sitting on a rock, facing into the trees, surrounded by soft grass and wildflowers. The peacefulness of the surroundings had calmed down her anger at her father. But there was still so much that was wrong.

Now that the museum gala was over, her schedule had been wiped clean. Her flight back to New York was supposed to have left that morning. It would've already landed at JFK by now, and she'd be in a car home.

Now, she didn't even know if the museum renovation would go forward. After last night's disaster, would the donors pull their contributions? Would the rest of the museum's board of directors revolt against her?

Would the damage spread to the foundation's other projects as well?

The media was probably in a frenzy over what had happened. They'd probably say she'd drawn too much attention to herself. Invited the attacks.

Maybe the foundation would be better off without her.

Danica hid her face in her hands.

Noah's footsteps approached. She looked up. He'd stopped beside her, hands in his shorts pockets.

"I emailed Gramps and Ginger. Told them to go stay in one of Ginger's condos for a while."

Because someone could go to the Vandermeer house looking for Noah and end up finding them. *Ugh.* This was so awful.

"Will they agree? Even Ginger?"

"She won't like it. But Gramps will convince her." Noah sat down in the grass in front of her. "You spoke to your dad?"

"My father admitted he's keeping secrets from me. But he said he won't tell me until I come home."

"That's progress, at least."

She shrugged. "I guess. I've been thinking about how Tori sent me that message last night, saying she needed to talk to me. About a sensitive matter."

"You think it was about your father?"

"Yes."

"It could've been about Blake."

"That's true. I guess there might be plenty of secrets to go around." She laughed without any humor.

"There's something else I should tell you, too," Noah said. "I asked Tanner to look into the blackmail threats you received about your father. Even though you'd told me not to."

She didn't know what to say. She just looked at him.

"I'm sorry that I went against your wishes. I shouldn't have. But I do think Bennett Security's researchers should investigate."

Danica nodded slowly. She pulled a piece of grass and rolled it between her fingers. "Okay."

"Okay?"

"Yes. Okay. I don't want to be mad at you."

"You sure? I suspect you like being mad at me."

"*You* might like when I'm mad at you."

"Maybe when you play mad. Not when it's real."

Wetness sprang into her eyes, a lump balling at her throat, and this time, she just couldn't hold it back.

At first, she and Noah had been pretending to be lovers, or dating, or whatever it was they'd been doing.

But she wanted it to be real. *All* of it.

She wanted Noah so badly that she felt the physical weight of all that wanting, and it was crushing her.

Even last night, she'd pretended that sex with Noah could be enough. But it would *never* be enough.

Noah reached out and smudged a tear away with his thumb. "Dani. Talk to me."

"I'm scared about everything that's happening. I'm scared all the time." Her voice was breaking.

"I know. I wish I could take that away."

"But you can't."

"Would you come here and let me hold you?"

She shook her head obstinately.

"Dani, *come here*." Noah gathered her up and pulled her into his lap.

She rested the side of her head against his chest and gripped his shirt in her fist. "I just couldn't take it if anything happened to you, especially if it was because of me."

"Hate to break it to you, babe, but that's what it means to be a bodyguard. I risk my life for you."

"Then you're fired."

He laughed. "No matter what I am to you, I'd still risk my life to protect you. Any day. That's what you mean to me."

"Don't be my bodyguard. Just be...mine." She lifted her face and found him looking down at her.

Their lips met, the kiss slow and tentative. Noah brushed her hair from her cheek.

"What about your family?" he asked.

The Foster-Grants... Their reputation. Their legacy.

None of it meant anything. Not compared to what Danica felt for him.

"When we lost my mom, it ripped us apart. We've spent all these years acting like we're still a family. But we're not. My father talks about love like he believes in it. But his love is always conditional. Soren hates our dad, yet he's also desperate for his approval. And I do nothing but work because that's easier than facing how empty the rest of my life is."

All the Foster-Grants had secrets, and that was hers.

"But when I'm with you," she told him, "I don't feel empty. I feel alive. I want to keep feeling that."

Her heart had never felt so fragile and exposed. He was holding it in his hands.

"So, be with me," Noah said.

"I don't just mean right now, today. I mean...something bigger. Something real."

"That's what I mean, too."

"You'd really want that? Even though it seems impossible?"

His eyes searched hers. "Dani, I've always wanted to be with you. How can you not know?"

She punched his shoulder. "I could've used a few more clues."

"Then let me show you." Noah pulled her against him and kissed her forehead, her nose, her cheeks. Showering her with affection. When their mouths met again, the first kiss was achingly slow. The tip of Noah's tongue licked at her lips.

"Let me carry you back inside," he whispered. "Let me take care of you."

It was so hard for her to rely completely on someone else. Not just physically, but emotionally. But with Noah, it was exactly what she needed—comfort and relief.

She wanted to trust him enough to see every side of her. Even when she felt so weak she might collapse and disappear.

He stood, cradling her. Danica sank into him, letting him bear her weight.

Noah took her through the door, kicking it closed behind them. He laid her on the mattress. "I could just hold you," he said. But the intensity in his eyes said he craved more. So did she. "What do you need?"

"You. Everything with you."

He pushed her shirt up and bent to kiss her bare stomach. "Are you asking me to make you feel good? However I want?"

She knew he wanted to go down on her. He'd made it abundantly clear. A thread of anxiety still wound through her stomach at being that vulnerable with him. That exposed.

But Noah was different from anyone she'd been with. The way she felt for him was different, and she didn't want to hold back from him anymore.

He already knew her so well. What was she really afraid of? "Yes," she breathed. "Anything."

Her clothes came off first. Noah's hands trailed over her skin as each new part of her was uncovered. When she was down to just her bra and panties, he rolled her over onto her stomach. The hooks of her bra sprang open beneath his fingers, and Noah kissed a straight line down her backbone.

He stopped when he reached the waistband of her underwear. Then he moved to the backs of her thighs, kissing and licking and caressing all the way down her legs. He kissed the sole of each foot, and then started his meticulous attentions back upward again.

Danica was suspended in a constant state of relaxation and arousal, like each nerve ending in her body was glowing with ambient light.

His fingers slid between her legs and over the crotch of her panties. Danica arched her pelvis, wanting him to keep going.

Noah chuckled. "Somebody's eager."

"I'm not denying it."

But he didn't escalate things yet. She was a little annoyed that he was teasing her, but she also couldn't complain. This felt way too good.

Noah turned her over and positioned himself above her, his elbows braced on the mattress to hold him up. He kissed her mouth with luxuriant care, taking long, slow pulls from her lips.

Danica worked her hands under his T-shirt, seeking out his hot skin and the firmness of his muscles. But Noah stopped her.

"Nope, this is my show. I'm the one doing the touching."

"Will you at least take your shirt off?"

"When I'm ready." His gaze dragged over her body beneath him, and she could see the naughty thoughts passing through his mind. A thrill of desire bloomed in her lower belly.

Noah got up on his knees, straddling her. He grabbed both of her hands and put her arms above her head. Her breasts pushed out toward him.

"You're going to keep your hands right up here for the rest of this."

She nodded, her breath hitching in her chest.

"Good." His head bent down. His tongue lashed over her nipple just before he sucked it into his mouth, then rolled it between his teeth.

By the time he finally kissed his way back down to her panties, Danica was rubbing her thighs together, desperate for some kind of contact on her clit.

Noah had already coaxed so much pleasure from all the rest of her skin. But the tension and need had been building. She wanted release. She wanted his mouth. And any trace of shyness or anxiety was gone.

"Give me your tongue. *Please.*"

Noah pulled her roughly to the edge of the mattress. She gasped at this sudden aggression. The heat and desire were nearly unbearable.

He held her knees, shoving her thighs apart.

His nose pressed into the crotch of her panties and inhaled.

"So sweet," he murmured. His tongue dragged over the fabric. He was driving her insane.

"Noah, *please*."

His eyes lifted, and his dimple flashed. "Did I just hear someone begging?"

Danica fisted the pillow behind her head. "Yes, I'm begging. All right? Are you happy?"

"Pretty happy. Yeah."

He stood up, grabbed his shirt, and yanked it over his head. His shorts were gone a second later, his erection bobbing and damp at the tip. Another flare of heat passed through her at seeing him naked. His thick thighs and broad chest and pretty cock.

Noah hooked her panties with his fingers and shucked them off. But then he was back on his knees. In one swift motion, he shoved her legs wider and dove forward.

His tongue went straight to her clit. Danica cried out. *Finally.*

He wasn't teasing or making her wait anymore. Noah sucked and lapped at her with abandon. The stubble on his chin and the callouses on his hands created the perfect amount of friction on her thighs. His moans were louder than hers.

It had been ridiculous to deny him this, because Noah's tongue was just as talented as the rest of him.

He'd told her to keep her arms over her head, but he wasn't the boss. Danica reached down and tangled her fingers in his hair. He just glanced up at her with a wicked grin as his tongue kept moving.

She sat up to see him better. Noah was stroking his own cock as he pleasured her, and oh did that ratchet up her arousal to an even higher degree.

Her worries, the fear and uncertainty, had all disappeared. Everything else was meaningless except him and what he was doing to her. Noah had stripped it all away.

He let go of his erection and thrust two fingers inside of her, and she was done for.

This was the release she'd needed. The orgasm took over her

body like pleasure was her entire purpose. She was an exposed, live wire, and she couldn't stop—much less control—the electricity coursing through her.

But she kept her eyes open, needing to see him. To know he was here, sharing this. He was hers.

My Noah.

Chapter Thirty-Four

*N*oah got up from his knees, licking his lips. He crawled onto the mattress and looked down at her. Danica gave him a languid smile.

He'd wanted to show her how much he felt for her, and he wasn't done yet. But first, he had to check in with her.

She'd been through far more than one person should have to deal with. Not just being targeted and threatened, but fearing that someone she cared about was behind it. If he'd taken away even a small amount of that stress, he'd done his job.

"You look relaxed," he said.

"Very." She scooted up higher on the bed. Noah lay down on his side, facing her, running his hand along her body. She rolled toward him, and his hard-on rubbed against her stomach.

Danica kissed his neck and his chest. "I want to feel you come inside me."

"Can't get enough of my cock, can you?"

"It's a tie. Between your cock and your dirty mouth."

She lay on her back and pulled him toward her, making absolutely clear what she wanted if her words had left any doubt.

Noah slid his shaft into her, burying himself to the hilt.

As his hips thrust, his heart started to do strange things in his chest. Sweat and goosebumps broke out all over his skin, but it wasn't just from the heat of their bodies meeting.

He ached for this woman. A feeling was rising up and inside of him, balling in his throat like it would choke him.

Noah dropped his face into her neck, breathing in the scent of jasmine. The glide of his erection in and out of her was everything he needed, and also somehow nowhere near enough.

Danica's hips rocked to meet his, and her panting grew more fevered. He loved how much she was enjoying this, and that just made the intensity climb higher for him. His balls drew up, tight and full, and the need to come sent lightning up and down his spine. Noah rose up onto his hands so he could watch her.

Danica's lips were parted, eyes hooded with desire. Her legs were tight around his waist.

So beautiful. *Take what's yours*, she said in his memory. And he wanted that. He wanted her to be his. Only his.

Noah pistoned his cock into her once, twice more, and he grunted as his orgasm ripped through him. Then Danica arched her back and cried out, legs shaking.

His arms wrapped around her, and Noah rolled them over so she was lying on top of him. They held one another as their breathing slowed. He was still inside of her, and every minute or two his dick jumped with an aftershock.

"I've never come in missionary before," she said.

He felt a lazy grin stretch over his face. "Hopefully, it won't be the last." That had sounded flippant, but the emotions flooding his system were anything but.

Almost nothing in the world scared him. But the thought of losing her, of letting her walk away not knowing, had him terrified.

Years ago, he'd let her slip away by failing to tell her how he really felt. He wasn't going to make that mistake again. And usually, he had no problem saying what he was thinking or feeling.

"Dani?"

Her chin propped on his chest so she could see him. "Yeah?"

"You said you want something bigger for us. Something real."

She nodded.

"I don't think it's impossible. I get that we live in different cities, and this might not be easy. But it's worth finding a way."

For a long time, Noah hadn't believed in happy endings. Maybe for other people, but not for himself.

But Danica made him want to believe. She made him want to fight for *their* happy ending.

"I love you," Noah said.

She lay her cheek on his chest, and he could *feel* her thinking. Danica was the type to push him away if she felt cornered, and he certainly didn't want that. She'd said she valued persistence, and he'd already gotten the impression that she needed to be wooed. Whatever that took, he was committed.

"Faith told me you don't seem happy," she said. "That you want more out of life and haven't found it yet."

Noah propped one arm behind his head. Faith had noticed that? He wondered who else had. "That's fair. I guess, since I left the SEALs, I've been...coasting. I like my job, and being a captain keeps me busy. But I'm not sure it's what I really want to do."

When he'd been in the military, so much had seemed clear. Now, he didn't know how to get that feeling back. How he felt about Danica made perfect sense to him now, but everything else? Not so much.

She sighed, rolling off him to lie flat on her back. Her arm was still pressed against his, but Noah missed the rest of their contact. "I told you that, when I'm with you, I feel alive instead of empty," she said. "Is that how you feel, too?"

"Absolutely. So alive it's almost too much."

"Yeah," she said in a small voice. "Exactly. It sucks to need someone else that intensely."

"That's true. But it makes the sex better."

She giggled. "It does." Danica turned her head toward him. "If you and I are...together, I think my father might come around eventually. But Soren really does hate you. He might never speak to me again."

"Does that bother you?"

"Yes, because he's my brother. But he'd be the one making the choice. Not me. And if I had to? I would choose you. Every time. *Every. Time.*"

She hadn't said she loved him back, but that was okay. For now, this was enough. "So we're together? For real this time?"

"Yes."

He put his hand on her cheek, unable to contain his smile. His whole body was shining with it.

Chapter Thirty-Five

*D*anica woke feeling nowhere near rested. But energy coursed through her all the same. Noah was snoring quietly beside her. The wound in his side looked red, but it hadn't opened up again.

She pounced on his shoulders and covered his face with kisses.

"Mmm?" His eyes squinted open, and his arms wrapped around her. "I was just dreaming about you."

"The real thing is better."

"So much better."

They'd been up half the night, talking and kissing and making love. Danica was riding high on euphoria.

It had been easy to pretend the rest of the world didn't exist, as if they could stay here forever and never go back. She bet she could even learn to tolerate the ice cold showers and the awful ready-to-eat meals.

For Noah, she could.

If only her mom could've met him. *You and dad said you were soul mates, and I think I've found mine.*

Of course, she wouldn't say that to Noah because it was way too sappy and over the top. But she still felt it.

He'd told her he loved her. She was pretty sure she loved him back, even though this was happening fast and she wasn't ready to tell him yet.

They didn't have to say goodbye. They had *time*. That was all that mattered.

They got cleaned up, ate terrible food, and spent the morning cuddling. At some point, she must've drifted to sleep, because suddenly her thoughts weren't making sense. Disturbing images were flying toward her out of the darkness.

Microphones being shoved into her face, so many she couldn't breathe.

The man with the eagle tattoo grabbed for her while blood poured from his neck.

A door yawned open, with faceless men waiting for her inside.

"Dani." Noah was gently shaking her. "Wake up."

Danica inhaled, opening her eyes. She grabbed his shirt. "Noah?"

"Were you having a nightmare again?"

"I—"

The phone rang shrilly, making her jump.

"Shit. I bet that's Max. I'd better get it."

Suddenly, she wanted to tell him not to answer. She had a terrible feeling about whatever news waited on the other end of that call.

But Noah had already gone over to the table to grab the phone, leaving Danica on the bed. She sat up as he answered.

"Hello?" Noah listened. "Yeah, boss, five minutes." He lowered the phone. "Max wants to have a video meeting. Detective Murphy is at Bennett Security headquarters. They have an update for us, both Max and the police."

"About the investigation?"

Noah nodded. "And Lana Marchetti is there, too. She's the West Oaks Assistant District Attorney. She's also Max's fiancé. We can trust her. Are you okay with this?"

"We don't really have a choice, do we?" Danica got out of bed. She wished she had nicer clothes to wear, instead of these borrowed ones.

Whenever she had a board of directors meeting that she expected to be contentious, she liked to wear a suit. Putting on her armor.

Noah set up the laptop. They both took seats at the table, and he started the video feed.

Detective Murphy was sitting in front of the screen, along with a woman Danica assumed was Lana. Max Bennett stood off to one side, hands in his trouser pockets. Tanner, Noah's fellow bodyguard, stood next to him.

Danica smoothed a hand through her hair.

"Ms. Foster Grant, I'm Lana Marchetti," the assistant district attorney said. "I'm sorry for not giving you more notice of this meeting. It came together pretty suddenly. But we have news that we need to share with you."

"Good news?" Noah asked.

Detective Murphy answered him. "We certainly think so."

Lana shifted in her seat and crossed her legs. She was wearing jeans, and Danica remembered that today was Saturday. She and Noah had been here two nights, and the time had blurred together. Incredible how much could change in so few hours.

"A total of six men have been arrested for trying to kidnap you," Lana said, "and the district attorney's office is in the process of filing criminal complaints against them. We also have two additional suspects who are deceased. One from the silver SUV that chased you and Noah on the freeway after the gala. And the other is the individual who attacked you inside the museum at the event. The man with the eagle tattoo, whom Noah killed."

Anxiety filled Danica's stomach, even though she was glad to hear confirmation that the man was dead. "It was self defense."

Lana nodded. "Of course. No one is disputing that. Apart

from your statement, Rosie Consuelo was also a witness, and she left no doubt that the death resulted from you and Noah acting in self defense."

Noah put his elbow on the table. "What about the man with the blue bowtie who was shooting at us? The one Tanner and I spotted inside the atrium at the museum during the gala?"

"He's in custody," Lana said. "He and the others aren't talking yet. But our office is amassing plenty of evidence. There's no doubt everyone we've arrested was involved in the kidnapping attempts. But we've also found the identity of the man with eagle tattoo. His name was Jason Gerrig."

Danica waited for this name to have some impact on her. It was strange to put a name to the almost superhuman image he'd taken on in her mind and in her nightmares.

But he'd just been a man. And now, he was dead.

"How did you find him?" Noah asked. "Fingerprints?"

"Fingerprints were part of it." A tiny smile appeared on Lana's face. "But we have Bennett Security to thank for filling out the profile."

"It was a joint effort," Detective Murphy corrected. "Between West Oaks police, LAPD, and yes, Bennett Security." Clearly, she wasn't happy about sharing the credit for this. "Gerrig was enlisted in the army, but received a dishonorable discharge for assaulting his commanding officer. That was almost ten years ago. Since then, he's been off the government's radar."

"Until Max's team helped track him down." Lana looked over to Max.

He cleared his throat. "Tanner, could you walk us through what you and Detective Sean Holt found?"

The bodyguard stepped forward, crossing his muscular, tattooed arms over his T-shirt. "It really started several days ago, with the drawing of the eagle design that Danica made. Noah sent it to Sean, and Sean asked around with some of his informants in the LA underworld."

According to Sean's informants, a hitman with an eagle neck

tattoo had been active in California for the last several years. He was a mercenary, available for hire to only the highest bidders for operations like assassinations and kidnappings.

Danica listened to this information with growing horror. She couldn't believe she'd gotten away from this man. But maybe he hadn't expected a woman like her to know how to defend herself. She'd caught him off guard.

"But even after we knew the guy's reputation," Tanner continued, "and his name, we didn't know where to find his base of operations. We were assuming he'd been using a fake identity, which turned out to be correct. But I spoke to several tattoo artists in the LA area, and one of them knew him. She'd done new ink on one of his arms recently, some sort of tally marks." Tanner shrugged. "Maybe for kills or ops completed, something like that. But the artist remembered the guy had a place right near Venice Beach."

"Our officers located that house this morning," Detective Murphy said. "We raided the residence and found a cache of weapons and equipment, including burner phones and a cell signal jammer. We also found evidence of the plot against you, Ms. Foster-Grant. Communications, plans, schematics for the museum, the works."

"But did someone hire Gerrig to do this?" Noah asked. "You said he's a mercenary."

Lana looked like she was hesitating. But Detective Murphy shook her head. "Usually, that might be how he operates—if the rumors can be believed. But this time, the potential ransom for Ms. Foster-Grant was incentive enough for him to act on his own. From what we've seized from his home, Jason Gerrig was the force behind this plot. He planned it all out. He brought in the thugs who tried to grab Ms. Foster-Grant. We have no evidence that anyone hired him to do it."

"But then how did he know I'd be at the natural history museum last week?" Danica asked. "The day of the first attempt?"

"That's been one of our top concerns," Max said, "and about an hour ago, we found the answer."

He cast a glance at Detective Murphy, who now seemed to be studying some interesting feature of the opposite wall.

Max continued. "Our research team was looking for any possible source for that information, either inside or outside your circle, Danica. We found it. A curator for the museum, Anderson Nobis, posted on a social media account a few days before your visit."

"*Anderson?*"

"He has an anonymous profile focused on Southern California museums. He complained online about how you'd be arriving that Friday afternoon to ruin the West Oaks Natural History Museum."

Danica couldn't believe it. Well—maybe she could believe Anderson's attitude. The man had spoken openly about his disdain for her. But to reveal her appointment so publicly? "Did he actually say I'd be there at six o'clock?"

"The post mentioned you'd be there just before closing. We haven't seen anything to suggest Anderson revealed this information intending you harm. But it would've been no challenge for Gerrig to find out the time and plan accordingly."

"My office is exploring whether Anderson violated any laws," Lana cut in, "but I doubt it. He was extremely careless, and the museum might want to consider terminating him. Especially considering that he tried to delete the post afterward, probably because he realized what he'd done."

Max nodded. "But by then, it was too late. If Gerrig had already been tracking you, looking for an opportunity? He would've been monitoring social media for each and every mention of your name."

Danica shivered. "Which I would never do, because it's awful. I don't need to see what people are saying about me. I hear it enough as it is." But she should've been paying more attention. Gerrig certainly had.

And Gerrig could've easily figured out that she ran every

morning, too. Would it have been so hard to construct a likely route around the West Oaks hills?

"Do you think Gerrig or his people could've been following me?" she asked.

Lana nodded. "We believe so, yes. We found photos in his apartment of you and Noah running together."

Noah turned to her. "We saw that white work van the first day we were running. It drove right past us."

Ugh. The thought made her skin crawl. Was that how Gerrig had gotten Noah's photo?

Detective Murphy grew animated again. "But the good news is, we know who was behind this, and we know they're either in custody or in the morgue." Her smile tightened. "Thanks to this joint effort between West Oaks PD and Bennett Security."

Noah's hand squeezed around Danica's. "Lana, do you agree with that?" he asked. "Everyone's been caught? Danica's out of danger?"

Again, Lana paused. She shared a look with Max.

"There are some loose ends we're still trying to untangle," Lana said. "It'll take some time to examine all of Gerrig's devices and documents. But we're hopeful. At the very least, now that Gerrig is dead, the primary force behind the plot to kidnap you is gone."

Detective Murphy stood up, straightening her blazer. "Ms. Foster-Grant, I'll be meeting with your father and your chief of security in about an hour. I'd very much like to have you on the phone at that time, so we can both assure them you're out of harm's way. And, I hope, heading back home?"

"I'll think about it."

So much had just come at her at once. She could barely get it settled in her mind.

Was it really over?

No, Lana had mentioned loose ends.

The altered video. That had to be what she'd meant.

Could someone within the police have been helping Gerrig?

"I'll have Mr. Bennett send over my cell number," the detective said. "If you could let me know as soon as possible? I'd also like to know your ETA for returning to West Oaks for a more formal interview."

Noah said goodbye and ended the video call.

Danica got up from her chair. "Could we go outside? I feel like I can't breathe in here."

Once they were out in the clearing, Noah pulled her into a hug and kissed her head. She sank into him. It was so much nicer letting him comfort her than going it alone.

"What do you think?" he asked. "Do you trust Detective Murphy's claim that all the bad guys have been caught?"

"I don't know. Lana wasn't convinced. There's still the museum video footage that I *know* was altered. Which means someone else could've been helping Gerrig."

"Right. I was thinking the same thing."

"But if they found out I'd be at the museum because of Anderson's post, I have no reason to think it was anyone in my family."

Noah twisted his lips. "It does seem that way."

She couldn't believe she'd suspected her family of trying to kidnap her. What kind of daughter was she, to think her father remotely capable of that? Or Blake, who was like an uncle?

Her father was keeping secrets from her. He'd basically admitted it. And those secrets had been her biggest reason for suspecting him.

"I have to go home." Her father had said he was willing to tell her the truth. She needed to find out whatever Tori had wanted to tell her, too.

She, Soren, and William hadn't really been a family in a long time. Now, Danica had a chance. She wanted to start healing the rift. Going home was the only way.

"Do you want me to come with you?" Noah asked.

She held his face in her hands. "I *need* you there with me. Whatever my dad has to tell me, he needs to understand what you mean to me."

They hugged again. Part of her regretted leaving the safe

house. It had become their refuge. But Danica wanted Noah to be a real part of her life. That would never happen if they stayed here, hiding away.

She had to go back into the world and figure out how to go forward—with Noah by her side.

Chapter Thirty-Six

*M*ax sent a car to the safe house to pick them up. With weekend morning traffic, they'd have a little over an hour for their ride to arrive.

Noah watched Danica send a message to her father, letting him know she'd be on her way to the house. But she'd chosen not to contact Detective Murphy, and he couldn't blame her. Noah still wasn't sure about the detective, either.

He and Danica picked things up as best they could. They'd pretty much just had their clothes when they'd arrived, but his tux and Danica's dress were ruined. After a quick lunch to keep their energy up, the two of them sat together on the bed, arms around one another.

"Does your father know I'm arriving with you?" Noah asked.

"I didn't give him that many details. But he probably assumes, given what I said to him the last time we spoke."

"Which was?"

"That I care about you and want you in my life. And that we're seeing each other."

Hearing those words made him indescribably happy. "I don't think we were *technically* seeing each other at that point. We'd gotten naked, but…"

She playfully punched his arm. "He knows how I feel about you, okay? And even if he didn't, he'd figure it out pretty quick."

Noah thought about his own family. Ginger and Gramps wouldn't be too surprised. But Noah couldn't wait to tell his mom and dad that he and Danica were together. Mom and Dad would want to know all the details of how it had happened. How Noah had finally won her over.

Twelve years apart and a lot of drama, and here they were. Together.

He didn't ask when she'd be leaving West Oaks. She had enough to think about at the moment. But it was an important question.

What if she asked him to move to New York with her?

He couldn't leave right away because he had responsibilities here. But maybe… Yeah. He thought he could. For her.

If she asked.

The car arrived, with Rex driving. Noah hugged him, and then Danica did as well. "Good to see you in one piece," Rex said. "Tanner said you got stabbed?"

"It was a scratch." He probably needed to have a doctor look at it, though. It would be dumb to end up out of commission from an infection.

Rex dug into his pocket and produced their phones. "I got clearance to return these. We found yours inside the museum, Danica. Even charged them up for you."

Noah thanked him, tucking away the device as they got into the car. He looked wistfully at his Ducati as they drove away. Max was going to send a tow service to bring it home.

That *had* been pretty fun. Pulling those moves on the freeway with Danica on the back. He'd never gotten to ride the bike that fast before, and it had been a thrill. One he hoped he'd never have to repeat.

Rex took them down the access road and along the route back to the freeway. Danica snuggled against Noah's side in the back seat, and they watched the trees fly past.

Noah didn't know what they were returning to. Was Danica truly out of danger, as Detective Murphy claimed?

He wasn't counting on it. Not until they knew who'd altered the museum security footage. But it did seem likely that her family had nothing to do with it.

They still hated Noah, though. He had no doubts about that.

Danica had said she'd choose him, but Noah didn't like the idea of becoming a wedge between her and her loved ones.

We'll figure it out, he told himself. *Somehow.*

THE CAR STOPPED, and Noah opened his eyes. He'd fallen asleep. Danica was blinking and rubbing her eyes beside him, so he guessed she'd done the same.

"We're at the Foster-Grant residence," Rex said.

"You ready?" Noah asked.

Danica reached for his hand. "I'd better be." They got out together, and her grip on his hand tightened as they approached the front door.

Just a few days ago, they'd made this same walk. Once again, Blake Halston waited for them, arms clasped behind his back.

But now, everything between Noah and Danica was different.

He wasn't her bodyguard anymore. But his protectiveness over her had only increased.

There was no bantering on the front steps. Blake and the house guards swept Noah and Danica immediately inside.

"Where's Rosie?" Danica asked, glancing around the entryway.

Blake clasped his hands in front of him. He was wearing his usual suit. "She's been fired."

"Are you kidding? That's ridiculous. Why?"

Blake gestured at Noah. "You've already got a bodyguard, apparently. So we no longer needed Ms. Consuelo's services. Mr. Vandermeer, I understand we have you to thank for saving Danica's life."

Before Noah could respond, William Foster-Grant appeared. "Danica." He grabbed his daughter into a hug. Then William noticed Noah and gave him a brisk nod. "Thank you for bringing her home."

Danica visibly bristled. "Coming home was my decision, Dad. Noah is just here to support me. We all need to talk."

"Detective Murphy already gave us an update on the latest developments," Blake said.

William was nodding, his usual confident demeanor on display. Was he really that unflappable? Or did he just hide his emotions well? "That's right. Let's sit down, try to relax. You must be starving and exhausted. Talking things through can wait until later." He said this with another glance in Noah's direction.

"No, Dad." Danica took a step away from her father, reaching again for Noah's hand. "You promised you'd answer my questions if I came home. So, here I am. Tell me."

Blake's mouth had pressed into a hard line, but he didn't look confused or surprised. The chief of security knew exactly what Danica was talking about.

He knew whatever William was hiding.

Her father looked resigned. "All right, if that's what's necessary. I suppose it's time. But this is a private family matter. Absolutely no exceptions."

"You're still doing this shit? Noah and I are together," Danica said. "Whatever your secret is—"

But her father interrupted her. "When you hear what I have to say, you'll understand."

Full strength had returned to his voice. He wasn't going to back down.

William pointed down the hallway toward his office. "I will tell you what you want to know, right here and now. But only you, Danica. I love you, and I've always tried to protect you. You will always have a place in my life. But this is the only way. We will discuss this in private, or we won't discuss it at all. Take it or leave it."

Noah could tell what she was about to say. She was about to

tell her father off and turn around, even though she needed to hear this. Whatever this secret was, it had been haunting her for a lot longer than the kidnapping plot.

Danica was stubborn. Noah didn't have a single doubt about that. But she'd clearly gotten that stubbornness from her father, and the two of them were at a stalemate.

"I'll stay here." Noah ran his thumb over Danica's wrist reassuringly, then let go. "I'll be waiting when you're done. I'm not going anywhere."

He knew he'd made the right call when Danica didn't fight him. They both knew this was the way it had to be. She could choose to talk with him later.

Noah still didn't completely trust her family, especially when it came to her emotional well-being. But if she walked away from them now, if she chose Noah instead, she might not be able to go back. He didn't want to be responsible for that. She would only end up resenting him.

With one last glance at Noah, Danica followed her father down the hall. The déjà vu was uncanny. But she'd been fine the last time they were here, physically at least.

After she was gone, Blake gestured at a doorway. "Why don't you wait in the sitting room? It's more comfortable."

"That almost sounded friendly."

"What makes you think it's not? I may seem like a hard ass. But I'm grateful to you for helping Danica. Her father and I both are."

"Could've fooled me."

Blake's mouth moved, showing a hint of a smirk. "I've heard that Bennett Security helped with the investigation as well. William will make sure your company is compensated."

"I don't want his money. Neither does Max Bennett."

"But you were fine taking Danica's." He shrugged. "I suppose that's your choice. Regardless, the case is solved, thankfully. We can move on from it. And Danica can return to New York."

The implication was clear. Blake was letting Noah know he

was a temporary fixture around here, nothing more. So much for being friendly.

Noah went into the sitting room and took a spot on a couch. "I'll wait for Dani. Thanks."

Blake nodded and left the room. Noah settled onto the cushions, crossing his legs.

He was sure Danica was safe right now. But he hoped that, whatever her father had to tell her, Danica would be all right after hearing it.

"Vandermeer."

Noah turned at the voice.

A dark-haired man stood in the doorway, the hard curl of a sneer at the corner of his mouth. A face Noah hadn't seen for twelve years. Not since they'd come to blows.

His former friend. Danica's brother.

Soren.

Shit.

Chapter Thirty-Seven

*D*anica sat in the chair in front of her father's desk. "Tell me what you've been hiding."

"Before I get into this, I need you to know——"

"Dad, enough. *Tell me.*"

He looked over at the engagement portrait on the wall. Danica's mother and father, smiling and happy. The Grant and Foster names, about to be united.

"It has to do with your mother."

"*Mom?* What about her?"

William picked up his desk phone and hit a button. "Could you come in here, please?" he muttered. "It's time."

Danica had no clue what to think. Her chest was growing tighter and tighter the longer she had to wait. *Especially* now that she knew it was something about her mom.

She wanted to reach out for Noah's hand, but of course he wasn't here. He'd stayed behind to allow her to have this conversation.

Danica was pissed at herself for letting her father win that argument. But her need for the truth was just too compelling, and Noah had understood.

Noah was waiting for her. That reassured her.

But she felt awful about Rosie getting fired. Danica would need to get in touch with her, make sure she was all right. Her father might accuse her of being disloyal. But Danica was more like Noah that way. She was loyal to those who deserved it.

The door opened, and Tori stepped inside.

Her head was bowed, eyes down. She slunk over to stand beside William.

So Tori *did* know William's secret. He'd shared the truth with his lover. Big surprise.

But why had Tori contacted Danica at the gala? To confess that secret, because William's poor daughter was hopelessly out of the loop? Taking pity on her?

Danica's confusion gave way to anger. "Dad, you said this was a family matter. That's why Noah couldn't be here. What does Tori have to do with it?"

"Because she *is* family," William snapped, his face turning red.

"What?" If her father had snuck off and married this woman, Danica was going to lose it.

"I'm your sister," Tori blurted out.

The room went quiet. Danica could hear blood rushing in her ears. *My sister? What the hell?* There was nothing to do but wait for an explanation, even though she wanted to run over to Tori and shake it out of her.

My sister.

William had covered his eyes with his hand.

Tori took a step closer to Danica. "I wanted to tell you. That's why I tried to get in touch with you at the gala. William didn't agree, and I didn't want him to find out. That's why I went through Lindley at the museum. William's my father. We have different mothers."

Tori was in her late twenties. But Danica's mother had died less than two decades ago. She could do that math, and she despised what it said about William.

How far do the lies go?

"How long have you known, Dad?" Danica glared at her father, who wouldn't meet her eyes.

"A long time."

The engagement portrait looked down on them all from its place of honor on the wall.

"For most of my life, I didn't know," Tori said. "After I found out, I tried to tell you last fall. I emailed you."

Email? Then it dawned on her. "*You* tried to blackmail me?"

Tori cringed. "I didn't think of it like that. I didn't want to blackmail you. I just…wanted your attention. And I needed help. *My mom* needed help."

"Go on." Danica's voice was low. Dangerous.

Tori came over to sit in the chair beside her. She seemed to be warming up to this conversation. "I never knew who my father was. But I figured it out last year."

"How?" Danica demanded.

"Well, it started when my mom and I saw you on TV. You were doing an interview. My mother, she's got a lot of medical conditions. Diabetes, emphysema. She's been deteriorating the last few years. That day, as we watched your interview, she started saying things about how *I* could've been the one on TV. I could've had what you had. She wasn't making any sense. But finally, I got enough out of her that I understood. And I just…I was angry. My mom needed better care, and we couldn't afford it, so the burden was all on me. I got desperate. I emailed you. I'm sorry."

"Blake got in touch with you?" Danica asked in a monotone.

Tori nodded. "He made the arrangements."

"*Arrangements.* He paid you off?"

"He offered me a job. As his assistant. And a chance…" Tori looked over at William. "To meet my father. To be part of your lives. Part of this family, even in secret."

"Has your mother gotten the care she needs?" Danica asked.

"Yes. She has. I'm grateful, even if I wish I'd dealt with it differently." Tori held out her hands, palms open, like she was begging Danica to believe her. To forgive. "I just wanted a little bit of what you have. Can you blame me?"

Why would you want any of this? Danica wondered. But the answer was obvious.

Tori and her mother had needed the money. So much ugliness came down to money.

"Why didn't your mother ask for a pay off before? She could have."

"I think she was proud. And I think she got some money before? Right after I was born."

William was nodding.

Danica felt sick. "Let me guess. Your birthday is January 17th? You're twenty-eight? Or probably twenty-nine now."

Tori glanced down at her lap. "Yes."

"Good old Dad paid off your mom when you were born. Because he was *married* to *my mother*." Danica jumped up from her seat, fists clenching.

"It was not like that," William said. "Your mother knew, all right? It was no secret. Not from her."

"So, what, she had to hide what you'd done? How is that supposed to make me feel better?" She wanted out of this room. Out of this house. But Danica had the feeling she hadn't heard everything yet.

Danica went to the window, and her dad followed her across the office. "Our marriage was all but arranged by our families. The Fosters and the Grants, uniting their fortunes."

"Yeah, that's what all the articles say. I know." How many times had she heard this story? "But then during your engagement, you fell in love, and..."

Her father was shaking his head, the saddest look on his face.

"No, sweetheart. We didn't fall in love. It was a business deal. Nothing more."

Danica felt like he'd slapped her. Like he'd taken a photo of their family—a representation of her perfect childhood before her mom died—and torn it in two.

This couldn't be right. If she accepted what her father was

saying, then everything about her parents would be a lie. Everything about her *mom*.

"You said you were soul mates. You loved her. She was everything."

"In a way, she was. Your mother was my best friend. But we lived separate lives."

"You're saying it was fake? You pretended to love each other? Why?"

"It was what our families wanted. Given our public profile, the business…"

"The business," Danica repeated. She felt numb.

"And then, you and Soren. We wanted to do what was best."

"You lied to us."

"Your mother and I made sacrifices. It wasn't easy. I fell in love with someone else. And so did she. But we did what we had to, and we kept our family together."

The Foster-Grant name. The Foster-Grant reputation.

"After your mom died," her dad went on, "I didn't want to tarnish her memory. I had to keep that…fiction going. For you, and Soren, and the family name."

This was too much. More than Danica could take. It was sick and twisted, and it couldn't be her life. "Does Soren know?"

"I think he suspects," William said.

"Am I supposed to tell him?"

"I'd rather you didn't speak about this to anyone. I'll handle Soren. But this has to stay in the family. Surely, you must see that."

"You mean Noah. I'm supposed to lie to him?"

She had to keep pretending that she didn't have a sister?

"This is why I didn't want someone like him involved in our lives," William said. "We can't trust his discretion."

Trust? Her father was talking about *trust*?

"I can't listen to any more."

Danica walked away from them in a daze, ignoring her father's requests for her to stay. She didn't want to hear anything else, and she couldn't offer forgiveness.

In the hallway, she swayed, catching herself against the wall.

"Danica, wait." Tori had followed her. "Our dad forgave me, and I forgave him. Maybe you could do the same. Can we talk about this? Please?"

"Not now." She had to get back to Noah, and she had to figure out what the hell she was supposed to say.

All her life, she'd held onto the private hope that she'd find a love like her parents had. Soul mates. All of it, lies. Fake.

And I made Noah lie for me, too. Didn't I?

Noah was so *good*. He deserved much better than this twisted mess of a family.

Better than me.

Chapter Thirty-Eight

"*Y*ou've got a lot of fucking nerve."

Noah stood up. "Hello, Soren. Long time."

Soren had grown his hair to his shoulders, and his cheekbones were prominent. He looked harder than he had in college. Crueler. It showed in the lines around his mouth and the gauntness in his face. The narrowing of his eyes.

Or maybe that was just the hate he was throwing Noah's way.

"What are you doing in my family's house?"

"I'm just here for Danica."

"You finally talked her into wanting you back? Makes sense you'd use this kidnapping mess as an opportunity."

Noah decided not to respond to that provocation. "What are you doing here? I thought you were in New York."

"I got here as soon as I could. I'm here to support my sister."

"That's thoughtful of you."

"Don't talk down to me, Vandermeer. You think anything's forgiven?"

"Did I ask for forgiveness? I don't regret anything. But for Danica's sake, I'd like to make peace."

Soren huffed a laugh. "So holier-than-thou. You act like

you're above it all. But you turned me in because you were *jealous.*"

Noah stuck his hands in his pockets. "And why would I have been jealous?"

"Because you wanted my life! I decided it would be cool to be a Navy SEAL, so you wanted to do it, too. You were an only child, so you latched onto my sister and tried to make her love you more than she loved me. You think I didn't notice how you looked at her? How you followed her around when we were kids? It was pathetic."

Noah's skin heated. He hadn't thought Soren could say anything that would get under his skin. But those comments had stung a little.

"It's sad that that's how you view the world," Noah said.

"I see plenty. I see that you're trying to worm your way back into Danica's life when she's in trouble."

"You sound like Blake." The chief of security had said pretty much the same thing.

"Because you're so obvious," Soren spit out.

Everything good became distorted in Soren's mind. He assumed other people were as manipulative and selfish as he was. Soren had always been a taker, even when they'd been in high school.

How had Noah ever considered this guy his best friend?

Noah had been blinded by Soren's charisma back then. But he'd still been a kid. Now, he understood a lot more about the world. He'd never be able to find common ground with Soren, so there was no use trying—except when it came to Danica.

She was this asshole's sister, and Noah would have to keep dealing with him forever.

Because that was what he wanted with her. *Forever.*

"I love Danica. I have for a long time. We're together. I understand that you're not okay with it. But you and I will have to find some way to get along."

Soren scoffed, shaking his head. "You honestly think you're going to end up with her?"

"I know it."

"You're confident. I'll give you that." Soren walked around the sitting room. He picked up a glass paperweight from a console table, then set it down again. "Since you and I were friends once, I'll give you some free advice. Because I'm generous. Danica is just like our father."

"And?" Noah asked. "What does that mean?"

"You know what a corporate raider does, right?"

"I'm familiar with the concept." Where was this going?

"William goes into a failing company, and at first? He's like a savior, offering to give them just what they need. More money. More chances. But you know what he'll really end up doing? He'll take them over, use them up. Tear them apart and feast on their insides."

"How dramatic," Noah deadpanned.

"William always talked about loving our mom, but it was all bullshit. If she hadn't died, they'd be divorced. Because all he loves is *winning*, and Danica's the exact same way. She might seem kinder and gentler because she's in the nonprofit world, but she's just as cutthroat as William. My father and my sister use people."

Soren walked toward him, advancing. Noah stood his ground, crossing his arms over his chest.

"So guess what, Vandermeer? Danica is going to chew you up, and when she's gotten what she can, she'll spit you out. That's what this family does."

"Including you?"

Soren shrugged. "I've never claimed to be any different. But if I were *you*, I'd cut my losses and run. Because you don't have what it takes to survive here."

"You have no idea what survival takes."

Soren pointed at him. "See, that's where you're wrong. I've survived nearly losing everything when my supposed best friend betrayed me. I survived being all but cut off by my father for being a fuck-up. I built my way back from it, and I've taken down far richer and more impressive people than *you*."

"Is that some kind of threat?"

"I don't need to make threats. If you choose to stick around, then you're screwing yourself over."

Danica appeared in the doorway. "Soren? I thought you weren't going to make it to West Oaks." She looked between the two of them. "What's going on?"

"We were just catching up," Noah said. He walked over and put his arm around her. He was gratified when he saw a vein twitching in Soren's temple. But Danica tensed beside him at his touch.

"I came because I was worried," her brother said. "Blake told me the police caught the kidnappers?"

Danica nodded. "That's what they say."

"Can we talk? You and me? It's important."

"Not now." She closed her eyes briefly. "I need a minute with Noah."

"Fine. You can find me in my room when you're done. But I'm serious, Dani. We need to talk about some things."

With one more glare at Noah, Soren pushed past them and left the room.

Danica shut the door behind him. "I'm sorry. I had no idea Soren was here."

"I'm not concerned about him," Noah said. "What happened with your father?"

Danica glanced up at the mirror above the sofa. Then she looked away.

"He told me the truth. The reason for the blackmail. The secret he's…" Her voice cracked. "The secret he's been keeping. My father asked me not to tell anyone else, including you."

As Noah had expected. "It's nothing that would endanger your safety, right?"

"Not my safety, no. And it's not anything illegal." But Danica's eyes shone, making it clear her father's secret put other things at risk. "It's the kind of thing that makes me second-guess everything I thought was true. About my parents, my child-hood…" Her breath skipped. She was trying not to cry.

Noah had never seen her this way. Not even when she'd been afraid of the kidnappers coming after her again.

Danica looked *lost*.

Noah could get her out of dangerous situations. But this? He had no idea how to help. "What can I do?"

She blinked, and the tears started to fall. Her fingers tried to brush them away, but they were coming too fast.

Noah went toward her, but she backed up, shaking her head.

"Even if I told you all of it, there's no way you'd understand. Your family isn't perfect, I know that, but at least you all have basic respect for one another. My family? Everything's on the surface. And somehow, I'm the only one who *didn't know*."

"That's their fault, not yours." Noah reached out for her again, but she pulled away.

"I heard what my brother said to you."

He was confused at first by the change of subject. "Just now?"

"Yeah. That you and I won't work out."

"He's wrong, obviously. I'm sorry you overheard."

"But that wasn't even the worst of it. Soren said I'd hurt you because I'm like my father." Tears kept streaking down her face.

"He's not right."

"In some ways, he is. The good, and the bad. I've never been ashamed of that before."

She was pulling away from him again. Noah felt it. As if the last few days between them hadn't even happened.

Danica sank onto the couch, wiping her hands over her face. "Noah, I can't do this," she whispered.

"Can't do what?"

But he was afraid he already knew.

"It wasn't real," Danica said. "We were always just pretend-ing." She gestured around her. "It just isn't going to work."

His stomach plunged.

Noah had been trained to ignore pain, shove it away, bear it. Leaving the SEALs had been tough, but most of his friends didn't even know how much it ate at him. The worst of his sadness, he still kept hidden.

But that disappointment had been nothing to what he was feeling now.

Danica was slipping away from him.

If he lost her again? Maybe he could keep going as if nothing had happened. As if his heart wasn't broken. But he'd have to act like Danica had never really mattered, and that would be the most unforgivable lie he'd ever told. Not just to the rest of the world, but to himself.

In college, he hadn't really tried to hold on to her, had he? Because he'd thought it was impossible.

But Noah wasn't the same man. He'd grown up, and he'd been trained to *overcome* the impossible. Maybe he couldn't do that when it came to his back injury, but this was different. Danica was worth *so much more* than a job.

This time, he refused to let her go without a fight.

Chapter Thirty-Nine

"I hate this," Danica said. "But I don't see any other way."

It had been awful to overhear what Soren had said about her. Never before had Danica been ashamed to be like her father. People made the comparison between them all the time, and usually, she'd considered it a compliment. Her father had his flaws, but he was tenacious and driven. Smart. Relentless.

But she'd also believed that he'd loved her mom. That had all been a fiction.

William had to have known that this day would come eventually. The truth about Tori being his daughter would come out. But he'd chosen to lie because it had been easier. Danica refused to live that way.

And Noah was looking at her like he didn't even know her anymore. It was the same thing she'd felt when she'd looked into that mirror hanging on the wall.

Who was Danica Foster-Grant? She didn't know anymore.

"I don't want to be like my father," she said. "I don't want to hurt you."

"So don't."

"You deserve so much better than my messed-up family."

She was sitting on the couch. Noah kneeled in front of her on the floor. "I'll take my chances. You're worth it. Don't do something rash just because of what Soren said."

"But I don't see how I can make this work." Every minute, she was more sure. The only way forward was to cut ties. Let go.

"I was never just pretending." Noah reached for her hands. His green eyes were pleading, but when he spoke, his voice was smooth and strong. "If you don't want me in your life, then say so. But I'm not giving you up for anything less. I lost you before because I didn't fight for you. I am *not* letting that happen again."

Danica was impressed by the passion in his words. But his argument didn't make much sense. Unless…

"Wait. Do you think I'm breaking up with you?"

"Isn't that what you've been saying?"

"No. *God*, no." That was the *opposite* of what she'd been saying. Though, granted, she hadn't been explaining herself very well.

Noah pushed out an exhale. "I really thought you were. Jeez, you scared me."

"But why would I break up with you? I'm crazy about you."

He smiled and laughed, still on his knees.

"Noah, I said I'd choose you every time, and I meant it. I choose you." Danica cupped his face, drawing him closer until their noses touched. "I choose *us*."

She kissed him, taking a second to revel in the softness of his lips, the scratch of his stubble on her chin. Her heart was so gone for this man. His kindness and honor, his humor and strength. The ways he was the same boy she'd fallen for all those years ago, and the ways he'd grown into the best man she'd ever met.

"Then what is it you have to do?" he asked. "Whatever it is, you're dreading it."

She sighed. This part truly did hurt. It was a terrible choice to have to make. "I need to cut ties with my family. I hope it's not forever, but I have to get some space. And…I need to tell you my dad's secret. Because I can't keep this hidden. Not from you. I just can't."

Danica needed to share the truth about her family. If she didn't, this secret would keep tearing her up inside. She wasn't going to spill her parents' dirty laundry to the media. But Noah was the man she cared about. She intended to share every part of her life with him. She *trusted* him. Her father knew nothing about real trust.

"Tori is my sister. My father's daughter."

Noah's eyebrows shot up.

"I'll tell you the rest of it later. But right now, I want you to take me to your place. I can't stay here."

Danica didn't recognize her family anymore. Whatever they'd become, she didn't want to be a part of it.

She needed Noah. The man she trusted. The man she'd fallen for all over again.

"Are you going to tell them you're leaving?"

"No. I'll explain it to them later." She'd have to figure out what to say.

"Soren really seemed to want to talk to you."

Danica was wondering about that, too. Maybe it was about Tori. Their sister. "I can't deal with him at the moment."

She was pissed at Soren for the things he'd said to Noah. As for her father, he wouldn't be surprised she'd taken off. William had seen how angry she was.

Noah took her hands and stood up with her. "We can go to my family's house. My grandpa and Ginger are still away, so we'll have it to ourselves. And if you want, tomorrow I can take you to my condo in town."

"I want to see it." She gave him another kiss. "I want to see everything that's important in your life."

She wasn't sure she'd ever come back here. Danica still felt her mom in this house, and she regretted losing that connection. Her mom wasn't around to defend herself, and Danica wasn't going to judge her mother's motivations. But she also had to do what was best for *her*.

She was choosing love over her family name—exactly what her parents should have done long ago.

DANICA WENT to her room to pack, leaving Noah in the front sitting room to arrange a ride for them.

She'd been hoping to avoid her brother. But Soren found her.

"Dani? Are you leaving already? You just got back."

She kept pulling items from her dresser and tucking them into the suitcase she'd brought from New York. "I don't see the point of staying just so we can pretend to be a family. There are no cameras here. If Dad needs a family photo op, his people can call my people."

"So he told you? About Tori?"

Danica stilled, a pair of jeans in her hand. "Yeah, he did. You knew? Why didn't *you* tell me?"

"Because you'd act exactly like you are right now. Freaking out over nothing."

"*Nothing?* Our parents living a lie is not nothing. Having a sister I didn't know about is not nothing." Under better circumstances, Danica would've wanted the chance to welcome Tori into her life. Maybe it would still happen. But Tori had tried to blackmail her, and had lied to her for the last several months. It was a lot to get over.

Soren leaned his shoulder into the door frame. "I'm sorry you're upset. But why are you taking it out on me? Because of Vandermeer?"

Danica bit the inside of her cheek. Was her brother truly that self-centered?

You're the one who's like Dad, she thought. *Not me.*

"You can't blame everything in the world on Noah," she said.

"But that's where you're going right now. To be with him?"

"Yep. And nothing you say will stop me."

She expected another argument on that subject, but then her brother surprised her.

"Shit, I'm really not trying to fight with you." Soren ran his hands through his wavy hair. "Look, this isn't how I wanted to ask. But I need a favor."

"What favor?"

A pained look crossed his face. "It's my company. Things… aren't going as well as they should. We're having a cash flow problem."

"Are you serious? You're asking me for money?"

He glanced away. "Some recent projects haven't panned out the way we'd hoped."

Her brother's appearance in West Oaks suddenly made a lot more sense. "You came here to ask Dad to bail you out, didn't you? And he said no."

"He's never believed in me."

"Then why should I?" She walked over to Soren, lowering her voice. "Because Dad and I are *so much* alike, right? We're cutthroat. We use people."

"You heard that? I was just…"

"Even if I hadn't? I still would've said no." She dropped the last stack of clothes into her bag and zipped it up. "I can forgive you, Soren, because you're my brother. But only if you grow up and start thinking of other people, not just yourself. Noah is a far better man than you've ever been. Why don't you try being more like him?"

Soren's expression shut down. Her brother had never looked at her this way before—with undisguised hatred. It was like a mask had been pulled away.

"So that's how it is?" he asked. "You're really going to choose sides against me?"

"I already did."

"You're making a mistake, Dani."

Without another word, she wheeled her suitcase past him and down the hall.

∾

NOAH CARRIED Danica's suitcase into the house. She followed, switching on lights in the entryway. She wanted to spend more time with his grandfather and Ginger, but at the moment, Danica was glad to be here alone.

It was past lunch time, but she wasn't hungry. She planned to get Noah upstairs to his bedroom and not leave for the rest of the day. Maybe even the rest of the week. Her schedule was shot anyway.

Noah closed and locked the front door. She gripped his shirt in her fist and pulled him down to kiss her. More than anything, she needed his arms around her, and her arms around him.

"Make me forget," she murmured against his lips. "I only want to think about you."

This trip to West Oaks had put her in danger and revealed truths about Danica's family that she'd never wanted to face.

Everything she'd believed had turned upside down.

But the past week had brought Noah back into her life, too. So it was impossible to regret anything that had happened, no matter how frightening it had been or how much her family had hurt her.

Noah could make it better. To be here with him, she'd go through it all again.

"We're back in civilization," he said. "We've got hot water now."

"Oh, thank god. No more cold showers."

"Should I clean you up?"

He scooped her into his arms and carried her upstairs to his bedroom.

While the water heated in his shower, they undressed each other. She put a kiss on the love bite at his neck. The past few hours fell to the floor with their clothes.

Danica pushed back to look at the wound in his side. "How's it feeling?"

Noah shrugged. "Forgot it was there." He stuck a hand in the shower to check the water. "Nice and hot. Come on."

His shower had plenty of room for two people and then some. They stepped under the spray. It pounded into Danica's back, massaging her tense shoulders. Noah's mouth slanted into hers, his hands on her hips, drawing her close. She grabbed his ass and squeezed the firm glute muscles. His erection was hot and thick against her stomach.

Danica broke their kiss to watch rivulets of water run over his pecs and down the ridges of his abs. Desire throbbed between her legs.

She was still kind of amazed that her little brother's friend had turned into the blazingly sexy man in front of her.

And he's mine.

She closed her hand around his hard-on. Noah hummed and smiled. "You want me to fuck you?" he asked.

Danica shook her head. "I want to watch you come and know it's because of me."

She stroked him slowly at first. Noah curved his hands at her neck and kissed her, their lips wet from the water of the shower. His tongue darted into her mouth and over her lips.

She could tell when he needed more. The rhythm of his breathy moans increased. This was so hot, being able to give him pleasure this way. Making this muscular, dominant Navy SEAL pant with need for her.

"Here." Noah grabbed a small bottle of lotion and squeezed some into her hand.

"Lotion in the shower? I can guess what that's for."

"You even need to guess? I'm a guy."

Her slicked fist moved faster on his shaft. Soft skin over steel. The head of his cock was a deeper shade of purple. So pretty. She had to bend down and kiss it. Noah breathed out a moan.

Danica stood up again. Her free hand went to his balls and tugged, her fingertips pressing into the sensitive skin behind his sac.

"Oh, fuck." Noah leaned back against the shower wall. "Dani, that's so good. I...I can't..."

He gasped, and his cock spurted in her hand, painting his stomach with his cum. She loved seeing the evidence of how good she'd made him feel.

Noah dug his fingers into her hair, pulling her into a searing kiss. Her fist pumped over him a few more times until she was sure he was spent. Then she moved slightly to let the water rinse off his stomach.

He looked down at her, chest heaving, eyelids heavy. His dimple appeared as he gave her a crooked smile.

"You're looking smug," he said.

She giggled. "I think I did pretty well."

"You did. But don't go thinking you're in charge."

"If I'm not in charge, who is?"

Noah spun her and pushed her against the tile. "Let's just see."

Chapter Forty

*N*oah's cock was still half hard, and he felt drunk on the high that orgasm had given him. But his girl needed some attention. In fact, he felt a little guilty about getting off first. He knew she'd enjoyed the power trip of making him come, though.

Now, it was his turn.

Danica wanted to forget about her family and her troubles. Noah was going to do his best. He wanted to wipe every worry from her mind and give her nothing but pleasure.

"Turn around," he said.

Danica obeyed, turning to face the shower wall. She braced her hands against the tile. Noah pushed her wet hair aside and trailed kisses across her shoulders, taking a moment just to admire her slender body.

He reached around her to squeeze her breasts. He loved how heavy and round they were, how they overflowed his hands. Then he dragged his palms down her stomach and to her hips.

All of this, for me.

He couldn't believe how lucky he was.

Noah brought one hand up to the wall. The other teased her inner thighs from behind, nudging so she'd spread her legs.

She looked over her shoulder at him. A new flare of arousal traveled down his center. He wasn't twenty anymore, so he couldn't get hard again just yet. But he was already anticipating it.

"Bend over a little?" he asked. Again, she obeyed him, and fuck did that turn him on. Especially because he knew how stubborn and strong she could be. He was the only one who got to have her like this. And she got the same from him—those secret sides of him that nobody else could see.

His fingers met the slick heat between her legs. Danica tipped her head back. "*Oh.*"

"Is that good?" he murmured, kissing the droplets of water on her neck.

"I need new words. 'Good' isn't enough."

He moved his fingers over her sensitive folds and clit and in and out of her opening. Danica kept her hands on the wall, her spine arching to give him better access as he finger-fucked her from behind.

They were both soaking wet from the shower, but the moisture between her legs was totally different, slippery and warm while the spray on Noah's back was starting to cool. He couldn't resist sucking that sweet wetness from his fingers, even though she protested at the loss of contact.

He groaned at the taste of her. He needed more.

Noah dropped to his knees behind her and replaced his fingers with his tongue. Danica cried out.

He sat back against his heels and pushed her thighs even wider with his hands so he could suck and lick just where she needed it.

The tile was hell on his knees. The water from the shower ran over her back and his face, making it hard to breathe. But he didn't care. He wanted to worship her.

His tongue pushed inside her, and his hands were tight on her hips. His mouth was unrelenting, taking as much as he was giving.

"*Noah.*" She shuddered, coming undone as she bucked against his face. More sweetness rushed over his tongue.

He really couldn't get enough of her. With Danica, there would never be enough.

Once they were dried off and dressed in fresh clothes, Noah carried her to his bed. He was hungry, but first, he needed to lie down with her and cuddle and just be together.

He was lying on his side, facing her. She put her palm on his cheek. He'd been waiting a long time to have her in his bed like this. His to kiss and touch.

To love.

Then Danica said what he'd been waiting so long to hear. "Noah, I love you."

Those words caught him off guard in the best way.

"It's scary to tell you, but in a way, I also love that feeling." She rolled her eyes. "I guess I'm twisted like that."

He leaned over to kiss her. "I get it." This was an adrenaline rush, every bit as much as rocketing down the freeway on his motorcycle. Or a HALO jump from forty-thousand feet.

"I don't know exactly how to make this work," she said. "But I want to try."

"We'll figure it out. I'll be right there with you."

They were free-falling together, and they couldn't see the ground yet. Didn't know when to open the chute. But he didn't want to miss a single second.

NOAH MADE them sandwiches for a very late lunch while Danica sat at the kitchen island.

"Do you still hate to cook?" he asked.

"Detest it. Even though I love to eat."

"Me too, on both counts. I foresee a lot of takeout in our future." He set a smoked salmon, tomato, and goat cheese sandwich on the plate in front of her.

She grinned at him and took a bite. "This is delicious! You

sure you don't know how to cook?"

"I'm told layering stuff between slices of bread isn't technically cooking."

"It's not? What about putting caviar on potato chips?"

"Well, that's just good sense."

They'd been talking for hours about everything and nothing. Neither had mentioned where home would be. Whether it would even be in the same place. He didn't love the idea of long distance, but if he'd still been in the Navy, long distance would've been a given for them.

It was going to work out. That was his new mantra. His days as a cynic were over.

Danica's phone chimed. She took it out of her pocket. "Lindley just texted." The executive director from the museum.

"Yeah?"

Her thumbs moved over the keyboard on her screen. "She asked if we could meet. I haven't seen her since the gala."

"I thought we were forgetting about the rest of the world for today."

She grimaced. "I know. But I hate that I left things so up in the air with the museum. I need to find out what's happening with our project, the donors... She offered to come here."

Noah rounded the island and kissed her forehead. "I was kidding. Lindley's welcome. I should check in with work, too."

Lindley arrived about an hour later. Danica opened the door for her. Lindley gave them each a hug and a kiss on the cheek.

"It's the boyfriend! You two have had quite the adventure, I hear."

"I'll let Danica tell it," Noah said.

Lindley put a hand on Danica's arm. "But was there really a car chase?"

"I was on the back of Noah's motorcycle."

"*What?*"

"If I told you every detail, you probably wouldn't believe it..." She took Lindley down the hall into the library to chat.

In his room, Noah sat at his desk and opened his computer.

He spent some time catching up on work.

But his mind kept wandering to Danica downstairs. He felt
himself smiling as he thought about her and all the things he
wanted to share with her. They both needed a *real* vacation.
Twelve years apart was a lot of time, and even though Noah felt
like he knew Danica at her foundations, there were so many little
details he'd missed out on. He wanted to know everything.

And of course, more sex. Lots of sex. *All* the sex.

He was a lovesick fool, like Chase had said. But he was a
blissfully happy one.

A text came in on his phone, jarring him out of his reverie.

It was a message from Max. *Call me.*

"Hey, Max. What's up?"

"News on Jason Gerrig," Max said, wasting no words. "The
guy with the double-eagle tattoo. We've been digging into the
documents found in his house this morning, including his other
aliases. We got a major hit on one of those identities. He worked
for Valoris Security."

Noah stood up from his chair. "Valoris?" The same company
that Rosie and the rest of Danica's security detail had
worked for.

What the hell?

"We've got a call in to Valoris's main office in New York.
Waiting on more details. But you needed to know ASAP. Is
Valoris still protecting Danica?"

"No. Her father fired her head bodyguard, and we didn't
bring any others with us. We're at my place now. But as far as I
know, some Valoris bodyguards are still at her father's house."

"Then maybe I should let Foster-Grant know," Max said.

"Probably."

Shit. Was Danica's family in danger? They weren't Noah's
favorite people, but he didn't wish them harm.

Noah's phone made a noise, and he looked down at it. Chase
from West Oaks PD was calling. Maybe Chase had heard about
the Valoris Security connection, too. Noah would have to call
him back later.

"You just watch out for Danica, and we'll keep working on this," Max said. "You're secure there? You're in the hills at your family's place?"

"Yeah, we're fine. Thanks, Max. Let me know what else you find out."

"Will do."

Quickly, Noah checked his Bennett Security app. He'd had a system installed on this house after he'd become a bodyguard. The motion sensors and cameras showed no activity outside. Doors all locked.

He exhaled. Danica was downstairs, chatting with Lindley. Everything was fine. The alarm was off right now, but when Lindley left for the evening, he'd reset it.

Noah wanted to tell Danica about this latest development. But he had to think it through first.

Jason Gerrig had worked for Valoris. That couldn't be a coincidence.

There'd been times in the past week that Danica had questioned whether to trust Rosie. Did that mean Rosie had somehow been involved in the kidnapping attempts?

That was hard to believe. Rosie had helped Danica escape from the kidnappers multiple times. She'd shot at the van that had tried to grab Danica in the hills. And at the gala, she'd shot at the guy with the blue bowtie.

At every step, Rosie had helped thwart the kidnappers, even if she'd sometimes been less than effective.

He remembered what Danica had told him. *She'd* insisted on hiring Rosie. No, there was no way Rosie had been in on it.

But what about others at Valoris Security?

And that meant—*fuck*. Danica's family had made the decision to hire Valoris. Did that mean William or Blake Halston really were involved, as they'd feared before?

Suddenly, the entire investigation was up in the air. Just moments ago, they'd believed Danica's family was innocent of trying to have her kidnapped. But now? Noah had no idea what to think.

Chapter Forty-One

*D*anica shut the door to the library. It was a cozy room, though the bookshelves looked like they were filled more with technical manuals and computer programming books than literature.

There were a couple of leather chairs in front of a fireplace. Danica curled up in one.

Lindley sat in the other, her purse tucked in at her side. Her red hair was back in a claw clip, and she wore no makeup. Danica had never seen her so casual. And her eyes looked swollen.

Poor Lindley probably hadn't slept well since the gala. That night had been a rough night for everyone, and Lindley didn't have a guy like Noah to pick her up and comfort her.

"I am so sorry about Anderson," Lindley said. "I heard this afternoon, and I absolutely couldn't believe he'd been so reckless as to post online about your visit. I feel like it's partly my fault."

"You couldn't have known."

"But I kept him on as a curator. I should've gotten rid of him months ago when he started complaining about the changes we envisioned."

"You don't think he posted my schedule on purpose, right? The police assumed he didn't."

"I can't imagine. Today, he genuinely seemed remorseful. But still, so stupid. I'm going to raise the issue with the board, but as far as I'm concerned? Anderson's history."

"I'll leave it up to you. But thanks." The damage was done. Danica was ready to move on from it. "Speaking of the board, I'm nervous about how they'll react to what's happened. Do you think the museum can come back from this? Not to mention the foundation. My reputation must be toxic right now."

Two dozen voicemails and far more texts and emails waited on Danica's phone. But she hadn't brought herself to go through them yet.

"I don't know about the foundation," Lindley said. "That's your wheelhouse. And it's got your name on it. That has to help."

She managed a laugh. "True." Though her association with her family was on rocky ground at the moment.

"But as for the museum board, I've already been getting calls from the other board members, and they're all behind you, Dani. They believe in you."

She couldn't describe her relief at hearing that. Danica had lost a lot in the past few days, but she believed she'd gained far more.

Most of all, Noah. But her friendships meant so much, too.

"I'm grateful for all you've done," Danica said. "You've had to deal with more than you ever signed up for." At the next board meeting, she was going to bring up Lindley's compensation package. She deserved a raise after all this.

Lindley's eyes darted away. "It really hasn't been that bad."

"Are you *kidding*? It's been terrifying. There's no shame in saying it." Danica had struggled to be open about her fears before, but she was trying to be honest about her feelings. Especially when it came to the people she cared about. "I'm so sorry you had to go through that because of me."

Lindley didn't respond, and Danica could feel the change in

her friend's mood, like a shift in the air. Maybe she'd said too much.

Lindley's hand went to her purse, squeezing the top of it. "What about the investigation into the kidnappers? Have they made much progress, aside from finding Anderson's post on social?"

"A lot, actually. They found the identity of the man with the eagle tattoo."

"The guy who was killed at the gala?"

"Right. He was behind the kidnapping plot. Some kind of hitman. He must've already been looking for an opportunity to go after me for ransom money, and when he saw Anderson's post about my visit to the museum, he decided on the time and place."

Lindley sat forward, eyes brightening. "So this hitman was behind the whole kidnapping plan? That's what the police said? Are they closing the case?"

"Closing it? I'm not sure. The detective probably would prefer that." Danica shrugged. "But Bennett Security, the company Noah works for, is still looking into it. There's a loose end. Someone altered the surveillance video from the museum."

Lindley's body went still. "Altered?"

She'd whispered this. Her lips hadn't even moved.

"I didn't mention it before because Noah and I were keeping it quiet. He's been helping me investigate." Danica felt a little bad about leaving her friend so far out of the loop.

And now, she was wondering if Lindley was ready to hear all this. Discussing the kidnapping had only seemed to make Lindley's discomfort increase.

Danica's phone dinged with an incoming text. She glanced down at the screen.

Noah: Are you done with Lindley yet?

"Sorry, it's Noah. Just a second."

Danica: We're still talking. Are you seriously that horny?

Noah: This isn't a booty call. Max had news on the investigation.

Danica: And?

Noah: Jason Gerrig worked for Valoris under another identity.

Danica's breath stopped in her chest.

"What's going on?" Lindley asked anxiously. "You look shocked. What happened?"

She forced herself to inhale. "Just got an update on the kidnapping investigation from Noah." Danica lowered her phone and rubbed her forehead. How much should she say? It might upset Lindley even more.

"What was it?"

Danica sighed. If Lindley truly wanted to know what was happening, she would tell her. "The guy I mentioned before? The hitman?"

Lindley hugged herself around the middle. "Yeah?"

"He used to work for the same security company that's been protecting my family in West Oaks. It's got me a little freaked out."

"Are you going to tell your family?"

"Yeah. I should."

And Valoris had provided bodyguards to her brother and dad in New York before as well. This was just...

Then a memory surfaced.

Her dad's office a few nights ago. The night she'd first seen him and Tori chatting, and made the wrong assumptions.

Danica had shown her father the drawing of the eagle design, and she could've sworn he'd recognized it. Since then, so much had happened that she hadn't thought much more about it.

But what if William *had* recognized the tattoo design?

What if he'd remembered Jason Gerrig from Valoris

Security?

More images bobbed up from the recesses of her memory.

A night out in New York. Had it been a year ago? Two? She, Soren and her dad had all been together, having dinner at Eleven Madison Park. They'd had a bodyguard detail that night. Not something Danica ever preferred, but when the three Foster-Grants were all in the same public place, it made sense.

She remembered a man in a dark suit, in many ways indistinguishable from the others on their security team that evening.

Except for the glimpse of ink just above his high collar.

Two curving heads, like snakes.

That was why the eagle tattoo had made such an indelible impression after that brief sighting inside the museum, though she'd struggled to place it. Too much time had passed. It had been a different city, a different context.

"Oh my god," Danica breathed.

"*What?* What is it?"

"He was a bodyguard for my brother in New York. Jason Gerrig. The man with the eagle tattoo."

Soren was the one who'd always hired Valoris.

Lindley's eyes widened. "You're sure?"

Danica nodded. She hadn't even meant to say that aloud, but the shock was too much. It had overwhelmed her, turning her numb.

But if her dad had recognized Jason, why hadn't he said anything? Had he been unable to place the memory, like Danica?

Or had it been something more?

While these thoughts spun through Danica's mind, Lindley had her phone out, texting rapidly. Which seemed odd. But Danica was too focused on what she'd realized.

"I have to tell Noah. And Bennett Security. The police."

"Wait," her friend said sharply.

Danica looked up.

One of Lindley's hands held her phone. But the other hand was buried inside her purse.

And she had the strangest look on her face.

Chapter Forty-Two

*A*fter he'd finished texting with Danica, Noah sat on his bed and called Chase's number.

"Noah?"

"Hey, man, sorry I missed your call."

"How's your client?"

"She's not my client anymore. She's...my girlfriend. In reality now, not just my fantasies."

"Damn. You pulled it off."

"Any luck with your love problems?" Now that he was a romantic, Noah wanted a happy ending for everyone.

Chase groaned. "I wish. But we'll have to catch up on my issues later. I have news about that surveillance video from the museum."

"Listening."

"I spoke to the patrol officers who responded to the scene. I found out who downloaded the surveillance video, and she's a friend. But she was out sick for a few days, so I only caught up with her this afternoon."

"Okay."

"My friend, this patrol officer, she said the scene that Friday night at the museum was pretty chaotic. They were focused on the vehicles that tried to kidnap Danica. So nobody thought to grab the surveillance footage that night. Sometimes there are delays, you know? Especially with gathering evidence after the fact."

"I understand."

"So my friend went back on Saturday to download the surveillance clips. It's just patrol who goes to get camera footage, not CSI or anything. When we can, we load them on a flash drive. It's the easiest way. When my friend got to the museum, she had to find someone with an access password first, then review the footage to confirm it was the right date and time."

"So she saw the videos right there? At the museum?"

"Exactly. First person from West Oaks PD to have any access. But when I showed her the copies you sent me, of that man in the ball cap? She said there was no difference whatsoever. She hadn't seen any neck tattoo on the original videos."

"You're sure she would've looked closely? It would've been just a short clip."

"Absolutely. To me, a neck tattoo is the kind of thing a cop would notice. And this friend of mine pays attention. She's good."

"That means the alteration had to have happened *before* the video left the museum."

"It's possible. But honestly, it looked a little like a technical issue with the camera. I think that's what Detective Murphy truly believed. Are you sure it was nothing like that?"

"Danica's sure, and I believe her. But wait, who at the museum would've had access to the security videos? Did your patrol officer friend ask? Could it have been a curator named Anderson Nobis?"

The guy who'd revealed Danica's schedule on social media. Maybe that hadn't been an innocent mistake after all.

"Not sure about that," Chase said. "Their surveillance system was encrypted with password-only access."

"And who was it who showed your friend the video? Who had the password?"

"Uh, hold on. I made a note… It was the executive director of the museum."

The executive director. Lindley Colter.

Who was downstairs with Danica right now.

Chapter Forty-Three

"*L*indley?" Danica asked. "Are you okay?"

Her friend was just sitting there, unmoving. Then she pulled her hand from her purse.

Lindley was holding a gun.

"Drop your phone, Dani."

"But..." She couldn't be serious.

"*Do it.*"

Danica let go of the device, raising her hands. The phone thudded to the rug.

"When I came here tonight," Lindley said, "I didn't know if I could go through with this. But now... I'm sorry. I don't think I have a choice."

Aiming the weapon, Lindley darted forward and snatched Danica's phone. She powered it off.

"Whatever is going on, we can figure it out." Thoughts flew through Danica's mind as she tried to put the pieces together. "Does this have something to do with Jason Gerrig? Valoris Security?" Lindley had seemed unsettled, but still okay until Danica had mentioned the Valoris connection.

Lindley flinched at the mention of his name. "He came to

the museum about three months ago. Threatened me. Told me if I didn't do what he said, he'd hurt me and my family."

Danica's hand flew to her mouth.

"But if I complied? I'd get paid. I never wanted to do it. I swear to you. If there'd been any other way…"

Danica tried to think. "Let's just calm down. Both of us. Whatever happened, Jason is dead now. He can't hurt you or anyone."

Lindley's knuckles went white against the gun. "All of this can hurt me. Don't you see that?" Tears spilled from her eyes. "Everyone's going to figure it out, and what then? What am I supposed to do? I gave those men your schedule. After they failed the first time, I stayed up all night figuring out how to delete part of the surveillance video. Even though it was Jason who messed up and let the camera see him, not me. At the gala, I disabled the alarm on the emergency exit for them."

"We'll explain to the police that you were under duress. We'll tell them—"

"*No.* Don't you get it? It was never just Jason Gerrig, Danica. He was hired by someone else. And if I report them, they'll kill me."

Someone else.

Who? she wanted to demand.

Noah was still upstairs. But if she screamed, Lindley might shoot. And she wasn't standing close enough for Danica to disarm her.

Do I even remember those moves? Shit. She hadn't seen her Krav Maga teacher in months.

This wasn't like with Jason at the gala, where Danica had been able to take him by surprise despite his training. Lindley was too wary of her. Too skittish already. Lindley's hands were shaking, and it would be easy for her trigger finger to squeeze. Or even slip.

Lindley gestured with the gun at the door. "We're going to walk outside now. I don't want to hurt you. But if you try to get

Noah's attention, I will. It's my life or yours, Danica, and I'm sorry, but that's not much of a debate."

"What then?" Danica asked quietly. "What are you going to do?"

"Give the people who hired Jason what they want. *You*."

Chapter Forty-Four

*D*read plunged through Noah's veins.

"Chase, could you send a squad car to my family's house?" He rattled off the address.

"I'll come there myself. But why? What's going on?"

He got up, heading for the door to his room. "I hope I'm overreacting. But the executive director of the museum is here with Danica. I need to go check on her."

"Yeah, do that. I'll call this in and head your way. Any reason yet to think Danica's in danger from Ms. Colter?"

Noah went out into the hall and jogged down the steps. "Only what you just told me. But I'd rather play it safe. We can ask Lindley to explain what happened with the video herself." He ended the call.

"Dani?" he shouted.

There was no answer.

The house felt wrong. He couldn't put his finger on it until he reached the library and saw that the doors were open, and no one was inside.

Cursing, Noah raced the other way through the house. He was starting to sweat.

He glanced at his phone, making sure she hadn't written any

further messages since they'd texted. Her last reply had been twenty minutes ago.

The back door stood open.

No. No, no, no.

"Danica! Can you hear me?" He ran through.

The sun was down, and the last remnants of the day's light were fading. Insects chirped on the lawn. The patio was empty, and the yard was shadowed.

He tried calling Danica's phone. It was off.

Heart in his throat, Noah opened his Bennett Security app again.

The motion sensors showed that someone had opened the door about ten minutes ago. Which was just a few minutes after he and Danica had been texting about Jason Gerrig and Valoris Security.

Why would she have left the house?

His mind was already grasping onto terrible possibilities.

He checked the video clips from the camera over his back door, and he went light-headed at what he saw: Danica, walking through with Lindley behind her.

Lindley had been aiming a gun at her back.

As he made a circuit of the exterior of the house, Noah held his phone to his ear. Max picked up.

"I was just about to call you," Max said. "I just got off the phone with Valoris's main office. They confirmed Jason Gerrig worked for them under his alias. But listen to this. It was *Soren* he worked for."

Noah filed away this information for a later moment. "I have something more pressing. Danica is gone. Lindley Colter was here, and I think she's involved in the kidnapping conspiracy."

Max didn't ask him to explain. Instead, he shifted immediately into operations mode. "Have you checked your cameras? Any idea which direction they could've gone?"

"The cameras picked them up as they left the house and got into Lindley's car. They backed out heading south. That's the way out of the neighborhood. It's been ten minutes."

Noah wasn't panicking, but he could feel his anxiety pressing up from his stomach, ballooning in his chest.

How far could they have gone in ten minutes?

"I'm going to call the gatehouse at the entrance to the neighborhood," Noah said. "I'll see if Lindley's car has passed through." This part of the hills was highly secure, and they would've had to go past the gate to exit. Just like that work van the other day after the second kidnapping attempt.

"All right," Max said. "Put me on hold and come right back."

He did. The guy manning the gatehouse said no car matching that description had gone by. Noah told him to notify the police if one did.

Then he switched back to the other call.

"Max? The gatehouse said Lindley's car hasn't passed through. They must still be here in the neighborhood."

And that meant there were only so many places they could be.

One location leaped to the top of the list.

His brain called up the information Max had shared, which had been processing in the back of Noah's consciousness for the last couple of minutes.

Gerrig had worked for Soren.

Noah was going to find out what the hell Danica's brother had to do with this.

"Okay," Max said. "I sent a message to the bodyguards we have on duty. They're about to head to your house."

"But I can't wait for them. I need to go to the Foster-Grants'."

He knew how important it was to have his teammates backing him up. But this was Danica. What if a single moment could make a difference?

"Hold on. Just wait for the other guys. They'll arrive soon."

"You said Gerrig worked for Soren. Danica could be at her father's house right now. If she's not, then I'll bet her family knows something. I'm going to pry it out of them."

"Don't go vigilante on me, Vandermeer. Don't do something stupid."

"Remember earlier this year, when you knew Lana was in trouble? Did you sit around waiting? Or did you get on the road and find the answers yourself?"

Max sighed. "I had my team with me when it counted. Just keep me apprised of your location and what's going on. Be smart."

"I'll be whatever I have to be."

Right now, Noah wasn't a Bennett Security bodyguard protecting a client. And he certainly didn't intend to answer to any governmental authority.

He was a man desperate to find the woman he loved. And he was going to do whatever it took to bring her home safe.

Chapter Forty-Five

*L*indley made Danica drive her car. "Pull in here."

At the horizon, the sun had almost disappeared below the ocean. They hadn't gone very far from Noah's house. Danica recognized this driveway. This was the Larsons' property. The neighbors who were gone all the time, who had the shortcut across their land.

"What are we doing here?"

"Just keep driving to the house."

She'd tried asking Lindley all kinds of questions, careful to keep her voice calm so she wouldn't agitate the woman too much. Lindley had kept the gun pointed at her, though always out of Danica's reach. But so far, Lindley had refused to explain.

She steered the car along the driveway, and the house appeared. All the windows were dark.

"Park around the side," Lindley instructed.

The gearshift pushed into park, and the engine switched off. Silence fell. All except the sound of Lindley's rapid breathing. Danica was terrified, yet she was also keeping herself steady.

But Lindley seemed to be barely holding together. Which was a major problem. Because Lindley was the one with her finger on the trigger of a gun.

"What are we doing here?"

"We'll have to wait."

"Wait for what?"

"For the exchange."

Exchange. Because Lindley was turning her over to the people behind the kidnapping plot.

Had Noah realized she was gone? Would he have any idea what was happening?

If there was some way she could get a message to him... Or get away from Lindley. She knew the way back to Noah's house from here. She could run, even in the dark.

She just needed to wait for the right moment.

"What now?" Danica asked.

"Get out. But slowly. Don't try to get away."

A chilly breeze blew in as Danica opened the door, and she rubbed her arms.

Lindley got out on the other side, slamming the door. She rounded the car, keeping the barrel trained at all times.

"Who are we waiting for?"

"Your family's a piece of work, you know that? If the world only knew the truth." Lindley shook her head.

"So tell them. Tell the world our secrets. I don't care. But you can't let them manipulate you like this. It isn't too late, Lindley. You can stop this."

Lindley dug the fingers of her free hand into her hair, knocking strands loose from her clip. Her eyes were wild. "That's what he told me last night. He said we were supposed to act like nothing had happened, not tell a soul. But I'm the one who's exposed."

"Who is *he*, Lindley?"

The gun kept pointing at Danica, but Lindley's eyes had gone distant. "When Tori contacted me at the gala, I thought she might be involved. That it was a way to get you separated from the crowd, somehow. Saved me the trouble of doing it. But then everything went wrong. And he acted like it was *my* fault. He's going to pin this all on me, I know it. And it'll just be my word to protect me—if I even live long enough to tell it. I'm not going to be the one to take the fall for this."

Headlights were coming toward them. The glare hit Danica's eyes.

A dark sedan with tinted windows rolled smoothly to a stop. Danica didn't recognize it, but that didn't mean much. It was probably part of the fleet owned by Valoris Security.

But who was behind the wheel?

Lindley was moving. "Step forward," she said to Danica. "Don't make me ask twice."

Danica went a few feet closer toward the sedan. It had parked at an angle, so she couldn't see through the windshield. Part of her told her to run, to find any possible way to escape before this situation got even worse.

But now that this car had arrived, she couldn't leave. She had to know.

Who was behind all this? Who had sent Jason Gerrig after her? Who had been terrorizing her for the past week?

The driver's door opened.

And Blake Halston stepped out.

Chapter Forty-Six

*N*oah skirted around a neighbor's house, keeping to the shadows between the trees.

He reached the brick wall that bordered the rear of the Foster-Grant property. Searching the ground, he spotted a rock about the size of a baseball.

He chucked it over the wall and waited. Nobody came running, and he heard nothing from the other side.

Noah scaled the brick and jumped down. He landed at the base of a lemon tree. Rotting, fallen fruit littered the ground.

Quickly, he checked his Ruger LC9 in his shoulder holster, then his phone. It was on silent, and he'd heard nothing else from Max or his teammates. But only about ten more minutes had passed since Max's call.

Noah had changed into dark clothing, grabbed whatever gear he could find at hand, and hurried over here. He hadn't stopped too much to think.

If he let himself think about what could be happening to Danica right now, he'd lose his careful composure. That was something he couldn't afford.

The layout of the Foster-Grants' house materialized in his

mind. He'd spent countless days here with Soren in high school, getting into all sorts of places they didn't belong.

Noah couldn't be sure if Soren still had the same room as back then. But Danica did, so that was a good indication.

He made for the north wing of the house, where Soren and Danica's bedrooms were located.

Voices carried, and Noah pressed himself against the side of the house. Security guards were out on patrol. Two of them.

The two guards went in the opposite direction across the yard, and Noah continued onward, crouching down as he ran.

At the corner of the north wing, he boosted himself onto a balcony. A glance through the window showed a darkened room. His knife sliced easily through the screen.

Shielding his face, he used his elbow to knock out a pane of the window. The glass tinkled as it shattered. Noah's long sleeve had protected his arm. Again, he waited for an alarm. Any indication that someone had detected the intrusion. But nothing came.

Just in case, he used the light of his phone to check around the edges of the window. He didn't see any sensors that would trigger when he opened it.

Reaching through the hole he'd made, he unlatched the window and pushed it up.

This was the room where Noah had slept as a kid when he'd stayed over. Soren had never liked sharing. But his bedroom was right next door.

Music blared through the wall.

He dropped silently onto the carpet. Waited. Then crossed to the closed door that would lead to the hall. Waited again.

When he heard nothing, he opened the door and looked out. Soren's bedroom door was open just a few feet away.

Noah ducked back into the shadows as Soren emerged, head bowed as he looked at his phone.

Soren passed by, and Noah stepped out behind him.

His arm clamped around Soren's neck, instantly cutting off

the air supply. Noah's other hand pressed the corner of his phone into the small of Soren's back.

It would feel close enough to the barrel of a gun. Soren wouldn't know the difference. But Noah didn't intend to shoot his former friend. Certainly not yet. So he wasn't going to draw his actual weapon.

Before the other man could start to fight back, Noah dragged him backward into the guestroom and used his foot to shut the door.

"Stay quiet and I'll let you breathe."

Noah's arm shifted just enough to let Soren take half an inhale, but then he closed the chokehold again.

Soren's body twisted wildly. His lungs would be seizing, trying to get air.

Noah had never hated Soren. Didn't even hate him now. This feeling was far colder and more calculating. It was the knowledge that he didn't care what happened to himself or what rules he broke, so long as Danica was safe.

Noah brought his mouth to Soren's ear. "You're going to tell me where she is. The longer it takes, the more pain I'm going to cause you."

Noah shoved him, and Soren went down on his knees. He bent over, retching as he gasped.

"I don't know what you're talking about," he hissed, barely able to speak. "I swear, Noah, I—"

Noah's fist grabbed Soren's throat, loosely this time, and the man started blubbering. "*Fuck.* Just give me a chance. Okay? Please. How can I tell you what you want if I don't know what happened? Something's up with Danica?"

"She's gone. Lindley Colter took her."

"Who?" His confusion seemed sincere, but Soren was an excellent liar. Noah couldn't accept anything he said at face value.

"The executive director of the natural history museum. She took Danica from my house at gunpoint, just after I found out Jason Gerrig had worked for Valoris Security. For *you*."

That name, Soren clearly recognized. He closed his eyes, cursing again. "Okay. Okay, okay. That's true."

"And you came back to West Oaks when Gerrig died. When your plan to kidnap Danica failed."

"*No.*"

"But you need money, right? Because your company's going to shit?" Danica had told him everything that Soren had said. How he'd asked her for help, and she'd refused.

"I wasn't going to hold my sister for ransom to get it! Do you see Danica here? Do I seem like I'm in the middle of a kidnapping? I was watching YouTube and going to get a snack. And— and think about it. Why would I ask Danica for money yesterday if I was going to have her kidnapped today? Huh? How does that make sense?"

"Show me your phone."

Soren grabbed it from the floor where he'd dropped it. He held it up, and the screen unlocked using facial recognition. The YouTube app was the first thing that appeared.

"Show me your messages," Noah said.

He did. There was nothing that mentioned Danica. Nothing that looked like it had come from Lindley. Noah scrolled back further in time and saw nothing suspicious. Of course, Soren could've used a burner for all of that.

He needed intel. *Now.*

"I'll accept that, *maybe*, you don't know where Danica is," Noah said. "But you know something. I'm going to find out what."

Chapter Forty-Seven

"You." Danica's dinner rose up. Bile stung in her throat.

Her father's chief of security strode toward her. His heavy shoes thudded against the concrete driveway.

"I want to know why."

"Don't get ahead of yourself. We have a lot to deal with first." Blake turned to Lindley. "I believe I told you this was finished. You weren't to contact me again."

The gun still pointed at Danica, but Lindley scowled at him. "You think you can destroy my life, and then walk away when your plan falls apart? They're going to trace back the things I did to help you. But you were supposed to help me in return. You're leaving me with nothing except the blame."

"So what is it you want?" Blake asked. "I'm willing to deal, even if you've now exposed me in turn and caused me any number of new problems. What does it take for you to go away?"

Danica's eyes darted left and right. If she could get to cover, hide…

"I want two million," Lindley said.

"That's far more than we promised you. It was supposed to be five hundred thousand."

"The extra is to compensate me for my emotional distress."

The gun had drooped. Lindley was getting distracted.

Danica shifted her weight to the balls of her feet.

"And how do I know you won't say something to the wrong person?" Blake asked.

"I just want to disappear. I'm going to take the cash and leave West Oaks forever. Leave the country, maybe."

"You expect me to have two million dollars in my money clip?"

Lindley pointed at Danica with the gun. "You're going to ransom her, right? Wasn't that the whole point?"

"Ms. Colter, I don't believe you thought this plan through. It would've been far better for you if you'd taken my advice and pretended none of this had happened."

Danica was going to make a run for it. In three...two...

Lindley kept growing more agitated. "But I already told you—"

Without warning, Blake put his hand inside his jacket, produced a long-barreled handgun, and fired. It emitted a small pop, and Lindley collapsed onto the ground.

Danica was too shocked even to scream.

Then her attention caught on Lindley's fallen gun.

"Don't even think about it." Blake turned his weapon on her. It had a suppressor on the end of it. He picked up Lindley's gun, hooking his pointer finger on the trigger guard. "Walk to the front door of the house."

"No. I won't."

"This is your one chance to live through this. You already know I'll shoot. I said, *walk*."

Chapter Forty-Eight

*S*oren glanced at the gun in Noah's shoulder holster. "Was that your phone in my back in the hall? Jeez, you're such an asshole."

"I don't draw a weapon unless I intend to use it."

Soren scooted across the rug, backing up until he could lean against the bed. Noah remained standing, blocking access to the door. The room was still dark, lit only by the light coming through the window. Nighttime sounds and cool air streamed through the opening.

"So you're not going to shoot me?"

"Not right now. Though I'm sure you wouldn't extend me the same courtesy if our roles were reversed."

"You're the one who nearly choked me to death. Do you know how much my throat hurts right now?"

"If you don't want it to hurt even more, tell me about Jason Gerrig. Eagle tattoo."

"That's not the name I used to know him by. But yeah, I'll tell you everything I can."

"If you lie to me? If you try to get your Valoris bodyguards here?"

"I get it. Pain and all that."

"Just start talking. You're wasting time that Danica doesn't have."

These words seemed to sober him. "Gerrig was a bodyguard for me. One of several Valoris used to send in New York. I didn't know him well, but he seemed really intense. And he had that neck tattoo."

Soren paused to rub his throat.

"Valoris stopped sending Gerrig at least a year ago. They have a lot of turnover, so I thought nothing of it. But then I heard about the kidnapping attempt at the museum, and how Danica had seen some guy with an eagle tattoo on his neck. It made me think of that same Valoris bodyguard from New York."

"And you didn't say anything?"

"I did! To Blake."

"You told Blake about the tie to Valoris Security? When?"

"It was days ago. He said it was a coincidence, and the police were already looking into it. That I shouldn't talk about it with Danica because she was already upset. And then, she took off with you."

"But the police had no idea until Bennett Security figured it out today. Blake was lying."

"I…" Soren's eyes bulged. "Oh. Shit." He started talking fast. "Blake visited me in New York plenty of times, and he would've met all the Valoris bodyguards. Jason included."

Noah studied Soren's response, looking for any sign Danica's brother was lying. But he didn't spot any tells.

"Is Blake working for William on this?"

At this suggestion, Soren laughed. "Are you kidding? No. William would never go after Danica like that. In some effed-up way, Blake must be doing this for *me*."

"*You?* Why would Blake kidnap Danica to help *you?*"

Soren's eyes raised. "Because he's my real father. Not William."

Chapter Forty-Nine

*D*anica walked toward the front door of the Larsons' home. It had an electronic lock with a keypad.

Blake called out, "Enter the code 3-8-9-9."

She punched in the numbers, and a motor whirred, unlocking the door.

"Open it," Blake ordered. "Go inside."

She did. The entryway was dark. "How do you know the Larsons' code?"

"They asked me to keep an eye on the house whenever they're away, which is most of the time. I do it for plenty of William's neighbors."

White marble made up the entry, with a few steps leading down into a cavernous living room. A huge bank of windows overlooked a pool.

"The Larsons will see the activity on the log for their alarm system," Danica said.

"Do you really think that's the biggest of my problems right now?" Blake closed the door and locked it. "Go into the kitchen."

"Why?"

"Danica, do not make this harder than it needs to be. I have no intention of hurting you if you cooperate. You were never supposed to get hurt."

"You sent masked men after me. Men with guns and knives."

"To show they meant business. If you'd been easier to capture, nobody would ever have been hurt, William would have paid the ransom days ago, and you'd be back safe and sound."

"So sorry I messed things up for you."

The metal of his gun winked in the low light.

Danica walked into the kitchen. It was an expanse of marble countertops, built-in appliances, sleek cabinets.

Blake reached into his pocket and produced a set of hand-cuffs. He tossed them to the floor at her feet. "Cuff yourself to the wine fridge. Do *not* argue with me. I've always been patient with you, since you were a kid, but I'm not at my best today."

The glass door of the wine fridge showed rows of bottles. Danica threaded the handcuffs through the handle and snapped them onto her wrists. She tried to leave some room, but Blake wasn't having it.

"Tighter," he barked.

She ratcheted them a little more. "Now what? You call my father with your ransom demand?"

"No. As I said to Lindley, those plans died with Jason Gerrig."

Never question Blake's loyalty to this family, William always said. All those years, pretending he cared. Or maybe Blake had cared once, but something had changed. She couldn't begin to fathom why he'd do this. Had her father not paid him enough?

"But you want money, right? That's what this is about?"

"It's about many things. But money is part of it." Blake set his gun on the kitchen table. From his pocket, he pulled the gun he'd taken from Lindley. He set this weapon beside the first.

"You're going to pay your own ransom. Fifty million."

"*Fifty million?* You think I have that lying around?"

"Don't be smart with me, Danica. You can pick up a phone, call your 24-7 banker, and arrange for a loan against your stock portfolio. It'll take minutes. Then you're going to transfer that money into Bitcoin and send it to the wallet of my choosing. Untraceable, unrecoverable. Be grateful I'm not asking for a hundred million. That's what I'd planned to get from your father. But now, I don't have to pay Jason Gerrig his cut."

"How do I know you won't just kill me afterward?"

"You'll have to trust me."

"Then you can *fuck off*. Because I will never trust you again."

He grabbed the weapon with a silencer and crossed the kitchen, aiming. "It's not just your ransom you're paying. It's Noah's. If Jason had done his job, Noah would be dead already. But I know plenty of people like Jason Gerrig. Noah's good, but he can't look over his shoulder every minute. Someone will sneak up on him eventually, and that sanctimonious prick will get what's been coming to him."

Fury surged through her, and Danica yanked at the handcuffs. Blake must've given Noah's picture to Jason. But it sounded like Blake's problem with Noah was personal. "What has Noah ever done except try to protect me?"

Emotion finally animated Blake's face. "Noah betrayed Soren. I was willing to let it go as long as Noah stayed away, but he hasn't. Unlike you, I'm loyal to my family."

"Loyal? How can you call this loyalty?" She raised her cuffed hands, sliding them up the fridge handle.

"Because Soren is *my son*."

Danica stared, her mouth open. "Your…son?"

"You already know your parents weren't in love. Their marriage was a business arrangement. They were involved with other people."

She was shaking her head. "No. You're lying." *My mother didn't love you.*

"Why else would I have stayed in this family so long? Put up with everything your father's done? When Soren was born, we made an agreement. Your mother, William, and me. William promised to treat Soren like his own child, but he never has. He's always favored you."

Danica searched for the words to deny it, but it was true.

Even when they'd been kids, William had been so much harder on Soren.

"That's why Soren is the way he is," Blake said. "Why he's struggled. I finally told him the truth after that scandal when he was in college. I helped him get back on his feet. But the damage was already done. He's always doubted himself, and I think he always will. The new company he's started? It's a fiasco, and once again he can't sort it out on his own."

"Did Soren know about this? The plot to kidnap me?"

"No, I kept him out of it. He has no clue."

"But he will. Everyone will know. If you leave me alive." She knew she was baiting him, but she was so sick of the lies.

"The moment I have the money, I'm going to disappear. Thanks to Lindley Colter, that's the only path I have left. It'll mean leaving Soren, but at least I won't have to put up with your father's demands anymore. A man can live well on fifty million dollars in a country that doesn't extradite."

With that, Blake turned on his heel and strode out of the kitchen.

Chapter Fifty

"*B*lake is your father?"

A cruel smirk appeared on Soren's face. "You sure you want to join this screwed up family?"

"You know what? I don't care. All I want is to find Danica. If Blake's got her, where is she?"

"How the fuck should I know?"

Noah drew his Ruger and pointed it at the other man's face.

Soren reared back, hands raising. "Whoa, whoa, relax."

"I'm not in the mood to relax." He was tired of talking. And he could tell Soren didn't have much more of use to him.

It was time to *move*.

Noah's teeth clenched as he spoke. "*Tell me where to find Blake.*"

He hadn't just been trained to use weapons. He was a weapon himself. What he needed was a place to aim.

"I swear I don't know," Soren said. "But somebody else might."

～

SOREN POUNDED on the bedroom door until it opened. Tori —Blake's assistant, and Danica's half-sister—stood inside, arms crossed over her sweatshirt. Her eyes were red like she'd been crying.

"What is going on?"

"Tori, we need to find Blake," Soren said. "Can you track his phone or his computer or something?"

They'd already confirmed Blake wasn't in his room or his office, and he hadn't answered when Soren tried to call.

Noah's phone had been buzzing, too. Chase, Tanner, and several other Bennett Security bodyguards had arrived at his house and had been asking for instructions. But he'd put them off with a text. Until he found out where Danica was, he had nothing.

And as each minute passed, the vise around his heart kept winding tighter and tighter, making him more willing to break any and every rule.

Tori's brow wrinkled. "Why are you looking for Blake?"

Noah stepped into the doorway. He'd replaced his gun in its holster, but Tori still gasped when she saw the weapon.

"Because we think he kidnapped Danica," Noah said. "I'll explain everything later. Please, just help find Blake. Can you?"

"I'd have to get into his office. But the security guards will see on the cameras. They'll probably try to stop me."

Then they'd need a distraction.

Noah lifted his phone, and Tanner picked up on the first ring.

"Noah? Do you have a location for us yet?"

"No, but I need somebody to cause a disturbance over here at the Foster-Grant residence. Entirely possible you'll end up getting arrested. Or shot by an overzealous security guard."

"Sounds like fun. When do we start?"

"How's five minutes?"

"Eh, give me seven. Rex is using the head."

Noah ended the call and lowered his phone. "Seven minutes."

He herded Soren into Tori's room. Soren had been cooperative so far, but there was no way he'd let Danica's brother out of his sight.

"Wait," Soren said, "the minute this distraction starts, William is going to storm out of his wing of the house and demand to know what's happening. Do you have any idea what a pain in the ass he is? He's going to blame me for all of this."

"That's just too bad. You'll do the honors of telling him how *your father* kidnapped Danica. You'd better hope I get her out of this. Otherwise, William will have a lot more to blame you for."

Six minutes and thirty seconds later, they heard shouts from another part of the house.

Noah opened the door to the hall. "Tori? You're on."

Chapter Fifty-One

*B*lake held the phone up while Danica spoke. "Fifty million," she instructed.

The banker made her repeat herself.

"Yes, fifty. I need it in Bitcoin."

There was a pause. "Of course, Ms. Foster-Grant. Just one moment while I process your request. Do you mind if I place you on hold?"

Blake had been right about her access to her bank at any time, any place. She also had a secret distress password that she could've used. It would indicate she was being forced to make the transaction, and the bank would notify the local police and the FBI.

But Blake probably knew about that, too. Danica didn't dare use it.

Besides, it was just money. If she could buy Noah's safety, she would. But Danica suspected that all she was buying was a few more minutes alive.

Blake was watching her with that same hard expression.

He was going to kill her. She knew it.

A plan. I need a plan.

The banker came back on. "Ms. Foster-Grant, it'll be about

an hour for the loan and currency exchange to go through. Would you like to wait on the line, or shall I call you when it's finished?"

"Call me at this number. Thanks."

Blake lowered the phone. Danica was still cuffed to the wine fridge, but the handle was long enough that she could sit on the floor.

"Was all of Valoris Security in on it?" she asked. "Even Rosie?"

He walked to the kitchen table and sat. An open laptop waited beside him, showing his cryptocurrency wallet. That was why Blake had left the house a few minutes ago—to get the laptop from the sedan.

"They only knew never to question my orders and to keep their mouths shut. The more people who knew, the more likely we'd have a leak. But I chose people whom I'd worked with before, who'd do what I asked. Then you insisted on adding Rosie. That did cause some complications."

"But Rosie acted like she didn't believe me after I saw Jason Gerrig outside the museum."

"Probably because I told her you were unstable. Prone to hysteria. I framed it sympathetically, of course, and she trusted me as someone who'd known you all your life."

Danica let her head fall back against the fridge door. "That's why she was suddenly so concerned about me. Why she doubted what I'd seen."

"I would've found a reason to replace Rosie earlier if I could. But by then, you were already suspicious. Then Noah was around you constantly, getting in the way, and Rosie barely mattered."

Noah. Was he looking for her right now? Was there any possibility he'd figure out where she was before the bank transaction was complete?

"How did you recruit Jason Gerrig? I thought he was Soren's bodyguard in New York."

"That's how I met him. I found out he'd been in the army,

and we got to know one another. Jason didn't like the constraints of working for the government, or even for a private company. I knew we were of the same mind. So when Jason was ready for a new opportunity, he let me know. He relocated to Southern California. We worked on a few ops together."

The police had said Gerrig was a hitman. A mercenary. Blake had basically just admitted to participating. His role as chief of security for the Foster-Grants would've given him all kinds of access and insulated him from suspicion.

"Did my dad know Jason, too? I thought he recognized the tattoo when I showed him my drawing. He seemed nervous."

"William? No, I doubt he remembered Jason on any conscious level. You're underestimating the stress your father's been under lately, keeping his secret about Tori. That was why he wanted you home so badly. To find a way to confess the truth, although the coward kept putting it off."

Danica shook her head. Her father hadn't known about the kidnapping plot, but his lies had still contributed. "Why send Gerrig to kidnap me? Why now?"

He sighed. "It was the IPO for Soren's company. I told your brother it was a bad idea, but he had his mind set, even if he had to falsify their financial data to make it happen. All to impress *William*, the man who wasn't really his father and had never loved him. Soren was just begging the Securities and Exchange Commission to go after him, maybe even send him to federal prison. After his brush with the law in college, they weren't going to be sympathetic. I couldn't let that happen."

"So you decided to make the money by ransoming me? You couldn't have ransomed Soren instead?"

"I'm not convinced William would've paid. And it would've drawn too much scrutiny to Soren. William told me you were coming back to West Oaks to work on your museum, and I saw the opportunity. After you hired Lindley Colter, I had Jason make contact with her to secure her cooperation."

"Through threatening her and bribing her."

"Of course. She wouldn't have agreed otherwise. She

helped Jason plan how the kidnapping would take place. She suggested the date and time you should arrive, based on Jason's request."

So Lindley hadn't simply informed Jason of Danica's schedule. She'd actually *manipulated* that schedule. That fact might've disappointed Danica in her friend even more. But Lindley was lying on the concrete outside, dead. No matter what she'd done, she didn't deserve that.

"If you hadn't arrived early to tour the museum that Friday," Blake said, "you would never have seen Jason in the exhibits at all. Jason was there to ensure Lindley didn't get cold feet and try to interfere. He was supposed to leave the museum just before you were set to arrive. He'd approach you on the sidewalk, help get you into the waiting SUV. It should've worked like clockwork."

Blake was chatting about the conspiracy like it was nothing more than a plan for a dinner party.

"I probably wouldn't have noticed him if not for the eagle tattoo."

"That stupid tattoo. I told him to have it removed, but it was his signature. Too much ego, and it got him killed in the end." He tilted his head thoughtfully. "It's unfortunate William ever decided to call Bennett Security. I was trying to get him to hire Valoris, but you know your father, he likes options. Earlier today, I gave Noah credit for saving you, and it's true. He's the reason our plan failed."

She almost laughed. As usual, Blake wasn't giving *her* much credit. She'd escaped the kidnappers multiple times, too. Without Noah's help.

But Blake had clearly never expected her to fight back.

"How did Lindley find out *you* had hired Jason?" Danica asked. "I would've thought you'd prefer to stay in the shadows."

"That had been my intent. I'd been trying to limit my communications with Jason as much as possible. Burner phones, encrypted messages. But after the first attempt got botched, Lindley was terrified, and she needed more convincing. Jason was only frightening her by turning up near the museum and her home. I stepped in to talk sense into her."

"You must be regretting that decision now."

Blake regarded her thoughtfully. "Lindley forced my hand. I might've done things slightly differently. But in the end, I'll still get what I need."

Even if Lindley hadn't tried to double cross him, Blake probably would have gotten rid of her anyway.

And there was no way he'd let Danica live, either.

Danica forced herself to sit quietly for a while, even though she wanted to scream. She thought of Noah, of the possibility that she'd never see him again.

She remembered her mom, whom she'd lost all those years ago. Danica felt like she was losing her again right now. Because she'd never truly known her mother at all.

Her throat swelled, and her nose burned.

"What was my mom really like?"

At first, Blake didn't react. She thought maybe he hadn't heard her. But then he turned back to face her, his expression softening for the first time that night.

"She was very special to me. We met because I was a bodyguard for your family. They hired me when you were born. It was right after I left the army. So she and I were a little like you and Noah, in a way."

Danica suppressed her revulsion at that comparison. What had her mother seen in this man? Had Blake been so different then? Or had her mother been fooled into loving him?

"She was the most beautiful woman I'd ever seen," Blake went on. He wasn't looking at Danica now. His gaze was focused in the distance. "It was no secret that your parents were married in name only. I asked her to run away with me, and I think she might've agreed. But she had you to consider."

"I used to think you cared about me."

"I do. Because a part of her lives on in you. But eventually, we all have to move on, don't we?"

Tears streaked down Danica's cheeks, and she let them fall.

Blake turned away.

He returned to his computer, tapping at the keys. Danica stared at the phone lying facedown on the table. When would it ring?

How many minutes did she have left?

Chapter Fifty-Two

*N*oah took the shortcut onto the Larson property, pushing past tree branches. The Larsons' driveway and the side of the house appeared. All the windows were dark, but he thought he saw a faint light glowing inside.

Chase tapped Noah's shoulder and pointed. A sedan was parked in front of the house.

And a body lay on the concrete, surrounded by a pool of blood.

Bitter acid rocketed up in his throat. Then he noticed how the moonlight caught the woman's hair.

Red. It was Lindley Colter.

Chase had already called for backup on their way here, which would include paramedics. Noah's team couldn't render aid until their target had been neutralized. But he imagined they couldn't do much for Lindley, given the loss of blood.

He signaled for Chase to take his left flank, and Rex the right.

Noah dashed out of the cover of the trees. He reached the side of the house and flattened himself against the stucco wall.

At a window, Noah looked for alarm sensors. He tried pushing the frame open. It didn't budge.

The room inside appeared to be an office. Through an open

door, he could see a dim light. It was like a computer screen, coming from somewhere else in the house.

He pressed his ear to the glass.

Voices.

They were close.

Chapter Fifty-Three

*D*anica used her cuffed hands to wipe the tears from her face, but she only succeeded in smearing them. "I need to go to the bathroom."

"You know I can't allow that," Blake said a monotone. "You'll just have to hold it, or do it there."

Danica let all her emotions overwhelm her. The terror and rage and fear. The agony that she'd lost her mother all over again, that she was losing Noah.

When she spoke, she was careful to allow just a hint of a tremor. "You can't even give me some dignity? After everything? For my mother?"

His fist clenched and unclenched. Finally, he stood up from the table. "You can use the bathroom down the hall. But I'm coming with you. If you try anything, you'll regret it." He gestured at the gun, which was once again aiming at her.

Danica nodded slowly.

Blake walked toward her, and he lowered the keys to the handcuffs into her open palm. He stepped back as she unlocked them.

"Go ahead. It's that way." He pointed with the gun.

Rubbing her wrists, Danica walked toward the hall.

In the bathroom, Blake stood in the doorway, averting his eyes while she peed. She kept her movements subdued. Head down. The tears continued to fall.

"I'm finished."

Blake moved out of the way. "Go back to the kitchen." He waited for her to pass.

Danica went down the hall. She reached the end of it, where the large room opened up. Living room on one side, kitchen on the other.

Her heart was beating so hard she could see it in her vision, like the room was pulsating.

As she stepped out of the hall, her pace slowed.

"Keep going," Blake said behind her. "I'm warning you."

The gun met her lower back. Just what she'd been waiting for.

With an explosive motion, she spun. Danica grabbed hold of the arm holding the gun, and kneed Blake as hard as she could in the crotch. He grunted.

The gun went off, the chambered round hitting the wall behind her.

She'd caught him by surprise, but Danica felt the strength in Blake's body. She had to get the weapon away from him.

Her knee jammed into his crotch again, and her hand closed over the gun, twisting it out of his grip.

But with a bellow, Blake charged. His weight slammed her into the wall. The gun went flying out of her hand. She couldn't see where it had gone.

His fist came at her. Danica pushed at his arm with the blade of her hand, deflecting the blow. She spun away from him when he tried to grab her.

His next punch landed painfully between her shoulder blades, knocking her off balance. She fell to the carpet.

Danica rolled onto her back just as Blake lunged at her, going to his knees. His fist retracted, his face a snarl of hatred.

He wanted to hurt her. Make her pay.

Then a deafening sound cut through the air.

Blake toppled forward, his body going limp.

Danica pushed him away, scrambling to get up. She saw blood on the carpet. Her brain was still trying to make sense of what had just happened.

"Dani?"

Noah. Noah was here, in the mouth of the hallway. Two other men stood behind him, though she hardly paid them attention.

She ran to the man she loved, just now noticing the gun in his hand. The acrid scent of gunpowder met her nose.

Noah's arms closed around her. She pushed her face into his chest. Tears were falling again, and this time, they were pure relief.

"Noah."

"I've got you," he whispered. "I've got you."

Chapter Fifty-Four

$\mathcal{I}$t took well into the next morning, but finally, all the police were gone. Noah shut the front door and walked into his family's living room.

Danica sat on the couch, eyes half closed. Noah wanted to scoop up his girl and hold her, but they had an audience. Both of their families were here.

Ginger sat on one side of Danica, an arm around her shoulders, while Tori was on the other side, holding Danica's hand. William Foster-Grant leaned against the wall, though from the angle of his body Noah guessed the man was ready to collapse from exhaustion.

The only person in the room getting any rest was his grandfather. Gramps was sprawled in his favorite chair, snoring at an astonishing volume.

Noah went to the center of the room, and the others looked up. "We should probably decide if we're going to get some sleep, or if we're going to be awake. If it's awake, I'm going to order coffee and lemon pancakes from Uber Eats."

Everyone else—except for Gramps, who continued to snore —waited for Danica to answer.

She managed a smile. At some point she'd showered and

changed her clothes, but Noah hadn't seen her sleep. "I need some rest. Dad, Tori, why don't you both head home. I'll talk to you later."

William jolted back to alertness. "Go home without you? After all that just happened, I'd feel much better having you close by." He quickly lifted his hands to cut off her protests. "I'm not ordering you back to the house. I know better than that."

Do you? Noah thought. He certainly hoped so.

"I am so sorry for everything, Danica," her father said. "For lying to you, for not believing your suspicions about Blake's behavior earlier. I've made so many mistakes in my life. But I love you. I love both my daughters, and Soren too, though I'm not sure that's a relationship I can repair. All I'm asking is for your permission to stay here with you." William nodded at Ginger. "Assuming I have the blessing of Noah's family?"

Noah hadn't imagined the man could be so contrite. But the revelations of the last several hours had taken their toll on everyone.

"I'm fine with you sticking around, Dad," Danica said. "As long as Noah feels the same."

Noah nodded. He doubted he'd ever be a fan of William, and the feeling was probably mutual. But forever was a long time. Danica needed her family. Noah would never stand between them.

As soon as Noah had left the Foster-Grants' last night, Soren had taken off, possibly to head back to New York. He'd sent a message to Danica, apologizing for his indirect role in the kidnapping. She hadn't decided whether to write back.

As far as Noah was concerned, and as guilty as Soren might be of other things, he was innocent of trying to hurt her. So Noah didn't really care what Soren did next.

His Bennett Security teammates, along with Chase Collins, had left hours ago after giving their statements. There'd been some talk about charges related to Tanner's efforts to distract the Foster-Grants' security guards. Reckless driving, property damage, trespassing… Thankfully, William had refused to pursue it once he'd understood the circumstances.

Tanner had driven his Jeep straight through the gate at the Foster-Grant residence. He'd acted like he was drunk and lost, a story that had been even more convincing because he'd stripped down to his underwear. A stroke of brilliance, Noah thought, because even the most trigger-happy security guard wasn't likely to shoot a drunk guy stumbling around in his undies.

He wondered if any security cameras had recorded Tanner's antics. That would've been fun to see. And it would've made a *great* screensaver at headquarters.

The commotion had given Tori the cover she needed to go into Blake's office and use his desktop to locate his other devices. Blake had taken all sorts of precautions to keep his secrets hidden, but he'd given his assistant access to most of his systems and passwords.

Blake had had a tendency to underestimate the Foster-Grant women. He'd never get the chance to do it again.

The paramedics had arrived minutes after the shooting. But Blake had been pronounced dead at the scene, along with Lindley Colter.

The Larsons' property would have to be repaired, including the bullet round to the drywall and the window Noah had broken to storm inside. Luckily, the family wouldn't return to West Oaks for a while, so the repairs probably wouldn't inconvenience them. The damage was minor in the scheme of things, but Danica had already been fretting about it.

Ginger clapped her hands onto her knees, then stood up. "It's settled. I'll show William and Tori to a couple of guestrooms. We'll all get some rest, and when we wake up, I'll match Noah's offer of pancakes, and throw in some mimosas."

She waived for them to follow her. Tori and William each gave Danica a hug.

Before he left the living room, William extended his hand to Noah. They shook, and William held Noah's hand in both of his. "I am incredibly grateful that you found my daughter. And I don't just mean last night. I'm sorry for any suggestions I've made to the contrary."

"Thank you, sir. I'm grateful she and I found each other, too."

"Take care of her?"

Noah could see her rolling her eyes in his peripheral vision. "I will. But Danica is extremely skilled at taking care of herself."

"I know that. But it's much harder to go it alone. I've learned that firsthand." William nodded at them both. "Until later. Looking forward to those pancakes."

"Bye, Dad."

After her father had left, Noah took Danica's hand. They went upstairs to his bedroom.

The minute the door clicked closed, she walked into his arms, and they held one another. He dug his fingers into her hair and breathed in the sweet scent of her. Like the jasmine that grew everywhere in the West Oaks hills.

"I love you," she said. "So much. When I thought I might never see you again, it was the worst thing I've ever felt."

"Same here. I love you, Dani. More than anything. I'm so thankful you're safe." His voice started to break.

Until now, Noah hadn't allowed himself to truly feel all the terror he'd been holding back. Even downstairs with their families, he'd been running on adrenaline and fumes.

"Thinking I might really lose you," he said, "that there was nothing I could do…" A tear streaked down his face.

He didn't cry easily. Maybe even less than Danica. But he wasn't afraid to show this side of himself to her. With Danica, he wanted to be open about everything.

She looked up at him and wiped at the trail his tear had left. Then she gave him that coy smile he loved so much.

"Well, it's a good thing I was busy saving myself. I mean, you helped speed things along by showing up when you did. But, you realize I had Blake in my guard when I was on the ground, right? I was totally about to break out some fancy moves on his ass."

"You saying you didn't really need me?"

"I always *need* you." She smoothed her hands over his shoulders and down his arms. "Especially to stand around looking pretty. You're really good at that."

With a growl, Noah grabbed her around the waist and lifted her in the air. Danica giggled, wrapped her legs around him, and held him by the neck.

She kissed him with soft pecks that turned deeper and slower. Her tongue licked into his mouth.

Maybe she *hadn't* really wanted to rest.

But when Noah took her to his bed and laid her down, Danica started dozing within seconds. Laughing, he snuggled behind her and stretched the covers over them both.

Then Lucifer jumped down from the bookcase and sauntered over. The cat leaped onto the mattress and curled up by Danica's other side.

"Thanks for looking out for her, Lucy," he whispered, and closed his eyes.

~

NOAH WOKE to Danica kissing his neck.

"No more resting." She straddled him, raining kisses on his face, hands snaking under his shirt.

"Don't you want me to brush my teeth?"

"No. I need you. Right now."

He looked around the bed. "Is Lucy…?"

"I put her in the hall."

This woman was not taking no for an answer. Not that he'd ever say "no" to her, anyway.

"You'll have to move so I can take off my clothes."

She kneeled beside him on the mattress. Noah pushed his pants down and off, along with his boxer briefs. His dick was just starting to perk up.

Dani's head dipped down, and she took him into her mouth. Noah made an incoherent sound, trying to stay quiet since they weren't alone in the house.

She swirled her tongue and sucked him until he was rock hard in her mouth, which took all of two seconds.

They took off the rest of their clothing, making out in between. They were both gentler with each other than they'd been before. Kissing and caressing. Taking care, even if Danica had still set a fast pace.

Every moment with her gave him a rush of energy and feeling. The sheer joy of being alive.

She lay back, naked, and Noah hovered just above her. Danica snaked her legs around his hips.

"You're not going to flip me, are you? Not sure my back can take it today."

"I want you to have me. Just like this."

Noah's skin flushed with heat. He brought the head of his cock to her opening. They both moaned as he slid inside, her body offering no resistance.

Then somehow, she tightened, like she was squeezing around him.

"Oooh."

"You like that?" Danica's body tensed again, her hips lifting as her legs gripped him.

"You know I do. Love how strong you are." Noah lifted his upper body so he could watch as he fucked her, his cock gliding in and out of her. This woman was so strong and beautiful. She could be rough on him and could take it when he was rough back.

But she was sweet, too. When she wanted to be. Noah wanted to earn all that sweetness. Every day, again and again.

"I love you," she whispered to him.

Noah lowered himself down to hold her in his arms. Then he didn't think about anything for a while except how good this was. How the universe might still laugh at him for being a romantic instead of a cynic, but he was going to love this woman with every part of his being for as long as he could.

Epilogue

Two months later

*D*anica had never seen so many people inside the natural history museum. Not even at the gala.

She walked through the crowd, shaking hands and saying hello in between answering questions.

Then she turned, and across the atrium she saw her favorite person in the world walking through the glass entrance doors.

Noah spotted her instantly and waved. A couple dozen teens and tweens trailed in behind him—the kids from his military mentorship group. Tanner and Devon pulled up the rear, herding the stragglers.

She hurried over to meet them. "Noah, I'm glad you could make it."

He winked at her. "Good to see you too, Dani. Been awhile."

"Introduce me to your friends?"

"I'd be happy to."

They'd woken up together that morning at Danica's new

house. She'd needed to leave early for the museum, so they'd had to choose between going for a run or making love.

Her cardio was going to suffer if she kept skipping workouts, but she'd started out the day more than satisfied.

Danica's new place was on the other side of the hilltop neighborhood from their families' homes. But she and Noah usually ended up visiting the Foster-Grants or the Vandermeers at least once a week. Brunches with Gramps and Ginger, where they sipped champagne and ate caviar, or just as often pre-frozen snacks warmed up in the oven. Dinners with William and Tori, which were a little stiff, but slowly improving.

Danica still traveled several times a month, often going back and forth to New York to meet with her foundation employees and her friends. Whenever possible, Noah came with her, and she'd loved showing off her sexy ex-Navy SEAL boyfriend to everyone she knew.

But she'd decided to make West Oaks her home base. Noah had been a big reason, but not the only one.

The revelations of two months ago had forever altered how she viewed her family. But that didn't have to mean losing them. It was a new chapter in her life. A new challenge that she was more than ready to face.

She'd been getting to know her sister better and reconnecting with her father. The three of them were even going to family counseling. It was going to take a long time to rebuild the trust between Danica and her dad, but she knew the effort was worth it.

But her brother was a more difficult subject.

Soren's company had lost most of its stock value after the truth about its financials had come out. The last she'd heard, he was under investigation by the SEC. She and William had both declined to fund his legal defense. But Soren had received some money from Blake's estate. Not fifty million, but enough to make a dent in his legal fees.

If her brother wanted to try fixing their relationship, she was willing. But she also wasn't holding her breath.

"Why don't you all come in and check out what's new," Danica said to the kids. "Our renovation isn't done yet, but our new exhibits are getting rave reviews. I can't wait to hear what you all think."

Noah headed toward the exhibit hall with his charges. But as he passed, he blew Danica a kiss. And of course, some of the kids noticed and hooted and hollered at him. Danica laughed, waving them on.

"You two just can't get enough of each other."

Danica looked over at Rosie, who'd just strolled over from the reception desk.

"Gives me hope for my own love life," Rosie added.

"If you need to be set up, just let me know." She'd made this same offer several times, without a firm yes or no. "There's one lady in particular I think you'd like, on the museum board of directors…"

Rosie's cheeks colored. "I'll keep thinking about it, Dani. But thanks."

Rosie was now Danica's chief of security. It hadn't been easy to convince her to permanently move to West Oaks from Northern California, which had been her home base with Valoris before. But Danica thought Rosie seemed pretty happy, too. Certainly more laid back.

Today, Rosie was in charge of the security arrangements for the museum's special event. They'd invited several school groups to get a preview of the new exhibits.

After the setback of losing their executive director and curator, combined with the problematic publicity from the gala, things were finally looking up around here. In so many ways.

~

NOAH WALKED OUTSIDE onto the deck. Danica was curled up in an Adirondack chair, working on her laptop.

He took a moment to admire her. Then he spoke.

"It's official. Fossils are now cool. Pretty sure the kids were making TikToks about the exhibits during their tour."

Danica glanced up at him, smiling. "I love it. I'll have to check the museum account later."

It was nearly sunset. Danica's view faced east, so they were missing most of the show. But sunrises on this side of the house were spectacular.

Especially when those first few rays of sunlight caught in her dark hair on the pillow. Noah had to wake up early to see it because Danica was the quintessential morning person. It wasn't always easy to slow her down. But those quiet moments together had become some of Noah's favorites of the day.

Noah sat in the chair beside her. "What's on your agenda for tomorrow?"

"Back to the museum to meet with the new executive director and debrief after the event today. Oh—I got an interview request from a journalist in New York. Some website, I think? She said it would be a chance for me to talk about the foundation's upcoming projects."

"Sounds great."

"But she asked if you'd be there, too. Wants to write about the whole 'love story' angle." Danica used air quotes. "You don't have to do it."

Noah shrugged. "I don't mind. I'll go."

He liked talking about how they'd fallen for each other twelve years ago, then reunited. There might be questions about Soren, but Noah would deflect them. He preferred to focus on the cuter parts of their story. After all, he was a romantic now.

Or maybe that wasn't right. Where Danica was concerned, he'd probably always been a romantic. Holding on to a secret hope, hidden even from himself, that they'd get their second chance.

Noah was living here with Danica, and his condo in town was on the market. He'd wanted to buy this house with her, but Danica had made some good points, primarily the fact that his income paled in comparison to hers.

Instead, he was covering their daily expenses. Like all those food delivery and takeout bills.

But he didn't mind being a kept man. Noah was secure enough in his masculinity that he had nothing to prove.

He'd decided to phase out eventually as a captain at Bennett Security. There was no rush to find his replacement. It would have to be a top candidate, someone who'd satisfy Max's demanding personality and vibe well with Tanner. He wanted to stay on as a bodyguard, but probably just part time.

Eventually, Noah planned to free up his schedule to do more with the Foster-Grant Foundation. Maybe even start a nonprofit of his own. Danica had already been helping him expand the military mentorship program.

He loved the idea of working closely with her, traveling with her. Truly being partners. Danica had helped him to see more clearly what he wanted—to dedicate his life to his ideals and to serving others. The same thing he'd done as a SEAL, just in new ways.

Every once in a while, he still felt anxious about losing her. But that risk was worth it. Each day with Danica was more vivid, more intense, than his last several years put together.

Time with Danica was more thrilling than anything else he could imagine. His Ducati probably felt neglected.

Noah had told Chase Collins something similar the last time they'd spoken. As far as Noah knew, Chase hadn't solved his love problems yet. But Noah had wished him luck.

The best things are worth fighting for, he'd said. A little advice between friends.

Noah hadn't even protested when Ginger made a gift of Lucifer as a housewarming present. That was how much he loved this woman. He was willing to put up with that demonic cat, who still enjoyed kicking him out of his side of the bed.

Danica set her laptop down, stood up, and stretched. "Want to go for our run? Since we missed it this morning?"

"I can think of better ways to use up that extra energy. We can put on one of your sexy playlists."

"You're such a bad influence." Danica laughed and shook her head. "I'm older than you. I can't afford to skip my workouts."

Noah thought *she* was the bad influence. Before Danica had returned to his life, he'd been the king of long runs and daily gym visits. Now? He just wanted to stay in bed.

"How about you run," he suggested, "and I'll catch you."

"Deal." She looked over her shoulder at him, a wicked gleam in her eye. "Let's see if you can keep up."

Don't miss the next book, HAVE MERCY—Chase and Ruby's story!

Also by Hannah Shield

THE BENNETT SECURITY SERIES

HANDS OFF (Aurora & Devon)

To keep her safe, he has to keep his hands off… But she has other ideas.

❧

HEAD FIRST (Lana & Max)

He's protecting his former flame… But can he resist falling for her?

❧

HARD WIRED (Sylvie & Dominic)

Can this bad boy find redemption in the arms of the enemy?

❧

HOLD TIGHT (Faith & Tanner)

He was supposed to be her wingman. She was never supposed to fall for him.

❧

HAVE MERCY (Ruby & Chase)

The only way to save his best friend's sister…is to marry her.

About the Author

Hannah Shield once worked as an attorney. Now, she loves thrilling readers on the page—in every possible way.

She writes steamy romantic suspense with feisty heroines, brooding heroes, and heart-pounding action. Bennett Security is her debut series. Visit her website at www.hannahshield.com.